Halfway Home

Jayce & Emma: The Complete Story

Barbara Winkes

Contents

HALFWAY HOME

When Emma first met Jayce Turner, she knew it would be better to stay away. Over time, her instincts had proven to be right, if futile.

Four weeks had passed since she'd moved in, four weeks that she'd been aware of the clock ticking, every single day, every hour. In a way, the surroundings weren't so different from prison, except for the fact that she was mostly free to go when- and wherever she wanted to. Emma used the skills she'd bene- fited from in the past months. Stay under the radar, try to make allies when you could, avoid making enemies at all costs, fit in. She was good at following the rules.

The outside world made her nervous in a way she had never expected when the gates of the prison first closed behind her and the fear eating her up inside flared up to the point she'd almost fainted.

Emma had learned that a little fear was a good thing. It kept you on your toes. Ironically, freedom had become a Damocles sword rather than the promise that had kept her sane and alive. She needed to find a job. She had expected the sentence on her record to complicate the task. What depressed her most were the suspicion and the pity she got from potential employers. Could they trust her near the cash register or official documents?

At times, Emma wasn't sure either, because she still had a hard time understanding the chain of events that had led to her conviction and subsequent prison stay. How could she have not seen the disaster about to happen? How could she have spent that much time with a person and not sense they were ready and able to kill somebody, just like that, for a few bucks?

Time had blurred the sharp edges of the memory, though she still woke up crying from time to time, from a nightmare in which she had blood on her hands that wasn't her own.

When Emma had frantically tried to stop the bleeding, to no avail, she hadn't been aware of the warm sticky fluid coating her hands, but her brain had stowed away the sensory details. The dreams had already become less frequent. She never missed group or individual counseling. The biggest priority at this point was finding a place to work. Emma had vowed to stay away from relationships in the future, because that would have served her well in the first place. All day, she hadn't been able to eat, anxious about the interview. Upon her return to the house, she headed straight for the kitchen to make herself some tea, running into Jayce.

"You're in a hurry?"

Tall, dark hair bound back in a ponytail, wearing jeans and a white tank top, she looked like every other woman who had gotten Emma into trouble. Then again, maybe it was time to grow up and take responsibility, because she'd been all too ready to be led into temptation, more than once.

"I'm Jayce Turner, by the way. I moved in this morning."

The tone of voice that sounded too intimate for a simple introduction, the handshake that seemed to last a little too long, all of those were familiar too. Emma backed off a step, uneasy with the woman's display of cocky self-confidence.

"Welcome," she said, clearing her throat. "I'm sorry."

Jayce gave her a wry grin. "No harm done. I guess I'll see you around." She walked away, a sway to her hips that Emma found impossible to ignore.

She touched her fingers to her cheek, the skin warm under her fingertips. With a sigh, she turned to the tea kettle. *No more mistakes, Emma.* She had also learned to identify the newbies and the distance to keep from them, based on the category she put them in. A threat. Will get into trouble at the first sign of confrontation. This one will fit in. This one is not going to survive without a friend.

Emma gripped the counter with both hands, her desire for the warm beverage gone. There was something about Jayce that deeply unsettled her. She hoped she'd be gone before suspicion turned to certainty. Emma wanted to be gone by Christmas. It was still possible.

❧

Idle hopes they were. Emma had woken up late, unable to decide whether her headache or hunger was more ravenous. In the kitchen, Jayce stood together with Meg, their conversation coming to a halt the moment Emma came in. If that was the company Jayce was seeking, Emma had to be even more careful about her. To Meg, the halfway house was high school, and she was the Queen B. She was the kind of bully who had never grown out the dynamic.

It was almost a miracle Emma hadn't gotten on her radar yet—another reason to find that job as soon as possible. Alison and Terri, the only ones Emma talked to on a regular basis, had warned her of Meg and her clique. They hadn't given her any specifics, but drugs were a good guess. Emma didn't need any more convincing to stay away.

"There's coffee if you like," Jayce said, prompting Meg to give her a sharp look.

"We weren't done here." Meg's tone held a note of warning that did nothing to impress Jayce. She shrugged.

"Come back another time. I've got to go to group counseling." That earned her another chastising look from Meg, before the woman stalked off.

With dread, Emma realized that Jayce would be in her group. Admittedly much of her lack of sleep had to do with the new addition to the house. Emma had enough to deal with, issues and people. She didn't care for another change—except it was not up to her. She'd see a lot more women come and go if her job search continued in the same way.

"There's no milk, sorry."

Jayce's voice jolted her out of thoughts, making Emma flinch. She clutched the hot mug Jayce handed her, only to set it down with a yelp.

"Wow, you're jumpy."

"It's all that black coffee, you know."

She could have sworn Jayce hid a smile behind her own cup. Emma wondered what she and Meg had to talk about. She wasn't going to ask. Not asking any questions had carried her through a lot.

"I see," Jayce said. "Group counseling, huh? Is it going to be as dull as I think? Half of the people telling their sob stories while the other half is asleep?"

"They want us to try. That's not too much to ask, is it?"

"Try what?" Jayce laughed. "Come on. We're running late." Emma hurried after her, trying to keep up with her quick step. They made it into the room just in time before the counselor.

Emma prayed it wasn't her turn today. Group counseling could be a minefield—you wanted to make sure to convey you were making progress, but not reveal too much to Meg's minions. Granted, there was only one of them in the group, Lynne. She put on a bored expression, but listened to every word in the hope she could bring something usable to Meg, and therefore get herself up in the hierarchy.

At least, that was Terri and Alison's theory. Emma didn't want to know, but she was careful not to reveal too much. When she left this place, she wanted to forget about it best she could, the same as with her previous address.

Meanwhile, Jayce took a seat next to her, looking as uninterested as Lynne.

When the counselor asked her to introduce herself, she countered, "What do you want to know? We're keeping scores? I had a friend who wanted to spice up her parties a bit. She got in bed with the wrong people and needed help to clean up the mess. One of us got caught. Here I am."

"Anything else you want to share with us is fine."

Jayce's eyes narrowed at the trace of sarcasm. "You mean about the people who broke down her door? Yeah, that was nasty. It's a good thing I had that gun. They took a few years off because the guy wasn't exactly a saint. Anything else you want to know?"

"Jayce, I hope you understand we are not the enemy here. This is a safe space."

Lynne rolled her eyes while Emma tried to make herself invisible. Under no circumstances did she want to be involved in this conversation. There was a screening process for the women who came here, but as anywhere else, there were the ones who played by the rules, and the ones who simply played. They were certainly not the majority, but they could do damage, to her future plans, everything she had envisioned.

"Okay," Jayce said. "Thanks. I'm done."

Emma wished she could have ignored her, but that was hard to do with the woman sitting right next to her. The voices of the other women faded, the air in the room feeling unusually stuffy. If only someone would open a window...She stumbled through her own report as if on auto-pilot, all but jumping to her feet when the session was over, her vision graying out for a moment.

"Hold on there. Are you okay?"

Awareness returned, alerting her of Jayce's concerned gaze, her hand on Emma's arm. All her conflicted feelings aside, she was grateful for the support.

"Emma?" The counselor had joined them. "You almost fainted. You should see the nurse."

In the corner, Emma could see Lynne whispering with another woman, the two of them laughing. Dr. Jeffries might be more polite, but Emma was afraid she might think the same.

"I was late, so I skipped breakfast," she finally said. "I just need to eat something."

"I'll come with you," Jayce offered. The warm tone of her voice and the gentle touch almost made Emma forget that Jayce had seemed pretty cozy with Meg earlier this morning. She didn't want to get in the middle of whatever was going on there.

"No thanks. I'm fine."

"Okay. Whatever."

Dr. Jeffries patted her arm. "I'll see you tomorrow, Emma?"

"Sure."

In the kitchen, Emma grabbed a piece of toast, feeling too exhausted to bother with putting anything on it. She poured herself a glass of water, trying hard to escape the thought that something bad was about to happen.

Oh, right, it almost happened. She'd nearly fainted in front of the group, giving way to innuendo. She hadn't eaten, she hadn't slept—no wonder she was becoming paranoid. Chances were, Jayce wanted to stay out of trouble and start a new life like the majority of them.

"Bread and water? I thought we were past that," Alison joked, closing the door behind her.

"I don't know about you, but that wasn't on the menu where I was."

"Have you met the new girl? Interesting one."

"Why do you say that?" Emma bit her lip. Curiosity might not kill her, but it led to complications. It always did.

"You can't tell? I thought she'd be your type."

"Come on. I don't have a type. I need a job." A few bites of the toast had calmed her stomach, and she got milk and jam out of the fridge, starting to make herself a real sandwich.

"Yeah, about that, how did it go?" Alison asked.

Emma lifted her shoulders in an uncertain gesture before she sat down at the table.

"They expressed their sympathy and then wondered whether I might rob their cash register. Not that they'd say it out loud, but I could tell."

"Sucks."

"Yeah, it does," Emma agreed.

"You'll find something."

Some days, Emma was less hopeful on the subject than on others. She glanced outside the window where the rain was coming down, still. It had been cold and rainy all week, leaving no doubt that winter was moving in. Lots of students had been pouring into town and were looking for jobs, and they didn't have any dark spots on their records. She'd made choices. She'd have to live with the consequences, wouldn't she?

"Maybe. I've got some skills." Her laugh sounded bitter, and yet, she shouldn't be complaining. At least, she wasn't deemed a danger to society any longer. It would take a lot more than a change of environment to leave the invisible prison.

"Honey, what's done is done. You can't turn back time. As cheesy as that sounds, you can get somewhere from here. If the folks here didn't believe it, they wouldn't have accepted you in the first place."

"I guess you're right." At this moment, Emma simply agreed because she wanted the conversation to end.

Still, when Marley called her into the office to tell her that the store owner was on the phone, Emma couldn't help the jolt of excitement. What if...? Next, there'd be the search for an apartment, but the social worker could help with that. Besides, it was much easier if she already had a job to show for. She could start over, leave behind the shadows of terrible mistakes and—

"I'm sorry, but we had to go with the most qualified applicant. We wish you all the best for the future."

The numbness encroaching on her made it hard to move, let alone answer the woman on the other end of the line. She wished she could rewind the moment, to that split second when she still had hope to be out of here in a few weeks. Not that she'd feel much safer, Emma wasn't fooling herself believing that she'd feel safe anywhere, anytime soon. Farther away from Meg would be a big improvement, aside from the fact that sooner or later, there would be pressure to leave.

"Ms. Curtis? Are you still there?"

"Yes...I'm sorry. Thanks. No problem." Actually, the woman had no idea how much of a problem she had created for Emma. No, that wasn't right. Emma had created the problem in the first place, and now she had to deal with the results. *Keep yourself together. Don't start crying until you're in your room.* Within a heartbeat, her skin was feeling so tight she wanted to jump out of it.

Emma didn't want to see or talk to anyone at the moment, but she also knew she'd feel claustrophobic within the four walls of her room. Maybe she could have a cigarette from Terri or Alison. Emma didn't even like smoking, but at a moment like this it would do wonders against the impulse to smash her hand against a brick wall. There was no alcohol allowed in the house since some of the women who came here were battling addiction.

No job. Starting over at zero. Against all odds, she hoped that someone had left some cookies in the kitchen, maybe brewed a fresh pot of coffee. Right, that was exactly what she needed, more caffeine. Of course, there was nothing sweet to be seen anywhere. The coffee pot was empty.

Emma gripped the counter with both hands, forcing herself to take slow, measured breaths, to relax some, but she couldn't stop the tears from falling. She wanted to be left alone. At the same time, she dreaded being alone. That's how ready she was to be a useful member of society, make her contribution.

"Try what?" Jayce had asked. She didn't seem to be worried much, but Emma felt like she'd been given that one second chance. If she kept screwing it up, at some point, there would be no more options, no more hope.

There'd be coffee in the back room that served as pantry. She needed the comfort, if only for the warmth. Emma closed the door behind her and sank to the floor next to one of the shelves, no longer trying to hold back the tears.

⁂

She wasn't sure how long she'd been sitting there when she heard voices. There was no end to her bad luck today. One of them belonged to Meg, so Emma's options were either running into her or waiting until whatever court she'd be holding in the kitchen was adjourned. Emma heard someone giggle—Lynne, maybe?—then Meg, chiding her in a sharp tone.

"Please do something to reassure me it wasn't a mistake to bring you."

"What, you're afraid someone could catch you? Girl, the food in prison wasn't that much worse."

"No," Meg shot back. "I'm afraid someone could kill me if they knew you couldn't be trusted to keep your mouth shut. I gave my word."

Emma froze, certain that she was about to witness something of the kind she'd done her best to stay away from so far. Wasn't it enough for one day? Her day got worse though.

"Who else are we waiting for?" Cherry, one of Meg's favorites, asked.

"Yolanda, and the new chick, Jayce," Meg said. She laughed. "Said she wanted to check out the logistics. I'm not so sure about her yet. I want to see if she can put up."

"And your 'cousins'?" Cherry sounded eager, stressing on the word in a way that told Emma clearly that it was code for something entirely different. "Do they have the product?"

"Damn it, watch your language! Are you stupid?" Meg exploded at her. "They are taking a big risk coming here, so the last thing I want is to make them think the police could show up at any moment. If that happens, it won't be just my ass on the line."

Emma wanted to cover her ears with her hands. Why didn't she go to her room right away?

"What about Jayce? How can you know we can trust her?"

"Connections. Grapevine says she is okay. She and the friend did a lot of prescription stuff before the shooting, so I figured she'd want to be in. We'll have to see if she can come up with the money."

It was none of her business. Emma had no reason to be shocked or disappointed for any reason other than her failed job interview. She had no reason to care about Jayce whom she had exchanged a few words with, or even be surprised that Meg was involved in shady, potentially dangerous dealings. Why couldn't she stop crying, damn it?

More voices, one male, two female. Emma recognized Jayce who introduced herself but stayed silent after that. The other two had to be the aforementioned "cousins" who were clearly taking over. When Meg talked, it was with a hint of unease in her tone. Emma pressed closer against the wall, as if she could make herself invisible. She should be safe for the moment.

What was she going to do? What could she do?

The attendants of the suspicious meeting were talking in hushed tones now, and whenever she could make out words, Emma wasn't too sure what they meant. What was going on right there on the other side of the door was probably everything Alison and Terri had warned her about. If she told anyone, would Meg come after her—would her "cousins"? What product had Cherry been talking about, and how had Jayce made her way into this group so effortlessly? There was an explanation, and Emma hated to go there.

If Meg had heard about Jayce through her questionable circle of connections, then she had to have a reputation. Just because she had shown concern earlier this morning, or her story at counseling had sounded like a lot of bad luck, it didn't mean she was innocent. Emma barely suppressed the hysterical laughter that was bubbling up inside of her. Innocent, none of them was. They were all halfway to...somewhere. Or nowhere. The direction was yet to be determined.

Ten minutes later, the meeting and any dealings it included, had obviously come to an end. Emma peered at her watch. She'd wait another ten or so to make sure everyone was gone, and then retreat to her room, try to distract herself, read or go over the newspaper ads again. She'd forget what she'd overheard. She didn't want to be drawn into anything that looked so clearly like trouble. The minutes ticked by, too slowly for all the nervous energy she still harbored.

Eventually, Emma got up and carefully opened the door, sighing in relief when the kitchen was empty. Maybe instead of hiding, she should take a walk, breathe some fresh air to clear her head. Emma might have done that, hadn't she found herself face to face with a furious Meg the next moment.

"I knew it. It's you!"

"Me? What?"

Meg pushed her up against the wall, hard enough to rattle her teeth. Emma understood in an instant that trouble was not a prospect of the future. She was already in deep.

"I didn't do anything!"

"Tell that to the cops you're snitching for," Meg seethed.

"I'm not..."

"Don't lie to me!"

Emma's heart raced, her fear skyrocketing when Meg's hand closed around her throat. Unable to speak, she could not give Meg the truth or lies, but the irony failed her at the moment.

"Hey! What's going on here?"

Meg's grip loosened, and Emma sank back against the wall, coughing. The room was spinning, but she could make out Jayce's concerned expression.

"What are you doing?" Her voice was tinged with anger.

"Well, I told you there was a snitch. Now we know who it is."

"Stop it. Leave her alone." Jayce groaned. "Great job. You could have just as well put up a sign and announce to everyone what we were doing."

"I don't know, and I don't care what you were doing," Emma offered after finding her voice again. "You leave me alone, and I do the same."

When Meg made another move towards her, Jayce held up her hand. "That's fair enough, I think. I'm sorry, Emma. Meg jumps to conclusions all too quickly. You shouldn't though. It's all good."

"I'm sure. Have a good evening."

All of a sudden, the need for fresh air had become overwhelming. Emma stopped in her room long enough to get her purse and a coat, and all but fled from the building. It wasn't until she made it into the park on the other side of the street that her breathing returned to normal. She was still shaking. Her throat hurt.

"Hey. Please wait."

She should probably be more grateful, but given the big picture, Emma had a hard time finding that sentiment. "Aren't you worried that Meg's going to find out?"

"Meg knows I'm here," Jayce said.

"Oh, even better. Did she send you to finish the job?"

To her surprise, Jayce started laughing. No, Emma wasn't just surprised. She was offended by the other woman's reaction.

"Care to tell me why this is so funny? She nearly strangled me."

"Yeah." Jayce turned serious in an instant. "She has no idea what she's doing, actually, and that can be pretty dangerous. Let me see?"

"Why?" However, she obediently brushed her hair aside for Jayce to inspect what was no doubt an ugly bruise. Emma might not have been in acute danger of dying, but she'd nearly fainted. In fact, the memory made her knees buckle and Jayce reach out for her quickly.

"Why what?"

She shivered under Jayce's careful touch, a reaction that wasn't entirely appropriate, and Emma was well aware.

"Why did you come to my rescue? You're in on whatever dealings she's doing. Doesn't that undermine her authority or something?"

"I don't answer to her." Jayce's quiet tone held a note of warning. Emma was more confused than ever.

"Then why did you—"

"Sometimes it's better not to ask too many questions, and no, this is not a threat. I don't want you to get caught up in any of this."

This time, Emma held back the question, if barely.

"Because unlike some of us, you have the chance to get this right," Jayce said softly. "Come on. It's getting late."

Emma paused on the job application. She knew she was stalling, and not only for the fact that she would have loved to work in the small bookstore rather than a fast-food joint. It wasn't like she had that many options, after all it was her fault she was facing this dilemma in the first place, wasn't it?

It was an entirely different dilemma that kept her from finishing her task. Ridiculous that Jayce was occupying her thoughts like this when she had a load of other problems to deal with. Get off Meg's radar, find a job and a place to stay.

This wasn't a good time or place to have feelings for someone, let alone act on them. In a way, it had been easier in prison, and a lot more messed up. She hadn't expected anything from either of the two women she'd had sex with. A trade-off against loneliness and paranoia—or justified fear, Emma didn't know, because she'd been constantly afraid from the moment that gunshot rang out. It had been a distraction from a dire reality.

Now, if she let somebody touch her, and maybe Jayce was even interested...She would make herself vulnerable again, to plans and hopes. The last time, it had nearly destroyed her. Emma didn't want to go down that road again, but when she lay down that night, the narrow single bed felt cold and empty. She couldn't get warm. She couldn't take her mind of the images, memory mixing with imagination.

She wanted to be close to someone who wouldn't use her, before all her ambitions of leaving the house, standing on her own feet—but Jayce wasn't that person. Jayce had her own troubles, and if Emma's instincts were worth anything, they were big enough to warrant some distance.

Her subconscious didn't think so.

In her dream, she was trapped against the bars of a holding cell by a hot body, wandering hands exploring her, the voice whispering to her all too familiar. Emma woke with a start, her heart pounding so hard it was almost painful, aching in a place she would have preferred to ignore.

A lack of prospects, being watched by Meg, and kinky sex dreams about the new girl—the list just kept growing.

The next morning, neither Jayce nor Meg mentioned what had happened in the kitchen, or after, for which Emma was grateful. She sat by herself for breakfast and went back to filling out applications afterwards. Going out to mail them would take her mind of more troublesome subjects for a while.

Standing at the bus stop, she was shivering in the cold wind, but nonetheless grateful to have escaped the claustrophobic feel of the house—at least it felt like that to her since last night. Thinking it was safe to hide out for a while had been a treacherous illusion. If Jayce hadn't been there...Emma felt her cheeks heat as the dream came back to her, and she was grateful when the bus arrived.

It was a ten-minute ride into town. In favor of saving money, she had planned to return most of the applications on foot.

Emma was almost swayed by the cold gust of wind in her face the moment she left the warmth of the bus, but she figured it was the equivalent to the cold shower she obviously needed.

When all her errands were done, her hands were pink with the cold, and with regret she realized she should have put on gloves. It was going to snow soon.

She wanted to be out of the house before Christmas. Emma wasn't so sure if it still could happen. To warm up, she stepped into a bookstore for a moment—not the one where she had applied—and walked along the shelves with jealousy.

Once upon a time, she would have filled her cart without thinking. The days before Maxine, when she was living an ordinary, mostly happy life, Emma had held on to a job and a reasonable amount of self-confidence. She had wanted a bit more excitement in it. If she'd been able to turn around to her younger self, she would have slapped her. Hard. Of course, she would have made the same fatal mistakes, because that younger version of Emma had not taken advice from anyone and walked right into the trap.

She shook herself out of her reverie and all but ran out of the store. Next door was a coffee shop, and for a moment, she wished back her old life with an intensity it hurt. The fancy coffees and cakes were beyond her price range, and maybe always would be. Emma only had herself to blame...and Maxine, but she preferred not to think of her as someone other than a faint shadow in a nightmare, a delusion.

Speaking of delusions.

"Are you following me?" she asked, irritated. "This is what you can report back to Meg. I don't care what she's doing, I won't rat her out. I was mailing applications. I want out of that house as soon as possible."

"I know." The corner of Jayce's mouth twitched, revealing that she was suppressing a smile in reaction to Emma's accusations. "Actually, I was following you, I admit it. I wanted to talk to you without the risk of running into someone from the house."

"Why?" At this point, Jayce had to think she wasn't capable of conversation other than monosyllabic questions or angry rants. Not the image you wanted to give someone...you had sex dreams about. Emma blushed hotly. "I mean, we're good. I'm grateful you came to my rescue. There's nothing to talk about." –or was there?

"What if I'd like to get to know you? Besides, it's freezing cold out here. Let me buy you a coffee?"

For the life of her, Emma couldn't figure out the subtext, her perception sadly clouded by thoughts that no cold shower or wind could have erased. She was frustrated enough at this point in her life that she was in danger of getting careless.

"You've been in the house for a few days. How do you have the money for this?"

She'd probably deserved the laughter. "How about 'Sure, thanks, Jayce'?"

Emma shook her head. "You're so full of yourself."

"Milk and sugar or black?"

They ended up sharing a cupcake, raspberry-chocolate, with a black coffee for each of them. The subjects between them were a lot less sweet.

"Sometimes I still feel like this is happening to someone else and that I'm only watching from the outside. One moment I'm thinking about backpacking through Europe, and then Maxine says 'hey, let's go for a ride'. She's been depressed for weeks, so I think this is a good sign. I didn't know she had a gun with her until we went into that store," Emma remembered, shuddering. "A couple of beers, sandwiches, and a bag of chips, and she shoots the guy. I didn't see it coming. I don't know, maybe, in retrospect, I should have. She could be erratic."

"How did you end up in prison?" Jayce asked. Her gaze was warm and without the judgment that Emma had come to expect. She had accepted that she deserved it. After all, a person was dead, which was partly because of her negligence, wasn't it? She shrugged helplessly. "Her word against mine, no witnesses. She didn't deny taking the shot, but she told them I was in on it from the beginning." Maxine in her despair could be convincing. "I didn't have the most motivated lawyer in the world...It could have been worse. Hell, from what I know now, I'm lucky. She could have shot *me*."

In answer, Jayce laid her hand over Emma's, let it rest there. *Don't*, Emma wanted to say. *I can't go there.* She didn't move.

"What about you?"

"You heard it all in group counseling. I've got nothing to add." Jayce's expression was guarded.

"Why Meg?" If anything, the answer might show her a picture she didn't want to see. Some people remained stuck in the same pattern, on the inside, on the outside. Steel bars and barbed wire hardly made any difference in the big picture. Emma didn't want Jayce to be one of those people. She wanted her to have a reason.

Jayce removed her hand as if she couldn't answer the question as long as they were connected like that. "I had an accident a while ago. I'm still on painkillers...sometimes."

With that explanation, there came a lot more questions. What kind of accident? Where did she get the money to pay off Meg? Why would any of this be Emma's business or concern?

"Be careful. You saw what kind of people she hangs out with." She shook herself. Jayce had been part of that meeting. How silly was it to try and warn her?

"I can take care of myself." Jayce squared her shoulders. "Let's talk about something more pleasant while we're here. What do you want to do when you get out of the house? With the first paycheck—or after that first job to get you back on your feet."

Emma wasn't so sure there could be a life for her beyond finding a job that paid the bills, a life that wasn't entirely tainted by her time with Maxine.

"I guess I didn't think about it all that much. I'll be happy to be in my own four walls, maybe have a cat, read a book with a cup of tea." Her face warmed as she repeated those words in her head—true enough for her, but she expected a woman like Jayce to laugh at them.

Jayce, however, didn't laugh. "Sounds nice. Would you be willing to accept visitors in that vision?"

Startled, Emma looked up at her. Jayce opened her bag and produced a new paperback, handing it to Emma.

"You wanted it so much," she said, as if that was reason enough. Before Emma could react in any way, she added, "I want to read it too, don't worry. I'm sure you'll be done before one of those applications works out for you."

"Thank you."

"You're welcome."

This time, she held Jayce's gaze, uncaring of anything she might reveal to her. If this wasn't a public place...if they didn't have to report back at the house where the walls were too thin for any secrets...The daydream ended abruptly. There was no point in playing the "what if" game. It wasn't up to them to make those choices.

"I think we should head home now, before anyone wonders where we are," she said. Home. The word seemed to mock her.

"What's going on with you and Jayce?" Alison asked when they were sitting over dinner. "You're not going to do something crazy, are you? Stick to the plan, remember?"

"Shh," Emma interrupted her, before she could continue her rant, blushing. The subject of their conversation was leaning against the counter, surveying the room with a speculative gaze. Fortunately, Jayce was out of earshot. "There's nothing going on."

"That's not what I'm hearing, and I'm telling you, it's coming up in all the wrong places. Be careful. Don't piss off the Queen B."

"What does that have to do with anything?"

"Everything. You know she's up to nothing good, but she's set her eyes on J, is what the grapevine says. She doesn't like competition."

"Well, I'm not trying to compete, in anything. I'm praying that one of those applications will work out, and I can get out of here."

Alison gave her a dubious look. "Don't we all, honey. Would you like to watch some TV later?"

Emma shook her head. "No, thanks. I've got a book to read."

"That's right, you were in town today. Gets better each time, doesn't it?"

"I guess." Emma wasn't that naïve. She guessed that Alison must have had some suspicions based on what had happened today—but who had told her? She should stop trying to answer questions, and more importantly, stop asking them in the first place. Take a shower, curl up in bed with a book, stay clear of any distractions or temptations. She cast an anxious look towards Meg who had walked in with her posse, ignoring Emma and Alison altogether. As long as Meg let her.

Jayce went to join them. Emma looked back at her plate and realized she had lost her appetite.

She spent a longer time than usual in the shower, trying to get warm, get a handle on her anxiety, and her hazardous desires. Hazardous, because they endangered every goal she'd managed to form since having to come to terms with her altered reality. Nothing worked. She read half a page, before closing the book again, staring at the cover for a long moment. The idea refused to leave her mind, and if Emma was honest, she didn't want it to. There was only one way to make her feel warm and relaxed, and if she was going to pursue that avenue, she'd have to ignore most of what she knew about Jayce. She knew nothing, really. No, that wasn't true. The way her heart was beating this moment told her a lot. Emma's life had been shattered before because she couldn't read the signs. At least this time, she was walking into disaster with her eyes wide open.

❦

Emma walked across the corridor, feeling watched though the space was empty. It was a little like going to town and freaking. She was always certain everyone knew, that she'd been to prison, that because of her, intended or not, a life had ended. She didn't deserve to be happy. She didn't deserve to feel this excited, but damn, she did. Raising her hand, she knocked.

"Come on in."

Jayce got up from where she was sitting on her bed, not even looking surprised it was Emma paying her a visit.

"Hey. You didn't like it?" she said with a quick glance to the book.

"No, yes, I...I needed an excuse to come here in case anyone would ask," Emma admitted. At least, she wasn't stammering like she had feared.

Jayce came to stand in front of her, too close. "An excuse for what?" she asked, a small, amused smile playing over her lips.

"This," Emma said and leaned in to kiss her. Jayce reached out, and for a moment, Emma feared she might push her away, but instead, Jayce's hands were warm on Emma's face as she returned the kiss. Finally, Emma was warm all over. She had done her best to keep the distance, to keep her emotions in check, but none of it could have made her forget how much she missed being held in a passionate embrace promising much more than a friendly hug. Being kissed by someone who wasn't looking back.

Jayce stepped back, regarding her for a long moment. "Are you sure this is a good idea?"

"No. Not at all, but it doesn't matter," Emma whispered, stepping into her personal space once more. "Please."

The last word might not have been necessary, because Jayce's hands were on her waist, sneaking underneath the hem of her sweater, pushing it further up. It ended up on the floor, moments later, together with her bra. For the span of a heartbeat, Emma felt self-conscious and a bit cold standing half-naked in the middle of the room, until Jayce pulled her close again. She couldn't remember the last time someone had undressed her like this, slowly, carefully explored her skin, and cherished her. Emma gasped as Jayce's fingers brushed over her stomach, lower, sliding beneath the fabric of her panties. Her eyes were on Emma the whole time, studying her, gauging her reaction. She might regret this not far from now, but at the moment, Emma had no reason to complain. She stumbled backwards onto the bed, tugging Jayce with her.

She wasn't feeling so self-conscious anymore when Jayce took off her sweater, halting for a moment before she leaned down again to kiss Emma's neck, then her mouth, as her hand slid up her thigh. Emma had made a decision in those past few moments. She might be safer trying not to feel anything, for anyone, but she might just as well not be alive at all. That way, she served no one, especially not the man who had lost his life. Emma might have been naïve hanging out with Maxine, but it was Maxine who had pulled the trigger. Emma had served her sentence.

"Shh, stay with me."

Oh, not a problem, she was right there. Almost. She had worked hard on keeping it together, for some time, but at this moment, she wanted to let go, to be swept away, no matter the consequences. "I'm with you." Her voice was breathless with anticipation, making Jayce smile.

"Good." Her hands were on Emma's thighs, gently opening her legs. Emma forgot to breathe for a moment. She let herself sink back into the mattress, pressing into Jayce's warm touch, hungry for more sensation. Tucking a strand of hair behind her ear, Jayce leaned down to brush Emma's thigh with her lips, working her way upward until Emma had to bite her lip to keep in the sound. The sensations held her captive, waves of pleasure washing through her body, a helpless moan she couldn't hold back.

Stillness followed.

Jayce lay down beside her, wrapping her arms around Emma's trembling body. Silence was all right with Emma, because every word would inevitably destroy what fragile connection was between them. They couldn't go anywhere from here, halfway nowhere.

⚓

Still typing on her report, Jayce was doing the best she could to hide from Lieutenant Chomsky when her superior passed by her desk. "Detective Finney? Have a minute?"

Depends on what you're going to tell me, and if you want me to come in for good, the answer is no. Instead, Jayce saved her file and got to her feet.

"Of course."

It was funny how undercover worked. Here, at her desk, life in the halfway house was like an elaborate, if real and potentially dangerous, dream. In the days spent there, however, Jayce Turner took over, a person who easily inserted herself into troublesome situations. Part of what had made the transition smooth, were some biographical similarities she could have done without. She hadn't expected the life of her undercover persona to bleed into her reality like this.

Emma.

Aside from the obvious reasons, Jayce was worried about her, because she was kind and curious, and hanging out with the wrong people. Jayce shook her head to herself, smiling wryly. Herself included.

"Something funny, Detective?"

"No. Sorry."

"Okay, have a seat."

"I can't stay long. I have to go back to the house," Jayce reminded her.

"That's what I wanted to talk to you about," the lieutenant said. "I think it's time to bring in reinforcements. The names you gave us...as you know, they are associated with some dangerous people. It's going far beyond the sale of a few prescription drugs and a bit of crack."

"With all due respect, Ma'am, I disagree. If you call in the FBI now, those 'cousins' are going to be spooked, and we'll never get to the suppliers behind them. We can go up all the way to the chain. Megan Connelly trusts me. I'll deal with the others."

"Are you sure?"

Jayce held her superior's gaze. "I am," she said, but they both knew she had hesitated for a moment. Jayce wasn't worried about the operation. She knew she could hold out until they had more than Meg's silly ideas of hooking up with small time drug dealer. They could get all the way to the top.

She hoped that when they did, Emma would be out of the house. She didn't want her in any danger, and seeing to that was the only thing she could do for her. Once Emma found out the truth...Jayce sighed to herself. It was all her fault.

"Is there anything else?" Damn the woman for being this perceptive. She hadn't made it into this office for nothing. Usually, Jayce appreciated a woman in power, but today she wished Chomsky would let her handle the situation without asking too many questions.

"There's someone...I'm worried about," she confessed. Lieutenant Chomsky regarded her intently.

"She overheard something. I don't think she wants to get involved in any way, but there's tension. I'd like to get her out before the takedown."

"Does she know anything?"

"Since when do we keep someone out of the line on fire only when they can help the case?"

Chomsky's expression told Jayce that her inappropriate outburst had revealed a lot more than she'd intended to. She made an attempt at damage control.

"She's young. She has no business being in the middle of this in the first place. Fell in with the wrong crowd. She got set up."

"Detective, can I be sure that your mind is a hundred percent on this operation? Because if it isn't, you shouldn't go back to the house at all."

"I'm fine."

"So you keep telling me. Okay. If you can't come up with that connection in forty-eight hours, we'll take the risk and go with the 'cousins'. They are low-level from what you're telling me. If we can get them to talk, there's no reason for putting more people in danger."

"Fine." She'd probably asked for this. The only way to turn the case around was to get the cousins' boss into the house for the deal, and preferably get Emma out before—all in forty-eight hours. Jayce was aware there was no way to do this without revealing herself.

It was already pitch dark when she stood shivering outside on the street. She didn't have a lot of time to make the transition into her character. Part of her wished she could have taken Chomsky up on her offer and get the hell out. Jayce wanted to get out, as far away from that house as possible, but she couldn't. Too much was on the line.

Not everything she'd told Emma was a fabrication. One of her omissions was that the accident had occurred at work, during a pursuit, when the suspect thought he could get away by ramming his own vehicle into her car, almost killing both of them in the process. A long and painful recovery had sent her into a downward spiral, on the verge of addiction. She had worked her way back out of the haze, dealing with part-time work and desk duty until she was finally back to claim her old job, a case that should have been cut and dried, but was starting to grow heads. There was the likely connection to a network of dealers they were about to tap into. Meg's little operation could blow up in her face any day—either way.

Then, there was Emma.

The bus finally arrived, and she could get out of the cold, find a seat close to the heating. Jayce leaned against the window, her thoughts troubled by the memory of last night. Unprofessional, came to mind. Impossible. She had needed to be with someone, her bad luck that it happened during undercover work, with someone she cared about.

From day one, she had found it hard to ignore Emma, wondering how someone like her would end up in jail for murder. She had done her homework on all the women, the ones she needed to get close to in order to get to the dealers. Emma wasn't one of them. From the day of her conviction, she had stayed under the radar, had been a model prisoner and was now working on leaving the halfway house as soon as possible. There were no friends or family to speak of, so she needed help with the transition. For sure, Jayce hadn't helped, but she'd been unable to resist either.

Marley greeted her as she pulled the front door closed behind her.

"Hey. Quick, close that door, it's freezing today, isn't it? Did you get all your errands done?"

"Yes, I think so."

"You got a job interview for Friday, right? Good luck with that."

"Thanks."

Jayce breathed a sigh of relief when she could finally escape the small talk and retreat to her room. The smell of food from the kitchen half-tempted her, but she didn't want to see anyone, especially not Emma. Nevertheless, as her gaze fell on the book on the bedside table, she had to smile. Emma had stolen out of the room and across the hall on her tiptoes, but not before she had fallen asleep in Jayce's arms. Feeling safe next to someone had become a privilege somewhere along the way, for both of them. She should do Emma a favor now and let it go. It was hard to stay away, almost impossible.

All conversations came to a halt when she entered the kitchen, something that Jayce didn't particularly like. Meg and Alison stood in opposite corners with their respective groups, not giving each other—or Jayce—the time of day.

Emma gave her a shy smile, unaware she was shattering all of Jayce's good intentions. In a way, they were both trapped. Who could blame them for trying to make that space a bit more livable?

"You're right on time," Emma said. "It's still warm."

Behind her back, Meg was rolling her eyes. Jayce had an idea why, but that was another thing she didn't want to contemplate at the moment.

"Good." She took a plate out of the cabinet, served herself and sat down across from Emma, the air of disapproval in the room chilling. Jayce didn't need any more hints to know that for the safety of both of them, she'd have to let her down gently, but she thought Emma deserved a warning at least. They sat in silence for a few minutes, before Emma spoke. "You've been away for a long time. Did you have a job interview?"

"Something like that." It wasn't one of the bigger lies. If she screwed up this case, she might not have a job anymore.

Emma sighed. "You've been here for a few days, and you already have opportunities lined up. Honestly, I'm jealous."

"Don't be. You'll find something."

"Maybe." Emma studied her for a long moment. "I finished your book," she said, and it wasn't hard to tell it was code for something else. The book had sat on Jayce's nightstand the whole day, where Emma had left it last night.

"Did you like it?"

"I'd like to read it all over again." Emma blushed a little, but she held Jayce's gaze. "I enjoyed it very much."

"You could give it another go. Maybe tonight." Jayce could hardly believe herself, saying, doing the opposite of what was the responsible, necessary thing. Tomorrow, she promised herself. Tomorrow she'd find a way to get Emma out of the house, after she'd learned the details of the new meeting. Everything had to happen quickly. She didn't want to go over the deadline

Chomsky had given her. After the arrests were made, maybe she could apologize to Emma and they could...*dream on*. Tonight would probably be all they had left together. She wanted to make it count.

"That would be awesome."

"Okay. I'll see you. I have to...go," she said awkwardly before getting up to rinse her plate in the sink. Alison followed her into the hallway, her buddy Terri not far behind.

"You and Emma seem awfully close lately," Alison remarked.

"You have a problem with that?" Jayce asked sarcastically.

"Personally, I think she could do better, but that's not my problem. Meg, however, isn't so pleased."

"I didn't know you cared about pleasing Meg."

"Just watch out. It's a friendly warning."

Jayce shrugged. "I appreciate it. Good night."

"You're going to bed already?" Terri called after her. "That must have been a stressful job interview."

Jayce didn't think she needed to comment on that. However, stressed, she was, for too many reasons.

"Here. If you actually want to read it this time," she said when Emma opened her door, a happy smile on her face.

All of Jayce's stress and worries were gone in a heartbeat, though, when she was the sole focus of Emma's attention. They didn't bother removing every piece of clothing, or even moving away from the door. Leaning back against it, Jayce gave up on reason and responsibility, enjoying the play of Emma's fingers teasing and tormenting her, the hungry kisses they shared. Eventually, Emma pulled down her pants completely, together with her slip, and got to her knees.

Emma didn't have any idea about what the urgency actually was, but she too seemed to sense that they were on borrowed time. After that first hurried time, they continued to undress each other, continuing at a slower, gentler pace on the narrow bed, until they collapsed in each other's arms. There was nothing left to prove. After the case ended, maybe they'd have a shot at happiness—and if they didn't, Jayce was all right with pretending for the moment.

Meg knocked on her door precisely at midnight. Jayce had expected her, but she hadn't expected Emma to still be there, curled up, sleeping soundly in her bed.

"Don't say anything about it, and make it quick," she warned. "We don't want to wake her."

Even in the dim light of the flashlight, Meg's pout was obvious. "So, it's true. Sheesh, you don't have standards, do you?"

"Nothing for you to worry about. Your 'cousins' coming over tomorrow or what?"

"Yes, of course, I told you. You didn't need to make such a drama of it. They got everything we want. As long as we bring them the money, everyone's going to be fine."

"Great. Make sure you check the pantry before we get started. We don't want any surprises like the last time."

Meg sneered. "I think you benefited from the last surprise, didn't you? Or maybe she isn't that good?"

"Screw yourself," Jayce said mildly.

Meg laughed. "Since you won't, I might have to do just that. Besides, we won't have that meeting in the kitchen. It's too dangerous to do it here. There's an abandoned house not far. Can't miss it. That's where we'll meet them. Quickly, in and out, deal done. If all works well, every other week from now." With a wry grin, she added. "We both know that you didn't go to a job interview, and you probably won't on Friday. We're all gonna stay here a little bit longer...and little Emma might just to warm your bed. Lucky you."

30

"Yeah. If that's all, I'd like to go back to said bed now?"

"Oh, sure, knock yourself out. If you strain anything...well, tomorrow is the day."

She closed the door, and Jayce winced. She had told many lies, but Meg's casual dismissal of Emma bothered her. *Hypocrisy much, Jayce Finney?*

She had thought, hoped, that Emma had missed the whole exchange, but no such luck. When she crawled back under the covers, Emma turned to her. "I wish you wouldn't do this," she said ruefully. "Anyone, but not Meg. I don't want you to get hurt."

"I'll be careful." Jayce was well aware that this wasn't what Emma wanted to hear. For a moment, she toyed with the idea telling her the truth there and then. She couldn't risk an operation that had started long before she'd shown up at the house, for a personal matter. She brushed her hand over Emma's cheek. "I promise." Whatever this promise was worth, because she would have to break it. Unlike other people in Emma's life, she had no choice.

In the afternoon, they had retreated to Emma's room with a cup of tea, trying to hide from the world and the inevitable. They were still hours away from the deal going down. Emma was blissfully unaware.

This could still work out for her, Jayce thought. When it all came out, she might be able to do something for Emma, ask around—Kitty, the wife of her partner Daniel, had recently opened a shop for stationary and greeting cards. It maybe wasn't what Emma had envisioned, but it was a start, something that might even give Jayce a chance to check up on her.

Her plans were altered drastically the next moment when the door sprang open, and a group of uniformed officers barged into the room. Jayce jumped to her feet.

"What the hell is this?" She'd been startled by the intrusion, but Emma looked shell-shocked as the cops started immediately to tear up the room.

"I'm sorry about this," Marley said. "We got a call...I don't know much either."

Jayce couldn't believe what was happening. These officers could easily undo her work of the past half year—gaining credibility with the players in question, the immense time and effort leading up to this day. If the deal was off, they'd most likely scare the higher-ups away, no matter if they had planned to do it in the house or not. She felt with Emma who still stood unmoving and pale, but at the moment, she couldn't help her. She would have loved to give the men a piece of her mind. She'd have to wait.

Their problems became even bigger a moment later, though, when one of the uniforms produced a package from underneath the mattress. Emma's eyes went even wider, her hand going to her mouth.

"No," she whispered.

Damn. Somebody had talked. Somebody had done this on purpose, or to create a distraction, because there was no way in hell Emma would hide this much cocaine—from the looks of it—in her room. The person who had done this also deemed their little stunt important enough to count in substantial losses. Why?

"You must believe me, I don't know how this got here. It's not mine." Her eyes filled with tears. "Please. I don't want to go to prison. I can't." Her voice rose with each word, in a near panic as the cuffs clicked around her wrists. "Marley. I didn't do this."

"Stop it. Let her go. I put it there. I'm sorry, Emma." The scene came to an abrupt halt. For a few heartbeats, no one spoke.

"Come on, it's me you want. I'll tell you all about where it's from, but leave her alone. She doesn't know anything. I thought it was safe. Oh well." Jayce held out her hands with a dramatic sigh. "Go ahead."

Marley turned away from the doorway, her body language clearly showing her disappointment. Emma wasn't disappointed, she was devastated. Jayce asked herself if the truth would make her feel any better. Probably not.

⁂

"It was an anonymous tip! What do you expect us to do, just ignore it?" The sergeant wasn't happy with either her or his officers. Jayce hated to admit that he had a point, which, unfortunately, did nothing to change the facts.

"What exactly happened there?" Chomsky asked. "I understand your frustration, but frankly, you took a big risk." Her voice was level, but Jayce knew from experience that her calm tone didn't mean she wasn't mad as hell.

"Someone set her up. Emma was one of the ones who tried really hard to keep her hands clean. She never did drugs."

"You didn't trust us to figure that out?"

Jayce bit her lip. There was no point getting into an argument with her boss, with the sergeant present. "Marley Peterson has been temporarily replaced. The new girl doesn't know anything about what went down, so if anyone asks, she can't tell them. No one knows! I'll go meet the others as planned, we make the deal."

"No, it's too dangerous." Chomsky shook her head, exasperated. "They don't even have to know you're a cop. Emma Curtis talks to anyone at all, word goes out you were arrested and set free so soon, they'll think you talked."

"About what? I have no idea where the cocaine came from. If anything, we could get an idea from tonight's gathering about who's behind this. I don't think it was Megan Connelly. She's in over her head as it is."

"Seems to me she's not the only one," the sergeant murmured.

"Hey. If your guys hadn't come barging in, we wouldn't be here, so your sarcasm is inappropriate. I'll take care of it. No one suspects anything, except they might if I stay here any longer."

"Okay, can I talk to my detective in private for a moment?" Chomsky's tone put a definite end to the argument. The sergeant shrugged and got up to leave the room. Chomsky waited until he had closed the door behind him. Jayce braced herself.

"You've been setting this up for months. I understand that you want the credit too, and you should have it, but I need to be sure you can handle it."

"I can." Jayce was well aware that she was talking about some of the things Jayce had told Emma that hadn't been lies. She'd been on the edge, one foot over it, and dragged herself back. She was going to see this through.

"What about the woman?"

"I don't think she knows anything at all, but I'd like you to keep her a little while longer, until the deal goes down. It'll be safer for her, and for me."

"I'll see what I can do," Chomsky promised.

"Thank you."

Before she left the station, Jayce went to the interrogation room, watching through the glass in the observation area. Emma sat in the chair like she was expecting somebody to hit her, curled up in on herself. Jayce hated to be the reason for her to feel this way, but there were too many things going on in and around the house at the moment. Most of all, she didn't want Emma to get caught in the crossfire.

"Wish me luck," she whispered before she turned to go. She'd need it.

The only way Emma knew how to keep it together was to shut off every emotion, make herself cold and numb. That instant reaction hadn't always been to her advantage, like during the trial when the lawyer told her she came off as arrogant to the jury when in reality, she was so terrified she could hardly breathe. Technically, she knew the cops were only doing their jobs, and that the package with cocaine had to have come from somewhere. Of course they'd have to investigate it.

However, her experiences had caused a deep mistrust of authorities and justice. Scratch that, she'd developed a deep mistrust of people in general—that was why she kept interactions at the house at a minimum, stayed to herself...

Not a good enough explanation for why she'd landed in bed with Jayce. Why she'd wanted to.

Emma sighed to herself. She wasn't sure whether to be worried about Jayce, or worried about herself. This could still go down the same way, someone she'd let her guard down with, turning against her. Not Jayce, right? She didn't know anymore. She jumped when the door opened.

"Ms. Curtis," the man in the grey suit said. "I'm Detective Walker. I just need to ask you a few questions, and then you can go home."

Home, she scoffed in her mind. *I don't have a home.*

"Okay," Emma said. Her strategies didn't work so well anymore, her voice sounding like that of a frightened child.

There was an eerie silence in the house when Emma returned. Marley wasn't at her desk. The woman who was sitting in her place looked up quickly, gave her a brief smile and went back to the file she was reading. No one in the group rooms or the kitchen. Emma's quick tour had only one reason—to delay the inevitable meltdown. No one had been telling her anything about Jayce, not that she'd expected them to.

They might never meet again. It occurred to Emma that Jayce had protected her from the day she came to the house, from Meg, from the unknown threat. Maybe they were the same? Had Meg planted the drugs because she was jealous? She and Jayce had been so careful. In her room, Emma sat on her bed, trying to clear her thoughts. She had vowed to stay away from any kind of confrontation, but she couldn't let Jayce take the blame for something neither of them had done, could she? She had to find Meg. Emma winced at the memory of Meg choking her in the hallway. That undertaking wasn't without risk. She had to do something. Sitting around here, with the book still on her nightstand, thinking of last night, and the night before...

With new determination, Emma got up. For a moment, she stood in the hallway, more than a bit frightened of what she was going to do, and what the consequences would be. Then she walked to the end of the corridor where Meg's room was and knocked.

When the door was yanked open, Emma was startled to see not Meg, but Alison on the other side. Before she could say anything, Alison pulled her inside and locked the door. "What the hell are you doing here?" she hissed, as if it was perfectly natural for her to be in the room that wasn't hers.

"They let me go. I wanted to talk to Meg. Where is she?"

Alison's eyes narrowed. "First of all, I think Queen B is up to no good. Who let you go? What happened here?"

"The police. They found drugs, in my room, I have no idea who put them there. Jayce said they were hers, but I don't believe it. They arrested her and made me go too. God, what a horrible day."

Alison regarded her long enough for Emma to become uncomfortable under her scrutiny.

"Maybe they let you go because they thought you could be helpful to them?"

"How?" Emma asked, confused. This had been her state of mind for too long. Life had become confusing from the moment she'd met Maxine. She didn't like the tone of Alison's voice though.

"Okay, whatever. Look, I'm going to come back later. I'm tired."

She turned to unlock the door, freezing when the felt the pressure in the center of her back, the unmistakable sound of a gun being cocked, tumbling her back into an ongoing nightmare.

"You wanted to talk to Meg, huh? Why don't we go find her?"

"What is this?" Emma felt herself tremble. She hoped Alison had better control with her finger on the trigger. This couldn't be happening. Alison couldn't shoot her. Emma was supposed to find a job and be out of the house by Christmas, start a new life.

"This is me staying on the safe side." Alison laughed, but it was Maxine's contemptuous, sarcastic tone that Emma heard. "Open the door, slowly. It's important that you don't make any mistake now, you hear me, Emma? If we meet anyone, you smile and say we'll go for a walk. Otherwise, I'll shoot them."

Emma nodded, after several moments in which she felt paralyzed, unable to move, unable to stop history from repeating itself. Her fault. Someone was going to spin the story, and if she didn't end up dead today, she'd be going back to prison. She couldn't hold back the tears.

"Get yourself together, damn it," Alison seethed.

All this time, Meg had been an obvious enemy, but by far not the worst. Emma thought that her instincts left a lot to be desired. She wiped her face, straightening. No one else was going to get harmed because of her.

❧

The attendants of the meeting were, so far, the same Jayce had seen before in the kitchen of the house, plus a couple of friends of the "cousins". The nervous tension in the room spoke clearly of the guest they were still waiting for, a man named Hammer, which, of course, wasn't his real name, but went with his reputation.

Jayce's undercover assignment had started months ago with getting herself arrested in a neighborhood on Hammer's turf, some jail time, and uncovering all the threads to the house, Meg Connolly's alleged cousins and a yet unnamed party.

All of this was supposed to lead them to Hammer whose dealing in prescription drugs was only the tiny tip of an enormous iceberg. The way they could casually write off the amount of cocaine found in Emma's room spoke volumes. Jayce shuddered, glad to know that Emma was safe at the department. It made concentrating on the task at hand a lot easier.

Almost comical, the silence that settled over the room once the car pulled up behind the house. Hammer was a man you wouldn't recognize on the street, rather unspectacular. The men who joined him made this more of a spectacle with their black clothes and stance that made concealed weapons very obvious.

Jayce stayed in the corner, hands in the pockets of her coat. She didn't have to pretend hard—she was freezing and wanted to get out of here as soon as possible. Impatiently, she waited for the inspection of the money and the merchandise. As soon as the deal was done, she could give the sign...

The scene came to a halt when rapid footsteps were to be heard, and Alison came running in.

With relief, Jayce noticed that all eyes were on the new arrival, so no one had caught her surprise. She sent a questioning look to Meg, who shrugged, just as much in the dark.

"We have a situation," Alison said.

One of Hammer's bodyguards came in after her. When Jayce saw who he had with him, everything changed in a heartbeat.

Emma looked frightened, and there was a bruise on the side of her face. She hadn't lost her courage though.

"It's a trap," she yelled. "Jayce, they know!"

Furious, Alison slapped her, while Jayce only had a split-second to alert her colleagues and duck behind some old crates before the place erupted in gunfire.

❧

It was somewhat of a miracle that she didn't get shot, Emma thought as she sat in the back of the ambulance, unable to stop shaking. It was a testimony to the quick and efficient work of Jayce and her colleagues.

She pulled the edges of the blanket around her even tighter, feeling cold and lost. Her aching head from when Alison had hit her—twice—wasn't even the worst of her concerns. Alison, and possibly Terri as well, had pretended to be her friend, when in reality, they were probably the most dangerous people in the house.

Jayce had pretended to be someone in Emma's life as well. She was a cop. Getting close to the women in the house and figuring out how much they knew about the drug deal was part of her job.

Stubbornly, Emma blinked back tears. She should have known. Even prison hadn't taught her. She was still too gullible, too trusting, the easiest prey. How lucky that this time, she'd only been fooled by one of the good guys—well, girl, in this case. Emma didn't feel lucky. She was feeling sick.

"Hey, are you okay? Thanks for saving me in there."

"No problem," she murmured.

Jayce lingered, fidgeting as she was probably searching for words. Emma didn't need an explanation. She was afraid that words would only make things worse.

"I'm sorry," Jayce said eventually.

"I feel stupid for telling you to be careful all the time." It went without saying that this wasn't the only thing Emma felt stupid for. "You were good. I believed everything you said."

"Emma..." Jayce sounded wistful and a bit hurt. "Not everything was about the job. What happened between us..."

"Oh, spare me. I get it. It can get lonely when you have to hide all the time. You take what you can get. I'm not complaining."

"Those were some dangerous people," Jayce said, as if Emma needed a reminder. The gunshots were still ringing in her ears. She wasn't even sure how she'd made it into the shelter of a nook in the wall, covering until one of the cops found her and got her out of the danger zone.

"What about Meg?"

"She was my informant pretty much from the start."

"Oh, great. She fooled me too. You all did—but don't make too much of it. I'm just easy to fool."

"That's not true. Listen..." Jayce cast a glance over to where a cluster of uniformed cops stood. "We need to wrap this up, okay? I was hoping—"

"No!" Emma interrupted her sharply. "I don't like the sound of that. Hoping is for losers. Whenever I tried that, it blew up in my face and...I don't want that anymore. I need to be by myself. I need to think about what happened."

"Okay. I understand." Jayce laid a hand on her shoulder, keeping it there for a moment. "I want you to have time to think. Maybe if you give it some time, you'll let me explain." Without waiting for an answer, she turned and walked away. Emma's vision blurred.

❧

Kitty, Daniel's wife, looked thoughtful. "If you say she can do the job, I'm sure it's true..."

"It is," Jayce insisted. "She caught a bad break, got screwed over. From what I learned, she could easily sue the city. Her lawyer was a joke."

"I didn't think you were hiring anyone fulltime yet," Daniel, who had walked in with large coffees for all of them, said. "You're going to get her a new lawyer too?" he addressed Jayce.

"I might," she said, trying not to sound defensive. "It's all in the serve and protect package. They system did her wrong. We can do something right."

"Well, I'm in." Kitty put a generous amount of sugar into her coffee, making Jayce wince. "Not just because I'm feeling generous, which I am, but I could really use the help. The time before the holidays is crazy."

"You're going to give her a call? I love you, Kitty." Jayce gave her partner's wife a heartfelt embrace, until Daniel said, "Okay, that's enough. That's my wife."

Kitty laughed. "I don't think it's me Jayce has set her eyes on."

"I want to make sure she has some support and can get back on her feet. She didn't deserve to get mixed up with all of this—and she warned me."

"Yes, and we're grateful for that," Daniel said, all bantering forgotten for the moment. "I can ask around, but maybe you'll make sure first she really wants to go to court. One step at a time. You don't want to overwhelm her."

Jayce leaned back in her chair, guiltily wondering if the steps she was taking already reached too far. She had something to make up for, no doubt. She remembered watching Emma browse the aisles of the bookstore, her longing so obvious. She needed someone to give her a chance. Jayce wasn't fooling herself. She was hoping Emma might give her another chance too, but that might not happen. They both needed to move on from the past. Jayce didn't yet want to give up on the idea that they could do it together.

⌘

Emma let herself into her apartment with a sigh of relief. She loved the normalcy of coming home from her work, having said work in the first place. Kitty was a pleasant person to work for, though not a day went by without a reminder that her husband Daniel was Jayce's partner, now that she was back to the regular job.

Jayce didn't come by the store, leaving Emma the space she'd asked for. Having some time to herself, room to breathe did her some good. She didn't have to worry about anyone in the next room, or the next cell. The small studio was all hers, and she had even decorated it for the holidays with a small tree. She had a pile of books from the library, food in the fridge...she should be grateful. She had everything she'd dreamed of in those long days in prison, and later, in the house. A paycheck, a roof over her head, and people leaving her alone. That was what she had wanted all along, wasn't it?

After a shower and changing into more comfortable clothes, she sat on the couch and opened the small envelope Kitty had given her, containing a little holiday bonus and...Emma sighed. She wanted to call that number, but she hadn't even thanked Jayce for getting her the job. Truth be told, she was a bit scared of talking to her, of having foolish hopes. Emma was sure that Jayce had long moved on. She wasn't dealing with all that baggage for real, it had been part of her undercover persona just like...At times, she'd like to curse Jayce for drawing her into that place, for making her think she could be with someone again and not end up getting hurt. Well, she was hurt and lonely now. Emma would have never thought she'd feel like that, once out of the halfway house. Marley had even sent her a card, congratulating her.

The doorbell jolted Emma out of her dire thoughts. She contemplated not opening, but maybe the person on the other side of the door was feeling just like her? A couple of hours ago, she'd been glad to escape the rush at Kitty's paper store. Now she wanted to hear someone's voice, even if that someone was trying to sell something, or asking for money for their charity. She opened the door to no one.

"What kind of joke is that?" Emma said out loud, then she heard the small sound, and her gaze was dropping to the floor. In the padded basket, something was moving. Something white, furry and...

"Oh my God." She dropped to her knees and picked up the kitten, amazed at how light and tiny it was. Emma couldn't quite make sense of the scene, but there was one thing that was for sure.

"Let's get you inside real quick, because there's no way I'm giving you back." It had to be Kitty and Daniel's idea, right? No one else would be so crazy as to put this tiny being in front of her door...but she'd never told Kitty or Daniel about that dream. She had only told one person.

"I had the hope that with her help, I could bribe you into letting me in," Jayce said ruefully.

"You...you are crazy. You already got me the job, for which I'm thankful, and I'm sorry I never called, but this is too much. I can't—"

"Please, don't freak out. I have a litter box and food in the car. Just to get you started."

Emma didn't know what to say without digging herself deeper, so she stood, clutching the kitten, staring at Jayce while she was trying to figure out what was happening.

"There's something else I wanted to talk to you about. You could have your case reopened, clear your name. Daniel knows someone who could help us with that. Emma, I know I told you some lies, but I had to, for your protection." Jayce laughed unhappily. "Which didn't work out so well after all. Asking Kitty for a favor was no big deal. I just wanted you to know...what I said about the accident and the time after, that was real, and everything between us was real too. I wanted to stay away from you, but I couldn't."

Emma knew she was at a threshold, in more than one sense. She could simply step back and resume her old ways, looking over her shoulder, running scared. She could do the opposite.

The fantasy had kept her going on some days, during her prison sentence, when she'd felt like there was no more reason to go on—the life she could have one day, working, a living space that allowed her the privacy she'd longed for, a pet and just maybe, someone she could be close to without feeling smothered. In her fantasy, that person had been shadowy and faceless. Not any longer.

"Can I come in?" Jayce asked softly.

"Merry Christmas," Emma said, holding the door open, her heart beating faster with the decision made, and all it implied. "What's her name?"

"Elvis."

"What? She's a girl. Oh—I get it. As in *Jailhouse Rock*?"

Jayce looked mortified. "I swear that thought never crossed my mind. *Blue Christmas* was on the radio when I came here."

"Okay."

The smile that lit up Jayce's face told Emma that opening doors on Christmas day was a good idea—even sometimes, against better judgment.

FAMILIAR PLACES

The sky didn't fall.

Almost three months after leaving the halfway house, Emma still worked at *Kitty's Greeting Cards & Stationary*, she lived in the same small but cozy apartment, and Jayce kept coming around. It was much better than she'd ever imagined, almost too good to be true which was why that bit of nagging worry always remained. Part of it was caution that had served her well in the past years, in prison and the subsequent months in the halfway home. The other part was naked fear that one simple turn of events could send her life into a tailspin once more.

At the moment, it didn't look that way—Jayce had come by in the late afternoon, and they'd had dinner together after catching up on each other's day and week. Curled up on the couch next to Jayce, she smiled, remembering details of the catching up that made her regret she had to sleep alone tonight. Jayce was about to leave for an all-night stakeout, except she seemed just as comfortable as Emma.

"I guess I really have to go," she murmured against Emma's neck before reluctantly moving to get up. "At least, this will be over soon. No more nights for a while."

Emma didn't ask. For one, she was still somewhat distracted. She didn't inquire more about Jayce's work than she was willing to share. It was safer for both of them, easier to forget it was because of Jayce's work that they had met in the first place.

"Thank God," she said. She got up as well to walk Jayce to the door, Elvis leaving her place in her favorite chair to follow them and brush against their legs. She didn't want Jayce to leave either, though in her case, it was probably about the treats Jayce brought her on a regular basis. "Do you have plans for Friday night? We could have dinner again." Sometimes, Emma still couldn't determine if she sounded hopeful or desperate, making suggestions like this. They spent time together on a regular basis, as much as their respective schedules allowed. They were dating. At some point she'd have to get over her doubts.

"Friday is fine, but can I take you out?" Jayce asked. "I'd like you to meet some friends of mine."

"That would be nice," Emma said a tad too quickly.

"Are you sure?"

"Yes, it's fine. You're going to be late."

"I know." Jayce turned to her to kiss her, deeply, and for a moment, Emma forgot all her reservations regarding aforementioned friends. They came back to her as soon as Jayce had left, and Emma walked back into her living room that now felt too empty and claustrophobic at the same time.

She had done everything she could to move on from a disastrous relationship that had ended with both Emma and her ex in prison, caught the lucky break she'd dreamed of during those never-ending days. That didn't mean everything was bright and easy now. Emma wasn't worried about history repeating itself, like when she first started hanging out with Maxine's friends, neglecting her own more and more, because Maxine was jealous and slowly isolating her.

Jayce wasn't that kind of person. Emma knew it for certain. Not just because she was a cop. Even in her undercover persona, when they'd met at the halfway house, Jayce had been kind. The problem was, most of her friends were cops too. After Jayce's last case, some of them had to know about Emma, her record, the sentence she'd served.

What they didn't know was how much Emma still wished she could turn back time. If she had found out about Maxine's plans, if she had been able to deter her…There was no point in going back there. She couldn't undo what had happened.

She could only cling to this brighter future with everything she had.

Emma was so deeply lost in thought that the sound of the telephone made her jump, which, in turn, made Elvis jump.

"Sorry about that," she muttered to the kitten and went to pick up. "Hello?"

There was a long pause. "Hello?" she tried again, shaking her head. "I guess not."

"Emma, is that you?" an unfamiliar voice asked a split-second before she had the chance to hang up.

"Who is this?"

"I don't know if you remember me. My name is Deirdre. I'm…"

"Maxine's sister," Emma said, as the world faded out for a brief, disturbing moment. "What do you want?" Wrong. She should have ended the call. Emma remembered Deirdre from the trial, and she didn't think anything good could come out of this interaction. Maxine had screwed her over. There was nothing else to the story.

"I heard you're out. I was hoping we could talk."

"Who told you?"

Deirdre didn't answer her question. "Maxine keeps asking about you. So—I wanted to see how you are."

"That's none of Maxine's business, or yours."

"Come on, after all these years, you still want to put all of this on her?"

This was going exactly into the direction Emma had feared it would. She had to remind herself that this time, she had options. One of them was not to listen any longer.

"All of this *is* on her. I'm sorry, I can't do this. Don't call again."

She went back to the couch, Elvis following closely, sensing that Emma was upset. She turned on the TV but didn't pay attention to the program. How had Deirdre found out about her, and why did she even care? Why did Maxine care?

Fear made her stomach clench suddenly and painfully. Maxine wasn't going to get out anytime soon, was she? No one had ever doubted Maxine had pulled the trigger.

Maybe she could ask Jayce to check for her, but then she would have to tell her about Deirdre's call. Emma would rather forget about it. Especially when she was about to meet friends of hers, she didn't want to remind Jayce of the past. This didn't have to mean anything. Deirdre and Maxine were trying to mess with her, nothing new there.

This time, she wouldn't let them.

It was still early, but Emma decided to turn in anyway. She had worked longer hours lately, as one of her co-workers kept cancelling her shifts, and there was some decorating for the next holiday to do.

Being around so many happy wishes and brightly colored paper would do her some good. She had to make it to Friday night.

Consoled by those thoughts, Emma curled up in the sheets they had shared earlier. Her life was back on track. It wasn't just her imagination.

There were a couple of more calls in the morning before Emma had even finished her coffee, Deirdre's voice sounding pleading and urgent on the voicemail. Spooked, she left fresh food and water for Elvis and then fled her apartment.

She had already filled a box with paper hearts and roses by the time her boss Kitty arrived.

"Oh, good, at least someone is taking this seriously. It looks like Samantha is not coming in this week—at all."

"I can do Saturday if you like." The words were out of Emma's mouth before she remembered that she'd made plans for Friday night which, she'd hoped, would include sleeping in on Saturday. Jayce would understand though.

Emma was well aware that Samantha thought she was cozying up to the boss. Her co-worker didn't realize how happy Emma was to have this job, and how important it was to her to keep Kitty happy. The other girl who took care of the online store didn't seem to have an opinion yet.

"Are you sure?" Kitty sighed. "That would be great. I don't know what's up with her lately. If she told me anything at least...We might be friends, but she's still officially on the payroll, so it would be nice if she showed up once in a while." She took a look around. "Wow, but you've been busy. When did you get here?"

Emma shrugged. "About an hour ago, I think."

"Everything okay? You look tired."

"Sorry. I stayed up a little too long."

"Hm." Kitty gave her a speculative grin. "Can I ask?"

"No, you can't," Emma said, relieved that the conversation was going into safer waters. Kitty's friendly curiosity about the state of her relationship with Jayce she could handle. "Are we doing St. Patrick's Day or heading straight to Easter?"

Kitty laughed. "All right, I get it. Let's do St. Patrick's—we might not have a parade, but everyone can use a little luck. I, for one, am very lucky you came to work for me. I'd like to make it up to you though if I have to keep you here on the weekend again. Why don't you and Jayce come over for dinner on Sunday?"

This was the old, new normal, before and after Maxine: A regular job, paying the rent, dinner with friends every now and then.

"I'd love to. I assume if Daniel is there, Jayce will have time too."

Daniel, Kitty's husband, was Jayce's partner at work, and the four of them had had dinner a couple of times before. When confronted with it in small doses, Emma was fine with Jayce's work environment. Daniel and Kitty had arranged for her to work at the store, and they knew the whole story. They wouldn't judge her.

"Yeah. Let's hope they will want to spend any more time together after this week."

They shared a smile, both of them having listened to their respective lovers complain about boring stakeouts for a few days now. There was something else they didn't need to say out loud, Emma thought. Boring stakeouts were good. Boring stakeouts meant no flying bullets.

Once opening hours started, Emma was busy advising customers on the most appropriate choice of greeting cards for all occasions, selling pens and stationary. While this wasn't the career she had envisioned at one point in her life, she was grateful to be working here—not just because it was a job to pay the rent, or because Kitty was the most easygoing boss she'd ever had. The people who came in mostly had something to celebrate, a happy story. Weddings, birthdays, Valentine's...There was the occasional condolences card, but even those customers meant to show another person they cared. The pay wasn't outrageous, but it was enough, and Samantha's increasing absences had put more money into Emma's bank account.

She had sold a card to the proud grandmother of a girl who had passed her driving test on the third attempt when Kitty came in from the office, her expression serious.

"Emma? There's a phone call for you. It sounds important...You can go in the office. I can take over here for a bit."

"Thanks." Emma's heart sank. It couldn't be, right? There was no way Deirdre could have found out where she worked, except...She had found Emma's phone number already. Emma had no hope that this could be anyone else, because everyone she cared for—Jayce, Kitty and Daniel—was accounted for.

"What the hell are you doing?" she asked, more resigned and scared than angry when she picked up the phone. "I told you not to call anymore."

"I have no choice. I need to ask you a favor, and I need to talk to you in person."

"No!"

Emma leaned on the wooden desk, desperately needing something to anchor herself in the present. Everything would be okay. She didn't have to do anything Deirdre told her.

"Emma, please, don't be like that. You're out. You have a life. Maxine will be locked away for a long time to come, so you could do me that favor at least. It hasn't been easy for any of us."

There were many things Emma could have said to her about how nothing had been easy for her from the moment Maxine came into her life. All she could do was sink into Kitty's leather chair and try to breathe, her eyes welling up with emotion, guilty relief. Maxine wasn't going to get out. Thank God.

"I still have no idea what we could have to talk about. I don't want you to tell Maxine anything about me. If you need money, I don't have any."

"Look, I know you're still pissed at Maxine, but I'm telling you, she had a lot of time to think about what happened. I'll come by tonight. You have it good now, Emma. It won't hurt you to be decent to someone who's not that lucky."

This time, it was Deirdre who hung up on her. Emma sat in the same place, staring into nothing for several minutes, trying to get a grip on her emotions, drawn back into memories that were never far behind. She had worked so hard to stay under the radar after the unthinkable happened—in prison, and in the halfway house. Without a doubt, some people had higher odds stacked against them. Maybe she should hear Deirdre out, if for nothing else, then for good karma. Emma didn't want to.

"Are you okay?"

"Yes, I'm fine. I'm so sorry about that. I told her not to call at work." She jumped to her feet and went past her boss, back to the store. Kitty followed her, locking the front door.

"What are you doing?"

"*We* are going to lunch," Kitty said, "and you're going to tell me what you're so worried about. You hardly ever take any breaks. It's okay to receive a call at work, especially when it's urgent."

"I...I really don't want to talk about it." Emma laughed unhappily. "It makes me feel like I'm jinxing everything. That sounds crazy, doesn't it?"

"Now I'm worried," Kitty admitted. "Who was that?"

"Don't tell Jayce. Deirdre is my ex's sister."

"Is she harassing you?"

"No...no, not really," Emma stumbled through the half lie. "She wants to talk, make amends maybe, I don't know. I guess I'm not that good a person, because I don't feel very forgiving."

Kitty regarded her with affection. "If you ask me, there's nothing you owe to anybody here, just the opposite. You should tell Jayce."

"Yes, maybe. I will," Emma added though she had no intention to do so. She couldn't risk Kitty taking matters into her own hands.

"Good. Now let's go eat. I'm starving," Kitty declared, laying an arm around Emma's shoulders. "Don't worry. Everything will be fine."

Emma didn't mean to be petty and jaded, but she couldn't help thinking, *I heard that one before.*

❦

"God, I can't wait for it to be Friday," Jayce exclaimed, for the umpteenth time trying to find a comfortable position in the passenger seat. After all those hours, tonight, the nights before, it wasn't going to happen. She was tired of waiting for their elusive suspect to show up, doubting he would anytime soon. Somebody might have tipped him off. He was probably long gone—but as a long as Lieutenant Chomsky thought the parents' house was still worth watching, they would be here for a while longer, until Thursday, starting again on Monday.

Not that she minded those delightful afternoons spent at Emma's apartment, but she would have liked to go back to a more regular schedule soon. Her muscles cramped from being cooped up in the narrow space, and her sleep cycle was as messed up as ever.

Well, the latter could have been from the musings that kept her up. Jayce was happy and in love these days, which was nothing short of amazing. As far as she was concerned, they still had a long way ahead. Emma had a good case if she wanted to sue for the injustice that had happened to her and clear her record. Jayce had conferred with a lawyer who was a friend of hers, ready to get started whenever Emma wanted to...

The problem was Emma tended to evade the subject as soon as Jayce brought it up.

"Something tells me you've had a pretty good week already."

She made a face. "Stop it right there."

"What?" Daniel asked, amused. "You were late, the second time this week. You're never late. It doesn't take a lot to put the pieces together."

Jayce couldn't deny that. "I'm getting increasingly more impatient sitting in this car for hours, with no result other than the need for a good chiropractor."

"Yeah, tell me about it. Kitty asks if you guys wanted to come for dinner on Sunday."

"Sure. Drinks on Friday?"

"Not sure. I think I'll want to spend the first night off at home."

"Just for an hour or so? I was going to bring Emma. I think she'd be more comfortable if there was another familiar face."

"I think you worry too much," he pointed out. "Emma will be fine."

"Yes, I know. I don't want to take any chances."

"All right then. An hour."

"Thanks," she said, relieved. "You're the best."

"Any chance the best is going to get some fresh coffee?"

Jayce was out of the car before she even answered. "Your chances are excellent. You have no idea how much I wanted to get out of here."

"Oh, I do," Daniel mumbled. "You only told me ten times or so."

Jayce held up her index finger in warning. "Don't push your luck. You don't want me to come back with decaf."

There was no other customer in the corner store on the other side of the street. Jayce thought it would be beyond irony if their suspect showed up right this moment. She got a black coffee for herself and a caramel latte, Daniel's favorite. Just thinking about the sweet concoction made her teeth hurt. She added a couple of donuts to her purchase, wincing at the cliché. Everything would be better once they were back to the day shifts, even their diet.

She paid for food and beverages to an exhausted looking store owner and turned to leave, nearly colliding with the customer who had come in, twenty-something, shaggy blond hair, hands buried in the pockets of his read sweater. Jayce couldn't believe her eyes.

Calmly, she put her bag and coffee back on the counter. "I realize I forgot something," she told the owner, before turning to the other man, badge in hand.

"Nathan Dolby, you're under arrest for the attempted murder of..."

He had nowhere to run, but that didn't keep him from trying. With the shelf behind him and the door his only possible exit to escape, he had no choice but to run right into her, tackling them both to the floor.

Being only mildly surprised by his desperate attempt, Jayce had time to react and put the cuffs on him before he could scramble to his feet. "Could have told you that wasn't a good idea. You're not that fast." He glared at her as she notified Daniel.

"I didn't do anything. You can't arrest me just like that."

"Oh, I can, but let's talk about that at the station. Thanks, by the way—for finally showing up. It's all right," Jayce assured the owner who stood, a few feet back, looking alarmed. "My partner is around the corner. We really need that coffee now...It's going to be a long night."

As Daniel walked in, she snuck a sip from her cup, wincing at the pull in her shoulder. A long hot bath and a couple of Tylenol would hopefully do the trick, sometime in the morning.

"Look, man, I did nothing," Nathan tried again during the drive back to the city.

"We will talk about this," Jayce said. "I could think of something not so smart you did ten minutes ago. Besides, trying to club your psychiatrist over the head on the day you have an appointment with him, and leaving the bat behind—also not smart."

He shook his head. "You got it all wrong. I only ran because I knew you wouldn't believe me."

"Well, that didn't help. Don't worry, you'll have a chance to explain all of it."

"You got the wrong guy. Dr. Simmons is the bad guy here."

They had arrived at the station where Nathan would be off to booking. Jayce wondered if Chomsky was still in the building and could be convinced that letting him wait a bit would convince him to do the right thing.

Five minutes later, she stood in Chomsky's office, trying not to fidget under her supervisor's critical gaze.

"I heard it got a bit violent. Shouldn't you have stopped by the hospital?"

"Oh, no, it was nothing. I'd just like to give him some time to think this over before we have the talk with him." Who had told her? She'd have to have a word with Daniel—but that could definitely wait until tomorrow.

"Has he asked for a lawyer?"

Jayce shook her head. At this moment, Daniel came in, quietly closing the door behind him.

"We're ready," he said.

"Let him know what we've got," Chomsky told them. "Tomorrow, we get in the DA, and his attorney, and we can wrap this up. Good work, Finney."

"Thanks, Boss."

Jayce suppressed a sigh. It didn't look like she was going to get out of here anytime soon.

"Friday…"

"Can't come soon enough, I know," Daniel finished her sentence as they made their way to the interrogation room. "Come on, let's get this done. I'm sure Kitty won't mind if Emma comes in a little later tomorrow."

Instead of rewarding the implication with an answer, she shook her head and smiled. It was a good thing she wasn't always this transparent.

Jayce felt only slightly guilty for keeping Emma up past her bedtime. Emma's hands, warm and gentle, felt heavenly on her shoulders, back, and everywhere they touched.

"I'll make it up to you. I promise."

Just not tonight, because she was already half asleep. A chiropractor wasn't necessary after all, not when she had a sympathetic girlfriend to come home to, something, Jayce admitted to herself, she could get used to easily.

"That's okay. I wasn't sleeping." That might be a little white lie. Emma had sounded sleepy over the phone, but once Jayce heard her voice, she couldn't help herself.

"You caught the guy. Congratulations."

"Yeah. Strange case. He didn't give us much of a challenge in the end, but he still claims he went at the doctor in self-defense, hitting him over the read right there at the clinic." Emma halted for a moment, reminding Jayce she was the first to know that things weren't always what they seemed to be. If someone looked guilty, it didn't always mean they were. Jayce was convinced though that Emma and Nathan Dolby had nothing in common. The statements of Dr. Simmons and his employees all pointed in the same direction. "I'm sorry. You don't need that kind of image in your head."

"It's okay. I'm glad you're here." Even exhausted as she was, Jayce couldn't ignore the forlorn tone of Emma's voice. She turned around, and Emma lay down next to her.

"What's going on? You're not still nervous about Friday night? We don't have to go if you don't want to. Dinner at home will be fine, since we have something on Sunday apparently."

"No, that's not it. I'm okay. Don't worry." Emma gave her a wistful smile. "I guess I'm a bit stressed whenever you're around people who swing baseball bats at others."

"Well, he's not swinging anything at anyone right now. Thanks for harboring me on such short notice. Let's get some sleep now, okay?"

Emma settled into her embrace without objection, and a moment later, Jayce slipped into the deep uninterrupted sleep she'd been hoping for.

Despite Daniel's reassurances, Emma was up early, already dressed for work when Jayce was barely awake, only now realizing why she wasn't in her own bed.

"I'm really sorry, but the other girl keeps cancelling, and we have to do her work too. Oh, I forgot to tell you, Kitty asked me to come in on Saturday. We can still go out on Friday though." Emma handed her a robe that was a little short on her—barely decent, in fact. "Breakfast is ready. I'm sorry; I'm in a bit of a hurry. I can sit down for a few minutes...Sorry, I know this isn't what you had in mind."

"Take a moment. Breathe. It's fine." Emma took a deep breath when Jayce laid her hands on her shoulders. "Let's have breakfast. I'll put on some clothes and drive you to the store, and if you're a couple of minutes late, blame it on me."

"You're a bad influence." Emma couldn't suppress the smile.

"Maybe. I learned that life is too short." Standing in the doorway, Elvis gave an affirming *meow*. "See? She agrees with me."

"I see. I'm outnumbered." Emma laughed softly. "Okay, girls. Let's get something to eat."

They had barely sat down when the doorbell rang, the sound making Emma cringe. She got up, hesitated, and then went to answer the door.

A neighbor on her way to work had decided to stop for a bit of chitchat and voice her irritation about the water being turned off for a few hours today due to construction on the street. Emma exchanged a few polite words with her before she closed the door again, looking relieved when she returned to the table.

"If this drags on, you can always use my shower," Jayce offered. "Or tub." She hadn't gotten to her hot bath yet, but it would be even better sharing it with Emma.

Sometimes, she had to make herself stop, wondering if she was moving much too fast for Emma who had been so careful and hesitant to trust, back in the halfway house. Jayce understood that it would take her a little while longer to feel certain that she had firm ground under her feet. Meanwhile, Jayce wanted her to know that things were good, between them, in the long run, even if they still had that lawsuit to discuss.

"I might do that," Emma said with a longing look.

Jayce ruefully admitted to herself that she might not have the same ideas. There would be time to find out. Soon.

❦

Much to Emma's relief, Deirdre seemed to have gotten the message. For a couple of days, she returned from work finding no new message. There was hot water—this, though, was almost a disappointment, not that she needed an excuse to take advantage of the comfort of Jayce's more spacious bathroom. No, because even though Emma's story might be a difficult sell, Jayce still wanted her to meet her friends, regardless of the fact that they might have questions.

Maxine had often mocked Emma in the presence of her friends for no reason. Looking back, Emma had a hard time understanding why she'd stayed so long. Maybe she'd given up on herself long before she found herself in an interrogation room, with a stranger's blood on her hands. For longer than Emma cared to remember, she'd been blaming herself, convinced she didn't deserve any better. That was making it so hard to accept that "better" had finally arrived. She still wasn't sure whether she was worth it.

Troubled by those thoughts, she went to fill Elvis's bowl when the doorbell rang again. Maybe it was Stacy from the other side of the hallway, complaining about the inconvenience of the construction site again.

Emma had a place where she could come and go as she pleased, lock the door behind her if she wanted to, with no one on the other side controlling the key. There was nothing much in the daily life that could truly inconvenience her.

Jayce showing up in the middle of the night had been a wonderful surprise—maybe she wanted to do it again.

Emma opened the door and immediately took a step backwards.

"Hey, Emma. I'm glad you're home." Deirdre came inside without waiting for an invitation and walked right to the couch where she sat down. "Nice place. You really turned your life around, didn't you?"

Emma tightened the belt of her robe. Deirdre was only a few years older than Maxine. The similarities in looks, body language and tone of voice were disconcerting.

"Why are you here?" she asked, aware of her voice going up a notch. "I have an early start tomorrow," she added, faintly hoping Deirdre would react the polite way, acknowledge that she wasn't welcome, or at least leave.

"Don't worry. This won't take long. I don't get it why you're so antsy. You have everything now. Maxine got the rougher deal."

"Because she killed somebody!"

"Well, yeah, I didn't come to talk about that. What's done is done. You could help me now."

This couldn't be good. If Emma hadn't known already, the uncomfortable hard beat of her heart would have alerted her. She might feel a tad awkward about being in a room full of cops, but Deirdre made her uneasy in a visceral way—maybe because she was related to the woman who nearly succeeded in ruining her life.

"Why would I do that?"

Deirdre's gaze was calculating. "One small favor and I'm out of your hair. That's not so bad, is it? I assume you want to keep all the pretty things that are in your life now. Look," she opened her bag and retrieved a wooden box about six by four inches, "You keep this for me for a few days, I'll come get it, and that's it."

"What's in that box?" Emma asked suspiciously.

"You don't need to know. In fact, it's better if you don't. It's not going to blow up on you."

"Why would I believe anything you say?"

"Believe it or not." Deirdre put the box on the table. "Maxine really cared about you. She says I can trust you."

Emma wasn't sure why she should take Maxine's word for anything. She didn't know what to say, other than she wanted Deirdre gone from her apartment, and Maxine from her mind, but the words didn't come out. She had felt like this before, like she couldn't do anything but watch the events unfold, numb, paralyzed.

"I can't. Why would you come to me?"

This was beyond ironic. Emma had heard the stories of other women who had served their sentence and then were contacted by former associates, dragged back into the life they wanted to leave behind. She'd been certain she wouldn't be one of them.

"Get out, now, and take your package. Whether it's drugs, or whatever, I don't want anything to do with it."

Deirdre smiled. "Maxine also told me you'd be difficult. She might have put up with this shit, but I won't. You have no idea how much trouble I can make for you in your little paradise here. You don't open it, you don't ask any questions. In a few days, I'll come pick it up. That's all you need to know. Nice talking to you, Emma." She leaned close enough for Emma to shrink back. "This box had better be in the same condition I gave it to you. Otherwise...well, you don't want to find out."

Long after the door fell into the lock, Emma stayed motionless in her chair, unable to do anything but stare at the conspicuous box as if it might jump at her at any moment. Maxine wasn't that kind of criminal though, and she had nothing to feel vengeful about. Something to do with money, drugs—Maxine had shared with her that she had dealt a little. She claimed she had stopped long before they started dating. Emma wasn't buying those reassurances any longer. Whatever was in that box, it was bad enough that Deirdre needed it out of her house for a few days and...what if she needed another favor after that? And another?

Oh God, what have I done?

Reality started to sink in, that someone could suspect her no matter how careful she acted from this moment on, if she got her prints on the object in question, or if she tried hard to avoid it. Given her past experience with Maxine, she had no reason not to believe Deirdre when she said she could cause her trouble.

She couldn't go back to prison, not for one day.

Maybe that nagging inner voice had been right, and she didn't deserve any better.

Work was helpful, but even in the cheerful surroundings Emma found it incredibly hard to keep the smile on her face. After a couple of customers in need of condolences cards came in, she excused herself and cried in the small kitchen.

"I'm sorry. It's like a conspiracy, they're all coming in today."

When she didn't get any answer, Kitty came closer.

"Emma, is everything all right? Is that person still bothering you?"

"Yes...no." She struggled to get her bearings again. "I am so sorry. I'll be there in a minute."

"Have you talked to Jayce yet?"

"There was no time," Emma said, praying that Kitty would buy her evasion. She wasn't so lucky.

"Make time. She can help you, and she will. There's no shame in asking someone who knows about these things."

"Jayce doesn't know everything." For one, she didn't know about the box Emma had finally hidden in the back of her closet, but that wasn't how Kitty interpreted her words. She pulled herself a chair and sat across from Emma.

"I won't pretend I know the first thing about everything you went through with that woman, but I want you to know we care about you. So, if you need anything, just say it. Whatever she told you, or the sister, you don't need to believe any of it."

Emma got up and washed her face at the sink. "I'm okay. I need to go back to work."

The steady stream of customers slowed down in the afternoon, allowing her to put up some more shamrocks.

Emma knew she'd been incredibly lucky. Most of the time, she felt lucky, but every once in a while, it seemed like all that luck was a house of cards that could come tumbling down any day. Deirdre and that stupid box could be the beginning, and what would come after that?

"That looks nice. You really have a knack for this kind of thing," Kitty observed.

"Thank you. About earlier..."

"It's okay. I made some coffee, for when you're finished up there." Kitty was silent for a moment, and Emma continued to fasten the garland.

"Can I ask you an awfully personal question? Maxine...was she ever violent?"

She could have made a flat joke right here, something like *"I was expecting that kind of question from the cop I'm dating,"* but instead, Emma was quiet, something that didn't go unnoticed with her inquisitive boss. The silence dragged on long enough for Kitty to become worried, Emma was sure. She needed to come up with an answer, any answer.

"Maxine got angry sometimes," she said. "Shoving people, that kind of thing. Not all the time, but...I guess you could call it that."

Emma was angry at herself, right this moment, for not seeing the signs when she still could have gotten out, before something terrible happened—for letting Deirdre in last night. She really did attract trouble, didn't she? She stepped down from the ladder, reluctantly facing Kitty. "How did you know?"

Kitty smiled wistfully. "Never assume that you're the only one who made bad choices once in their lives. You can come back from that, no matter what anyone says." She hugged Emma gently. "Talk to Jayce. You have the right to protect yourself. That Deirdre person needs to understand you don't want anything to do with her or her sister."

"Thank you so much. Everything is such a mess right now."

"It doesn't need to be, believe me."

It was with a lighter heart that Emma arrived at her home, off work half an hour earlier, with more than enough time to get ready for an evening out with Jayce. Maybe Kitty was right, and Jayce could really help her. She didn't take Deirdre's threats lightly, but this time, she had people in her life that cared about her and believed her.

This time would be different.

As she went through her closet in search of a suitable outfit, the box never quite completely out of her mind, Emma's gaze fell on the dress she'd worn on New Year's Eve, the first real date she had gone on with Jayce. Never mind that this little blue dress came from a thrift store and the shoes had been marked down three times. Emma had made some adjustments to the dress and spent a wonderful night in, and later, out of it, filled with hope for the future.

Was that feeling still true? Could she *dare*? Emma picked a purple dress that Kitty had given her a few weeks into her employment with the store.

"Please, don't think of it the wrong way," she'd said. "My friend Clare has a bit of a shopping disorder. Some of the stuff she gives away has never been worn. She's your size, so I thought...Just try it on."

She'd been on her own for a few weeks only, and already there were people in her life she owed so much to. Deirdre was not one of them—Kitty was right about that.

"You look beautiful." Jayce greeted her with a kiss. "I can't tell you how glad I am this week is finally over!"

Emma had to smile at her enthusiasm, amazed how different she could be from the undercover persona Emma got to know at the halfway house, enigmatic and troubling. Back in those days, Emma had admitted the instant attraction, even though she wasn't sure she could trust Jayce Turner, a woman who obviously had secrets and was hanging with a dangerous crowd.

Detective Finney's story was a different one. Emma knew she was safe with her—so why didn't those words come over her lips?

"I can imagine," she said instead.

"Are you ready? I promise you won't have to make small talk all night. Besides, Daniel will be there too."

"I'll be okay. Don't worry." If she said it often enough, maybe she'd start believing it? After tonight, they would go to either Jayce's or Emma's apartment and make time to talk. If not tonight, then sometime tomorrow.

With a bit more confidence than she'd had earlier, Emma stepped inside the bar a few minutes later, Jayce holding the door open for her. She hadn't expected the cheers, freezing.

Jayce shook her head. "Stop it, guys. I made a coffee run and he walked right into it. That's all."

"Well, Finney, you saved us from having to stake out that house for all eternity," a tall blond man all dressed in black said, patting her shoulder.

"Don't listen to what he says," a brunette woman advised. "We're just really happy for you since you're dating again. I almost thought you made her up."

Jayce laughed. "You're embarrassing me. Emma, let me introduce you to the comedians. Ray and Tanya, with whom I have to put up on a daily basis. Meet Emma."

There were friendly smiles and handshakes, and yet Emma felt a tad overwhelmed. Jayce seemed to sense her state of mind. She took Emma's hand. "Come on, let's get a drink. I know the place might not look like it, but they have fabulous cocktails, and the best wings in town."

"I can't wait. I'd like a beer though."

Her relief at how Jayce's friends had greeted her didn't entirely do away with her unease. She still wasn't sure how much they knew, any of them except Daniel. For Jayce's sake, wouldn't it be better to pretend Deirdre's visit had never happened, just sit it out? In any case, Emma didn't want anything stronger than beer tonight, in case she'd still find that courage.

In the course of the evening, Jayce introduced her to more of her colleagues, in a manageable dose. However, when she excused herself to the bathroom, Emma sat on the barstool, clutching her half empty glass and hoping no one would talk to her. Daniel came by to make an order. He lingered, and it occurred to Emma that this might be Jayce's doing.

"I'm okay," she said. "You can go back."

He shrugged. "That's fine. I'm not in a hurry." She gave him a grateful smile.

"So, Emma, what do you do?" Tanya, who had joined them at the counter, asked.

"Why don't you give her a little more time before you start interrogating her?" Daniel stopped her line of questioning. It might be the beer she'd had, or maybe this comment was the last straw. Emma felt irritated with everyone's attempt to shield her from the world, because it was telling her how much she still needed that kind of protection.

"It's not a problem," she said. "I work in Kitty's store." She assumed most co-workers knew about their spouses—if they knew who'd been dating, and who hadn't.

"Oh, I see." Tanya didn't elaborate what she was able to conclude from the piece of information. "That's how you met, I assume?"

Jayce returned this moment, saving Emma from having to answer. "I was afraid this was going to happen." She slapped Daniel's arm. "You didn't do a very good job here, partner."

"Me? I'm waiting for my order...and here it comes. See you."

"I'm sorry, I didn't mean to be nosy," Tanya said. "Okay, I did, but I was nice about it."

"She was," Emma confirmed. "It's not a secret, after all." She searched Jayce's gaze, wondering how many secrets she had kept from her co-workers. They probably didn't know everything that had happened during the undercover assignment.

"I'm sure you were. That's why she always gets to be the good cop."

Tanya laughed, shaking her head. "Don't make her think that all those clichés are true. All right, I get the hint. See you on Monday, Jayce. Have a great night."

It could be, if only Emma was a bit braver.

The harshness of the pressing questions mellowed some, later that night, when they had retreated to Jayce's apartment, and all of Emma's troubles seemed far away indeed—the mysterious package as well as the friendly curiosity of Jayce's co-workers.

"See, that wasn't so bad, right?"

"Not at all," Emma said. "You're pretty good at this." They both laughed. Emma thought this was definitely many steps up from the narrow single bed they'd shared for a couple of nights at the halfway house—with the danger of someone walking in on them. Jayce's place was safe from unwanted visitors and trips down memory lane.

Mostly.

"Thanks for the flattery." Jayce placed a soft kiss on her shoulder. Emma shivered. No, this wasn't like anything she'd experienced in the past years. Deirdre was right, she'd do whatever possible to keep it. With every passing moment, telling the story would only make it worse. Jayce would be mad at her for not coming to her right away, and maybe worse than that…

"Can we talk about the lawsuit?"

Emma stiffened. Jayce interpreted her reaction correctly.

"All I'm asking of you is to meet the lawyer and hear what she can do for you."

"This is over. I don't want to be in a courtroom ever again."

"I don't understand." Jayce sat up with her back against the headboard. "I know it's not easy for you, but you have people who support you now. Just one appointment and we go from there."

"I can't," Emma insisted. "What if I lose? I'd owe legal fees for the rest of my life."

"You won't lose. You know what happened. Maxine lied and she got away with it. Somewhere along the way some people weren't doing their jobs. They owe you. I'm sorry, but that's the only way you'll ever clear your name completely, make it official."

"I served the time," Emma said tersely. "That's official enough for me. I'm sorry if that isn't something you want to tell your friends."

Jayce shook her head. "Forget about my friends. What happened in prison? Did you hurt someone?"

"No! Of course not!"

"What else then? Did you do drugs—use, or sell them?"

"No, I didn't. What are you getting at?"

"I'm trying to figure out why you think you don't deserve this. Any of it. You served your time, yes, but for something you didn't do. You didn't pull the trigger. You didn't even know about that gun."

"Nobody believed me. I don't want to think about this anymore. Can't you get that?"

"I get it, I really do." Jayce pulled her close, and despite the uncomfortable exchange, this was still where Emma wanted to be, close to her. "Once we're through this, you'll have more options."

She didn't elaborate, but Emma could fill in the blanks just the same. Her job in the store had been, and still was, a blessing. No one could say exactly how long it would last. With Samantha showing up one in five of her scheduled days, she was safe for now. She didn't have the impression that Kitty wanted to make any drastic changes soon. A few years from now, things might be different.

"I like working in the store," she said anyway. "You have no idea how happy I am you made that happen, and Kitty gave me a chance. It's good work, and I can't worry about what happens five or ten years from now."

"Will you think about it?" Jayce asked. "If we meet with the lawyer, and it's too much, I'll let it go. I swear."

"I'll think about it," Emma promised, feeling even worse with the additional pressure. "I will."

"It doesn't have to be tomorrow. Emma. Please don't cry."

It certainly wasn't the idea of meeting the lawyer alone that broke her composure. In only a few hours, she'd go back to a job that wasn't as safe as she'd hoped after all. If she was honest, Emma had known, she'd just successfully repressed the thought. Kitty would be asking again—Kitty who at least understood, because she'd made bad choices of her own.

There was no way out of this conversation. She was scared of the moment when Deirdre would return, but more so of what Jayce would think once she knew.

"I made a mistake," she said, the tone of her voice enough to alert Jayce on how serious this was. Emma took a deep breath. She was going to tell all.

Jayce kept her tone soft and reassuring, knowing that she couldn't afford a mistake in this situation, or they would both be in trouble. Part of her was hurt, for Emma, because she had been more afraid of Jayce's reaction than the consequences of this little agreement with her ex's sister—a term to use loosely, because Deirdre had threatened Emma.

She felt a bit irritated with Emma, too, something she couldn't let show at the moment, but mostly angry at a system that had cracks wide enough for good people to fall through them.

Emma wouldn't though, have one mistake determine the rest of her life. Jayce made that decision as a cop, because it was so much easier, clearer. As the woman who had fallen in love with her...She wanted to simultaneously shake her—not a good idea—and protect her, hide her away from the world.

No, being a cop for now would serve both of them better.

The information Emma could give was fairly sketchy, even though it was her apartment in which something likely illegal was hidden, her future on the line. Jayce was certain that Deirdre's antics were a lot more serious than a harmless prank. Finding Emma, her phone number and address, and bothering her after all these years, all of this was obviously part of a bigger plan.

She would find out why Deirdre had gone to these lengths.

"Okay, this is what we do," she said, aware of Emma's anxious gaze on her. "We'll go over there right now and get the box, check what's inside, and then we'll go to the station. You'll call

Deirdre and ask her to come, and depending on what we find, we'll ask her questions. You'll be out of the crosshairs." Jayce didn't realize her rather inappropriate choice of words until Emma flinched. "Sorry. Come on. Let's get this over with."

"Do we really have to go there?" Emma asked, her voice small.

Jayce could imagine that a police station didn't harbor the best of memories for her, but she couldn't think of any other way.

She wasn't naïve. Emma might be innocent in every unexpected twist life had thrown at her, the criminal ex, getting caught up in Jayce's undercover operation at the halfway house, and now with Deirdre. Sadly, most people wouldn't see it that way but find something suspicious about the situation and the string of unlucky coincidences. That was why they had to think ahead.

"It won't take long," she said, hoping she wasn't promising too much.

The box had a simple lock, one that didn't resist much. They had found themselves an empty room, and this early in the morning no one had even stopped to ask. Most of Jayce's colleagues were either finishing their shift or weren't here yet.

Emma stood in the corner, looking as if she still couldn't believe what happened in the past hours—or days. Finally, the lock gave way, and Jayce carefully lifted the lid with gloved hands.

Her jaw must have dropped a little at the content: Neatly rolled bills, altogether a few thousands, she guessed. The box itself was a cheap fabrication. She easily identified and removed the false bottom. Underneath, she found a selection of rings, bracelets and watches.

"Holy sh—" Jayce stopped herself just in time. Emma took a stumbling step forward, steadying herself on the back of the chair.

"I had no idea! This can't be hers, right? Why did she do that? Maxine? Is someone going to come after me for this?"

"Emma. Relax. Sit down." Emma reluctantly obeyed. "Nothing's going to happen to you, okay? I have to make a few calls. We need to get someone in here who'll find out where these pieces came from, and we have to check everything for prints."

"I don't think Deirdre has a record."

"Well, she didn't do this on her own. We'll think of something, I promise. First, we need to know what we're dealing with. Give me a moment. Everything will be fine."

Emma pulled her cardigan tighter around her, and Jayce laid a hand on her shoulder as she punched in the numbers. A Detective Jackson answered. Good. She had met him on a few occasions, and she felt safe trusting him with Emma's predicament.

"Jackson, hi, it's Jayce Finney. I could use your help." She described the pieces found in the box, and he interrupted her right away.

"Can't say for sure until I've seen them, but that sounds like some of the items taken in the recent home invasions on Park Street. I'll be right there. Thanks."

Jayce was hopeful that they could wrap this up pretty soon. She could only imagine how Emma had to feel hunched over in her chair.

They were good. Everything would be fine. Though it was completely irrational, Jayce wondered if Emma might regret that the first woman she dated, back in freedom, was a cop.

"Once we're done here, Deirdre is not going to bother you anymore. That's a good thing, right?"

"It is. Thank you." There wasn't much conviction behind her words. Jayce attributed it to the fact that it wasn't yet 5:00

a.m., and Emma might miss her shift. She was probably exhausted. Keeping secrets did that to a person.

True to his word, Jackson knocked on the door and stepped inside about ten minutes later, his eyes widening when he saw the content on the table.

"My ex's sister brought it to me. She asked me to guard it for her for a few days."

"And you didn't think it was strange?" he asked in disbelief.

"She asked me not to open it. I didn't." Emma sat up straighter, cautious. Jayce hated that she had to put her through this, but with the time already gone since Deirdre's first approach, it was even more important to do everything by the book.

"I wanted to come here," Jayce explained. "There were some threats, and we thought the content might be something that warrants getting the police involved."

Jackson looked from the open box to Emma who was fidgeting in her chair. "She was threatening you? With what?"

"I went to prison because of her sister. She...I don't know if she blames me for everything and wanted to get back at me, or if Maxine told her to do this, I don't know!"

"If you were worried, why didn't you tell anybody?"

"She told *me*," Jayce cut in. "Slow down. Emma is not a suspect. She came to me because she felt something was wrong—which is a good thing. Let's have these processed and we'll see what we do from here."

"What's going to happen to Deirdre?" Emma asked, timid.

"These pieces here," Jackson said grimly, "they come from a string of violent home invasions. The last owner is still in the hospital. Your friend will have a lot to answer for."

"She's not..."

"I'll need your statement too. Finney, can you do that? We'll go find Deirdre in the meantime. Got a last name, Ms. Curtis?"

"I'm not sure. I think she married once. Maxine's last name is Brown."

"All right. Let's see what we can do."

⁂

Before taking Emma's statement, Jayce got them both a coffee from the vending machine, keeping Emma with her the whole time. "This is good news," she said. "You did the right thing."

"I don't know. I don't feel like I've done anything right in a long time. The owner of that store is still dead, and the people who were robbed…"

"Emma. Hey. You're aware that none of this is your fault, right? Yes, you should have told me right away, but it doesn't matter now. The home invasions still would have happened. If Deirdre is involved in any of this, we'll find out, and she'll be held accountable. I know," she added when Emma didn't say anything. "It's not fair. That's why we'll get you out of this as soon as possible and get on with our lives."

"No. I can't." Emma shook her head. "Can't you see that it's always going to be this way? I saw the way he looked at me, and if you weren't here with me, he wouldn't have believed a word I said. I'm not sure he did anyway."

"What are you saying?"

It was early. They hadn't slept all night. It wasn't a good time to have this conversation.

"People are going to ask questions, and not all of them will be as nice as Tanya. It's going to impact your career. I don't want that." Emma shuddered, from cold or emotion, Jayce didn't know. She couldn't believe what she was hearing.

"My career is just fine. You don't need to worry about that."

"I don't think we can do this any longer. I was fooling myself into thinking that after all this, things could be normal for me. I'm sorry."

"Emma, stop. We'll talk about this later."

"There's nothing to talk about," Emma insisted. "I...I'm really grateful you're helping me with this, but when it's over, I won't see you anymore. It's better that way. I should call Kitty. It doesn't look like I'm going to make my shift."

"Emma..."

"Detective Finney, would you join us in my office for a moment?"

When she saw the lieutenant's serious gaze, Jackson standing next to her, Jayce knew her problems had multiplied.

"Can I go home?" Emma asked.

The sympathetic look the lieutenant gave her made Jayce wince.

"We have a few more questions, Ms. Curtis."

Emma nodded, as if she had already expected this turn of events and resigned to it. Jayce got to her feet so rapidly she almost knocked over her chair, and followed Chomsky and Jackson into the lieutenant's office, slamming the door for good measure.

"What the hell is going on? She had nothing to do with any of this." If she was honest, her frustration and worry had a lot less to do with her colleagues than with Emma's suggestion. What would it take to make her see she got this all wrong?

"Deirdre Brown wasn't at her apartment," Jackson said. "Clothes, everything personal is gone. She ran."

"So? Place got a little too hot for her. She knew you were investigating the burglaries. That's why she came to Emma in the first place, I assume."

"Possibly—thinking she could trust her. Why would she risk that amount of money with someone if she didn't expect them to keep their mouth shut?"

Jayce threw her hands in the air in an irritated gesture.

"Emma was scared, because Deirdre Brown threatened her. I know she wasn't specific, but...Lieutenant, you know the story. Em...Ms. Curtis moved out of the halfway house a few months ago. When Brown said she could pin something on her, get the police involved, she believed her. It's not that odd. She didn't want Brown to ruin everything she worked so hard for, and that's why she told me. We came here right away. Now let's find Brown."

"That's the plan," Jackson said. "I was hoping Ms. Curtis could help us with that."

❦

"Did you call Kitty?" Jayce asked when she could finally drive Emma home.

Emma shrugged. "It was okay. She said Samantha wanted to come in after all. No idea what's up with her."

"Okay. You remember everything we said?"

"I do, and I really think it would be better if you weren't involved in any of this. I can handle it. The next time Deirdre calls, I ask her to come. Someone's going to watch the building in case she shows up unannounced again. It will be okay."

How can you say that when you just broke up with me?

"Let's get you home then. Maybe we're lucky and Deirdre resurfaces sooner than later."

Part of her was hoping that when they had a moment alone, Jayce would be able to convince Emma that her idea was a bad one. Sure, this was an unexpected detour, but it wasn't enough to give up. The plan was solid, and it didn't require more from

Emma than telling Deirdre that she had followed all her orders, have her come back to pick up the box. The empty apartment worried Jayce, though she didn't think Deirdre would leave this much money behind. She was looking forward to a time when they would leave Emma alone, Deirdre, Maxine, all of them.

It was no surprise that Emma wasn't thinking too clearly at this point.

"Kitty was right," Emma said ruefully. "If I'd told you right away, at least they wouldn't have doubted my story. Or maybe they would have anyway."

"Wait. You told Kitty about the box?"

"No, of course not. Deirdre called at work once, so I told Kitty who she was, and that she'd contacted me. Don't be mad with her. I said I'd tell you—which I did. It's not her fault that it took me a while."

"Why?"

Emma cast her a quick worried glance. "Why what?"

"What did you think would happen if you told me? Why didn't you trust me?" Okay, now was not the moment to dump her own issues on Emma, the lingering guilt that she had to lie to her in the halfway house, or that it had been other cops that had messed up Emma's case in the first place, all those years ago. "I'm sorry. I think I know the answer. I need to run a quick errand, but I'll come back as soon as I can."

"Sure." Emma got out of the car, standing on the sidewalk for a moment, looking so lost that Jayce was tempted to delay the "errand." She didn't give in to the lure. They couldn't have a fresh start until all the questions were answered—and Kitty had a lot to answer for.

Emma's hesitation and trust issues, Jayce could understand, even if it was painful to learn she, their relationship, wasn't completely excluded from them. Kitty, however, should have known better.

Kitty and Daniel were both home. Jayce remembered that another employee, Samantha, was minding the store for the moment.

She wasn't going to spend a lot of time.

"What the hell were you thinking?" she asked. Kitty's defiant look told her she knew exactly what Jayce was talking about.

"I guess this is about something Emma told me in confidence," she said.

"About family of her ex threatening her. You didn't think I should know? Kitty, what's wrong with you?" The lack of sleep and the stress of the past few hours were creeping up on her.

"Oh no, Jayce," Daniel intervened. "You don't come into my house on a Saturday morning and talk to my wife like that."

"It's fine. Give us a moment?"

He glared at Jayce but turned around and left the spacious kitchen.

Kitty sighed. "Okay, from the beginning. Emma got a few calls at home, and one at work, so we talked about it. This woman seemed annoying, but not dangerous. I told her to talk to you, so you could put a stop to it. I assume you found out."

Jayce felt a lot less righteous than she had minutes ago. She wiped a hand across her forehead, unsure about what to say.

"Frankly, you don't look so good," Kitty offered. "Would you like a coffee?"

"She yells at you, and you offer her coffee?" Daniel, who hadn't gone that far away after all, asked in disbelief.

"I'm sorry about that. That woman didn't just call, she asked Emma to keep a box for her, and not look inside. Well, we did. There were over five grand and jewelry that came from the burglaries on Park Street. It's going to be okay, but Jackson and his guys had a lot of questions. You can imagine this morning wasn't so easy for Emma, and much of it could have been avoided if we had known right away."

Kitty exchanged a stunned look with Daniel, before she picked up her own cup.

"Wow. I'm so sorry. I had no idea it could be anything like that."

"Nobody did. Daniel…could you leave us alone for real? Just a few minutes, I have to get back anyway. I promise I'm done yelling."

"I hope so. Fine. I'll be outside," he said to Kitty, not entirely placated. Jayce couldn't blame him.

"I'm so sorry. This was uncalled for."

"You're both under a lot of pressure. I understand that."

"Emma broke up with me." Jayce hadn't even meant to say it, but the words came tumbling out anyway, in all their gravity.

Kitty looked shocked at the revelation. "Why?"

"She thinks being with her is harming my career, now, in the future. I didn't have a lot of time to convince her otherwise."

"You will." Kitty pulled herself a chair and sat next to Jayce. "Give yourself some time until all of this is sorted out. Emma has been through a lot—the jealous, criminal girlfriend, prison, everything that happened in the halfway house. Give her a break."

"What about me? When do I get to have a break?"

Her guard wasn't just down, it was in pieces. In some ways, she needed a fresh start, a do over, just as badly as Emma. She had hoped, at first, then lost all doubt that Emma could be sharing this new life with her, the second chance after her accident, but that glorious future hinged on too many uncertain factors now.

"In time," Kitty said softly. "Remember you have a different set of options here. Emma's scared and confused right now. I would be if my violent ex's family showed up on my doorstep, and you know what I'm talking about. You can work this out. In fact, I'd be disappointed if you didn't, because I still want you to come for dinner tomorrow. Go talk to her."

"Yeah, I guess I can't avoid that. We are still waiting for Deirdre to contact her."

"Keep her safe, will you? I don't want to lose my best employee," Kitty said with a wink. "She sells those cards faster than I can restock them."

The joke did little to alleviate Jayce's fears, but she managed a small smile for Kitty's sake. "Thanks for the coffee—and pep talk. I appreciate it."

I don't want to lose her either, she thought.

The pain traveling down her back when she sat in the car wasn't entirely psychological. She'd have to stop at the pharmacy on her way back to Emma's.

There was something disturbing about Kitty's narrative that had stuck in the back of her mind, *my violent ex*. Jayce knew what Kitty had been talking about. She was troubled by the thought that there could be a parallel in Emma's story.

During her undercover assignment, Jayce had pulled Maxine Brown's file in order to get a feel for the case, and to determine if Emma was telling her the truth. Brown had shot the owner of a small grocery store point blank, apparently because she didn't want to pay for a six pack of beer and a bag of chips. No priors, but unfortunately abusers didn't always show up in police reports.

She was only a block away from Emma's apartment building when she got the call from Jackson.

A couple of uniformed officers had picked up Deirdre near a bus station. This part of Emma's nightmare was finally over.

⁂

Jayce hadn't returned yet, and even if she had, Emma wasn't sure what else she could tell her. Few people were willing to give someone in Emma's situation the benefit of the doubt. The scarlet letter left a stain on anyone who got too close, and she didn't want that to happen to Jayce, whose life and career had been on the line before. Clinging to her would be...selfish.

Emma wanted to, hold tight, but she knew it was only a matter of time before another situation like this would arise, putting a spotlight on the woman who had served time for being an accomplice in a murder case, and, by association, Jayce.

Unless she went through with that lawsuit supposed to clear her name and let the world hear the truth. Emma was tired, too tired to cry even. She would lie down for a bit, escape the world and its cruel realities. If Deirdre called, she would do as she'd been told.

Sleep pulled her in almost immediately, leading her into dark and oppressive dreams. The sound of the gavel, the prison cell lock, *"I need to ask you a favor,"* and then there was Alison in the halfway house, holding a gun on her. Waking up in a place she didn't want to be, with Maxine, within walls that were closing in on her, days, then months, years...

Emma woke, gasping for breath, disoriented for a few moments. The sound that had jolted her out of the dreams came again, a firm knock on the door. She got up from the bed, hit with a wave of dizziness.

Hopefully, this would be Deirdre, and once the cops got her, she'd never have to see her again.

"Coming!" Emma straightened her clothes and went to answer.

Maybe it was Jayce, and she could tell her that she had changed her mind, and if it was selfish, she didn't care, they'd find a way...

The man pushed his way into the apartment, kicking the door shut behind him. Emma shrank back, painfully aware that there was nothing in reach she could use as a weapon.

"I believe you have something that belongs to me," he said.

Deirdre Brown glared at her with self-righteous indignation.

"I moved," she said. "It's not illegal. I don't know anything about a box. I called her because Maxine wanted to know how she was doing. You gonna arrest me for that?"

"No, but try breaking and entering. There were enough prints in the house, and on the box. We can also have the owner of the last house come in and identify you," Jackson suggested. "Or you could simply tell us the truth."

"Emma is a liar. I don't know what Maxine ever saw in her. Sweet-faced bitch almost convinced the jury that she never knew Maxine brought that gun into the store."

Jayce wanted to slap her. Obviously, Jackson could sense that she barely held back the impulse, because he shot her a warning glance. This wasn't her case. She hadn't even planned to be here on this day, but enjoy a lazy afternoon with Emma instead.

Sometimes, it was better not to make plans—at all.

Jackson sat across from Deirdre.

"This isn't about Emma and Maxine though. We know you weren't by yourself in those houses, and what you took from them was far more than what we found in this little box. You took that, a little cut for yourself? I could imagine someone's really pissed by this."

For the first time since Jayce had met her, Deirdre looked uncertain.

"The owner would have died if he hadn't managed to trigger the alarm. Once those fingerprint results come in, it'll be you we can place at the scene, and you will be the only one to take the fall. Are your buddies really worth it? They'll come visit you in prison?"

"I have no idea what you're talking about," Deirdre spat, but the tense set of her shoulders spoke volumes. She was afraid, Jayce realized.

"I think you do," she said, "You better start talking, Deirdre. You're helping us, we're helping you, that's how it works. In fact, it's your only option. Speaking of prison visits, it would be a long time before you see your sister again."

Deirdre looked at her hands on the table, shaking her head.

"You can't protect me. I don't trust you."

"Who do you trust? Believe me, they screwed you over, and they're getting away with the bigger part, laughing about you," Jackson said.

"My sister doesn't belong in prison. She shot somebody, yes, but she gets these weird spells—she needs help. Can you do that?"

"Oh no, you got that wrong. You're not making any demands here." In light of Kitty's revelations, Jayce couldn't care less about Maxine's fate at this moment. Deirdre sounded oddly sincere whenever talking about her sister, but she also hated Emma.

"Detective Finney, why don't we hear Ms. Brown out and then see if we can do something for her sister?" Another pointed look from Jackson.

Jayce shook her head, but she remained silent.

"Of course, in that case we need something from you first. Names. Who was with you in that house?"

"He's going to kill me." Deirdre sighed heavily. "I told Maxine that bitch is trouble, too high maintenance..."

"Ms. Brown," Jackson warned.

"I broke up with him, okay? Ted's been messing around with other women, and I had enough. You won't find my prints in any of the houses, because I was never with them. I thought since the bastard's been cheating on me from day one, I deserved something in return, but he went ballistic when he realized some of the goods were missing. He thought his cousin had taken it. That's when I realized I had to get away. I can give you the next two addresses they staked out, his cousin's name, whatever, if we can talk about Maxine. I want her transferred."

"We can suggest an evaluation and go from there. Do you know where Ted is now?"

"Well, since I'm gone and five thousand dollars, I assume he'll go looking for both."

And Emma, Jayce thought with sudden alarm. He might have even followed Deirdre to Emma's apartment the first time.

"Ted's full name and address, now." To Jackson, she said, "I'm going to call Emma. We need to send a unit."

She knew that Jackson had called off the surveillance the moment they'd found Deirdre.

Jayce's call went to voicemail.

❦

"I told you, Deirdre already picked up the box. I don't know what was in it, or what she did with it. Please, believe me. If you leave right now, I won't tell anyone. I never saw you."

Emma could barely breathe, but apparently, fear hadn't made her loose her speech. This couldn't happen, not now, after everything she'd survived. She wouldn't have the chance to tell Jayce that she'd been wrong.

"Tempting." The man laughed. "No, I'd rather have my money, and you're going to give it to me."

"I don't have that kind of money!"

Emma knew she'd made a mistake before he slapped her hard enough for her to stumble.

"You never opened the box, but you know what kind of money was inside? Stop bullshitting me!" He grabbed her arm and pulled hard, dragging her behind him into the bedroom. For a split second, Emma thought she might pass out.

There was a knock on the door, and an unfamiliar voice shouted, "Ms. Curtis! Are you okay?"

"Help! Somebody—"

Her voice was cut off by the hand clamping over her mouth.

"Shut up," the man hissed. "I have a gun. You don't want me to use it." She could only signal with a tiny movement of her head that indeed, no, she didn't want that. "All right. I want you to go back to the door, don't open it, but say that everything's fine in here. Make him go away. You do something stupid, I swear you gonna regret it."

Emma wasn't sure if she'd be able to speak or walk at this point, but she nodded.

"It's...it's fine," she said, clearing her throat when her voice was barely audible. "I was watching TV. I'm sorry if it was a little loud."

It had to be the officer watching the building for Deirdre to arrive, but hopefully the intruder would think it was a neighbour, and not hurt anyone. Emma had seen enough people get hurt while she could do nothing but stand by.

No more.

"Okay. Must be a good show. I suppose you can't talk then."

"No," she whispered. "Sorry."

"That's okay. See you soon, Ms. Curtis."

"Now where were we? You know, Deirdre will come crawling back sooner or later. Why don't I wait here until she does, and meanwhile..." He gave her a hard shove. "You start talking? I don't want to hurt you..."

Liar, she thought. *You already did.*

"...but I will if I have to."

Emma had a split-second, enough for all the horrible possibilities to enter her mind before the front door came down, and policemen filed into the room, handcuffing the man who had invaded her home. She dropped to the floor by the window, blocking out the sounds around her until a gentle touch to her shoulder startled her back into reality.

"You did good," Jayce said, giving her a reassuring smile, even though she looked as exhausted as Emma felt. "We got Deirdre too. It's over." Even in her warm embrace, Emma couldn't stop shaking, because part of her was still afraid "it" would never be over.

There was comfort, though, in knowing that Maxine would never get out. Emma had been given a second chance to be brave, and selfish.

Jayce kissed her cheek softly before she got up, offering her hand to Emma. "Don't get me wrong, but I really hope this will be the last time we have to take your statement. You might want to pack up a few clothes and Elvis."

"What? Why?"

Jayce stepped aside, and for a moment, Emma could only stand and stare. "Oh. Right. I don't have a front door."

"I'll have someone take care of that," Jayce promised. Emma hoped her gratitude was self-evident, because she was too overwhelmed to react in any appropriate way. "Hang in there for a bit longer. I have a little surprise for you later."

Emma managed a weak smile at that. "I'm not sure how many more surprises I can handle."

"This is a good one...unless you'd be more comfortable in a hotel. We can arrange that too."

"No. No, this is okay." This was hardly the place and time for the conversation they needed to have, soon, so Emma hoped that Jayce had heard all the words that were left unsaid for the moment.

She wasn't sure how much longer she could hold herself up.

Jayce didn't prod or ask any of the questions that must have been on her mind. Instead, she went out of her way to make Emma comfortable in her home, including offering a hot bath which Emma gratefully accepted.

She wasn't sure if she could ever feel comfortable in her own home again, no matter how much everyone had tried to reassure her—but maybe it would happen with time. The past few days had provided her with a harsh lesson. They had also made some things clearer.

She would meet the lawyer Jayce had talked about, if only to gauge her chances. She'd be able to tell Emma if the hope of clearing her name was more than a waste of time and money. If it wasn't...Emma assumed that could make a lot of things easier for both her and Jayce. She had to try, at least.

A soft knock that nevertheless made her jump preceded Jayce into the room.

"Hey. I wanted to make sure you're not falling asleep in here," she said softly.

Emma had to admit the possibility, though there was too much on her mind to relax that much. At least she wasn't shaking anymore.

"People will always ask questions, as soon as they know I served time. One way or another that will reflect on you."

"Emma, please."

"I know. You're an adult, and you know what you're getting yourself into—I hope—but I want to do my share too. I will see the lawyer."

The surprise was visible in Jayce's face. "Are you sure?" Behind that question was another, her tone so hopeful Emma wished she'd never given her any reason for doubt in the first place.

"I'm sorry. I didn't sleep, I was scared no one would believe me, and...I don't want you to get into any trouble because of me—but I hope you still want me, even if I said all those things."

Jayce wrapped her arms around Emma, regardless of the fact that she was still fully dressed, and then they kissed, all the answer Emma needed.

When Jayce pulled back, the bathwater had turned her white shirt see-through.

"I do," she said, laughing. "I guess you figured that out by now."

"Good, but you should get out of those wet clothes."

"I should. Would you mind...?"

As badly as the day had started, it couldn't get much better than this, Emma thought, sharing a tub with Jayce in this softly dimmed room, warm scented water enveloping their bodies.

There was a time when Emma had been convinced that there was no safe space left for her. Maybe she'd been wrong after all.

✦

"You don't have to see the lawyer for me though," Jayce reminded her when they had retreated to the bedroom. In here, the dark seemed no longer frightening, and the truth didn't come with a heavy weight. "I'm sorry if I pushed too hard."

"You didn't," Emma said. "You were right. I should know what my options are. At least Deirdre told the truth, and she's not going to harass me any longer. I'm sure Maxine had a good laugh about me getting tangled up in all of this."

Jayce silently found her hand in the dark, entwining their fingers.

"I know you want to ask, why did I stay with her? Sometimes, I don't know either...but other times, I remember I felt like I had nowhere left to go. That sounds silly, right?"

"No, not at all. Some people are clever manipulators. Did she ever hurt you?"

Emma wasn't too surprised about the conclusions Jayce was coming to. She didn't want to mislead her either, but it was hard to find the right word to describe the train wreck that her relationship with Maxine had been.

"Not physically," she said, because that was the truth. There was no saying what could have been, if things hadn't gotten out of control that one day.

"I'm so sorry. You were right—it isn't fair. Would you want to talk to somebody? Maybe a lawyer isn't the first person to contact after all."

"No, not right now. As you recall, there were lots of opportunities for that in the halfway house."

"Yeah. Emma...I know you worry, but you don't need to. If my career was ever at risk, I was the only one who did that. Not you."

"You can tell me," Emma whispered. "It's impossible that you messed up worse than I did."

"I'm not sure, but I think you deserve to know. The story I told in group therapy was obviously just that, a story, but some of it wasn't too far from the truth. I was in an accident, and on painkillers for some time."

Emma had seen the faint scars, but she wasn't going to ask until Jayce wanted to share. "You stopped at some point though."

"Not when I should have, but yes, I stopped. There was a time when I thought...well, let's say I don't look back on that with pride. I want you to know you did everything you could, that time, and today. That's all we can do."

"Thank you."

Jayce laughed softly. "I'm afraid those words of wisdom aren't all mine. I saw a shrink I actually told the whole truth."

"I mean, for listening...and understanding what I want to say, even if I'm saying the opposite."

Emma leaned in for a kiss, meaning a lot more. Fortunately, Jayce understood that too, without words, until there were no more doubts, just pleasure. Even back in the halfway house, with an uncertain future and too many secrets between them, Emma had found she was safe with her, could give herself into her hands with ease.

She craved those hands on her body, the gentle caresses and a firmer touch, sensation taking over, chasing away the worrisome thoughts. Jayce moved between her thighs, fingers tightening on her hips as she continued her intimate explorations until Emma had no choice but to surrender, trembling with the intensity of the moment.

There was no time to waste. Her hands were still shaking when she touched Jayce in return. She needed to.

"You can take your time." There was a smile in Jayce's voice, but her tone was dark and warm with lust. "Or not. That's fine with me too."

It had been a long time since Emma had longed to forge a connection with someone, for reasons other than not being lonely, to satisfy them beyond the physical. She was still amazed that with Jayce, it was so easy to go there.

When the world returned to a slower pace again, she wished they could have stayed in the comfort of the dark and quiet forever, with nothing between them.

Elvis, having no problems adjusting to her temporary new surroundings, jumped onto the bed and curled up at its foot.

No ghosts would be haunting them tonight.

I love you. She said those words only in her mind. It might be much too early to say them out loud, but that didn't make them any less true.

⁂

Crisis averted. They'd been so damn lucky, Jayce thought, wide awake at 4:30 a.m. and well aware that Emma sleeping by her side tonight wasn't something she could take for granted.

She had seen the rap sheet of Deirdre's boyfriend Ted, shuddering at the thought of this man in the same room with the woman who had come to mean so much to her. Meeting Brianna, the lawyer, was only the first step, and of course, no one could guarantee a positive outcome. Except...Deirdre wanted to do something for her sister. Nothing Jayce had learned about the case suggested that Maxine wasn't able to determine wrong from right. She understood that she was committing a crime by shooting a man because she didn't want to pay for snacks bought in his store. The evaluation would show this without a doubt, but still Deirdre seemed to think this was the way to go.

Jayce got out of bed, slowly and carefully so she wouldn't wake Emma, and sent a text to Detective Jackson. This was probably the best opportunity they would ever get, and it would give Brianna something to work with.

She slipped back under the covers, curling around Emma's sleep warm body for a few more hours of blessed peace.

⁂

When the phone rang, it was still much too early for a Sunday morning. Jayce wasn't worried though when the caller ID showed Kitty and Daniel's number.

"Hi," she said. "Don't worry, we're still coming to dinner. In fact, we could both use the distraction. It's been a few wild days."

"Jayce." Kitty sounded uncomfortable. "Is Emma with you?"

"Yes, and she's still sleeping. Can't this wait?"

Kitty sighed. "You're going to find out anyway. In fact, I hope you might help me with this and find someone who can look into it without causing a stir and more of a headache for you two. I'm aware that this is not your typical case."

"What are you talking about?" Jayce was wide awake now, and none of Kitty's words offered any reassurance.

"Samantha. She came back to work yesterday, and she found some irregularities in a couple of receipts, so the numbers don't add up. That happens sometimes, but now she already told another girl in the store and...I don't want any rumors to start."

"They don't believe Emma took money from the store? That's ridiculous!"

"You and I know this, but people are bound to talk. I wanted to give her a heads up, and frankly, I need this problem solved yesterday."

"*You* don't believe she did it, right?"

"Are you kidding me? Of course not. Emma takes this job more seriously than any of the others." Kitty's response was swift and without any ambiguity.

"Okay. Good. I can send you someone to do this discreetly. Thanks for the warning."

After making a couple of calls, Jayce prepared breakfast, the scent of coffee finally coaxing Emma to wakefulness.

When she walked into the kitchen, looking a bit worse for wear from yesterday's incident, Jayce had the instant impulse to keep Kitty's call a secret. Emma didn't deserve this, the distrust, the innuendo—but she deserved the truth.

"Good morning," Emma said, making a surprised sound when Jayce pulled her close. "You missed me?"

"Yeah. I'm afraid...There's something we need to talk about, and don't worry, we will fix this."

They would, once and for all, Jayce vowed silently.

Emma sat at the table, wrapping her hands around the mug Jayce set in front of her, the resignation in her expression heartbreaking. It was no wonder she had trouble believing that this was the start of a new, better life, when the bad news kept coming.

"All right. Hit me."

Both of them winced at Emma's choice of words. She listened impassively, her only reaction gripping the mug even tighter.

Jayce sat across from her, wrapping her hands around Emma's.

"It's a good thing Kitty let us know. She believes in you. We all do. I'll have someone look into it, and meanwhile, don't let that kind of gossip bring you down."

Emma shook her head. "You don't understand. That's how it always starts, and all of a sudden, everyone is looking at me. It's only a matter of time. God, at this rate, I should have stayed in prison. At least I knew what to expect."

"I know you don't mean that. I promise we'll figure it out."

"I hope you're not suggesting I sue her too."

Her smile was a small success, Jayce decided, something to build on. "I could ask Brianna about that... No, come on, I'm kidding. You'll be okay. There will always be people looking to exploit somebody. I wouldn't be surprised if Samantha had something to hide, and if that's the case, we'll find out."

Emma didn't have anyone in her corner for a long time. Jayce was determined to make sure she'd get used to it—after all, they'd dealt with worse than a gossip-spinning co-worker.

"I talked to McAllen today," Daniel said when they were having a glass of wine in the den before dinner. Kitty was off with Emma to show her some new designs. Jayce felt grateful that they weren't around for this part of the conversation. Emma probably couldn't care less about the shop talk. "There was a drug overdose at Marks Hospital. A thirty-six year old woman."

"Suicide?" Jayce winced.

"They don't know yet. It's odd, in any case..."

"Wait...That's the place where Nathan Dolby hit his shrink over the head."

"It is. I think we're going to hear a lot more on this. If there was indeed foul play involved, Dolby's story doesn't sound crazy at all, and maybe Chomsky will want to send someone in."

Jayce took a sip of her wine. "You want to volunteer?"

"I don't think I'd be her first choice," he said, and all of a sudden, Jayce understood where he was going with this.

"Tanya could do it. There's a lot going on in my life right now. I'm not sure it would be a good idea to add a psych ward to the experience."

"Everything worked out all right at the halfway house," he reminded her. "You don't have to worry anymore."

"That I can't trust myself around drugs? No, I don't worry about that. I'd like to stay under the radar for a bit, enjoy life, you know? If Chomsky wants to go there, I won't be the first to raise my hand. I think Ray and Tanya have got this."

"Okay. I thought you'd like to know."

"I appreciate it." Much had changed in the past months, Jayce reflected. When she came back to work after the accident, she would have jumped at any chance to prove herself. Shutting down the dealings at the halfway house and arresting a high-profile dealer and most of his crew in the process had made her regain her confidence in her abilities, but she had gained something else as well. Her priorities had shifted.

When Emma and Kitty returned to the den, it was clear that stationary and greeting cards weren't all they'd been talking about. Jayce had never been more grateful for her friends. The time to come might still be difficult, but she and Emma weren't alone in any of it.

⚬

"Can you imagine? Ria and I have been working here from the start, and this girl comes in and takes all the hours, basically takes over...and what do I hear? She was in prison. Her girlfriend killed somebody."

"Wow," the new employee said. *"That's quite the story. I'm not sure if I'm comfortable around someone like that. She seems so nice."*

"Well, looks can be deceiving," Samantha said. *"We can't trust her."*

"What can we do?"

"We are protecting ourselves, make sure Kitty will kick her ass out on the street."

On the video that showed the kitchen in the store, Samantha rambled on, trying to convince the rookie cop on her first undercover assignment that she'd been righteous, stealing money from her employer and pinning it on a co-worker.

"Wow, indeed," Kitty said. "I'm feeling a little sick right now. Thanks, Jayce, for setting this up. Emma, I don't know what to say. This is terrible. I'll make sure it's her ass that'll be out on the street the moment she comes in, and Ria too, if she knew anything about it. I'm so sorry for not catching this earlier."

"It's okay," Emma said, her throat tight. It was one thing to assume what some people thought about her, another to hear it point blank, even if one of the women was a young officer drawing Samantha out.

Those who matter know the truth. Maybe it wasn't enough after all, which was why she had agreed to the appointment with the lawyer. Emma was curious, and she was dreading it at the same time.

"You're sure that young officer wouldn't like a career in greeting cards?" Kitty asked, half serious. "She was pretty good."

"I'm sorry, I don't think so." Jayce laughed. "She said the boss was nice though. Speaking of which—I would love to take your employee to dinner now. You'd think you can let her go a few minutes early?"

She would need more time to let reality sink in, Emma realized as they were walking to the restaurant through the park, holding hands. Back in the halfway house, her only focus had been finding a job and an apartment, something to show for. She needed to work on a lot more than that to find her balance again, a confidence she'd lost even before her prison sentence—that sometimes, things could turn out the way she hoped, that she could trust, and even love someone.

Jayce's cell phone rang, and she managed to answer without ever letting go of Emma's hand.

"I see," she said evenly after listening for a few moments. "Yes, that's good news. Thank you."

It was work. Most likely. With this new, hopeful perspective on life, Emma also had to realize that the world wasn't revolving around her, not even Jayce's. This call wasn't about her. There was no need to panic.

"I should let you sit down first," Jayce said after finishing the call.

Another lesson: Don't make any assumptions one way or another, Emma reminded herself, her heartbeat accelerating in anxious anticipation.

"Don't be scared. This is good."

"I have a new front door, and my landlord is not canceling my lease?"

Jayce shook her head. "Better. Besides, if he did, you could always come live with me—too soon? No, that's not it. You remember Detective Jackson. He told me that Maxine is changing her initial statement."

The world vanished for a moment, and Jayce quickly steered her towards the closest park bench. In a heartbeat, the questions multiplied. Emma had hoped for this day to come for so long, and eventually given up on it. She had no illusions about Maxine's motives. Certainly, she'd want something in return.

"Why would anyone believe her after all these years?"

"Remember, it's what you said all along, and she's finally confirming your story. She agreed to do this even though it places the blame solely on herself—the way it should have been in the first place. I'm sure that will make sense to any judge. Don't over think it. This is something to celebrate. It will make our case easier."

"That sounds great." Emma got to her feet when she was sure she could trust her legs to hold her up again, still not finding all the words to express the turmoil of emotions, but thankfully, she didn't have to.

"It is. Believe it," Jayce said, kissing her softly.

It had been a long time since Emma had dared to dream of anything other than what was expected of her, to hope for something more than what would satisfy the parole officer. She hadn't felt free once she got to live in the halfway house, imprisoned by guilt and fear of failure.

Freedom, inside and out, was no longer a faraway dream. It was right here, within her reach, and the best was, she had someone to share it with.

NEW ROOMS

S he had one more night with Emma before her assignment started. That didn't leave Jayce with a lot of time to take care of some important matters. She was glad Brianna had agreed to meet her in her office. She didn't mind the latte from the fancy coffeemaker either. Perhaps she had chosen the wrong profession after all. Emma's case was pro bono, to right a wrong. Neither of them could have afforded Brianna's services otherwise. They'd been lucky.

Jayce's visit today was about everything but the money Emma would hopefully soon see in her bank account.

"You two have nothing to worry about," Brianna said, taking a sip of her own latte. "The Powers That Be want this over, the sooner, the better. Obviously, it's an embarrassment to them that Emma's case was handled so badly, and they want as little exposure as possible."

"Sounds good. I came here to ask you something though."

"Anything."

Jayce took another look around the fancy office, wondering how she could break her request to her friend without sounding awfully patronizing. It wasn't likely.

"Thanks. You know I have to go away for a couple of weeks—for work. I wondered if you could check in with Emma every once in a while, because I won't be able to."

Brianna regarded her for a moment, silently, though the surprise showed in her expression.

"She's aware you're going, right?"

"Yes, of course. I just don't want her to be alone that long."

"And it would be too obvious if you asked anyone at work, right? I understand. I could give her a call once in a while, but I'm sure Emma will be fine. She's been through a lot and made it out on the other side, not to mention she'll have some financial security soon. I don't think you have to worry about her."

That might be true, but Jayce worried anyway. Since the days in the halfway house, she and Emma had gotten close. While Emma seemed okay with the prospect of a temporary work-related separation, Jayce didn't want her to think she was letting her down. She worried, because, truth be told, Emma had a knack for attracting trouble without meaning to. Yes, that sounded patronizing. She had to turn it down a notch.

Maybe Emma wasn't the only one she was worried about. In the past, Jayce had accepted undercover assignments without thinking, because she had only herself to take into consideration—not anymore. This time, she wished someone else could have done the job, but Lieutenant Chomsky had zoomed in on her right away.

"You might be right," she said. "Thanks for the coffee and...everything. I appreciate it."

"You're welcome. Good luck on whatever it is you'll be doing."

"Thanks."

Jayce could use some good luck—lots of it, actually, to wrap up this case soon and be back to what passed for a normal everyday life, on the job and with her girlfriend.

When she arrived at the apartment twenty minutes later, Emma stood at the stove in her tiny apartment, Elvis the kitten brushing against her legs. Jayce found that the domestic scene made her ridiculously happy.

"I'd be willing to chop something in exchange for a glass of wine," she offered after embracing Emma from behind and placing a kiss on her neck.

Emma laughed. "You're a little late for that, but you can still have a glass. It's almost done. How was your day?"

"Same old." Jayce shrugged. She got another glass out of the cabinet and helped herself to the open bottle of red wine. On second thought, she grabbed a spoon and stole a taste from the pot on the stove, where the stew, vegetables, potatoes and meat, was simmering. The wine would go well with it. For the next few days, she'd have her meals provided for her, but she doubted they'd be this delicious. Alcoholic beverages would be out of the question. "What about yours?"

"It was good. We got a couple of weddings today." Emma sounded a tad wistful at that. She had been working at the greeting cards and stationary store for a while now and would probably continue to do so after the payment came through. First of all, it wouldn't be that much. Brianna had often said they could go higher, but like the aforementioned Powers That Be, Emma wanted it over, and Jayce could sympathize.

Two weeks, three max, it didn't seem all that long. The prospect loomed, all this time of not letting her guard down, always watching her back. Maybe she should look into a possible transfer to another unit. She had always liked working with the people on her team though, Daniel, her partner who was married to Emma's boss Kitty, long-time friends. Lieutenant Chomsky, who was one of the most skilled cops and the best supervisor Jayce had had in her career.

Those would be two weeks of slipping back into the mind of J. C. Turner, who couldn't seem to get her life together. J. C. kept hanging out with the wrong people and had a dangerous habit of abusing prescription meds. The dangerous part here was how close she'd come to being that person at one point in her life. It helped make the undercover persona real, but it was also a trip down memory lane she didn't like taking.

"You're quiet," Emma observed. "I hope it's not me mentioning the weddings." If there was a hint of concern to her voice, it was because she knew exactly what Jayce was thinking about. They had talked about it at length.

Jayce pulled her close in response. "No, it's not. I'd marry you in a heartbeat. Especially now that you're going to be a wealthy woman...I'm kidding. Not about the marrying part, but...you know."

"Yeah." Emma went into her embrace eagerly, wrapping her arms around Jayce in return. "It's going to be fine."

She had heard that a lot today. Jayce had no reason to believe otherwise. She'd had worse assignments before, and most importantly, she had one more night left before she had to become J. C. for a while.

A woman had died in a psych ward for patients who had committed criminal offenses, an apparent suicide that was highly suspicious. If someone else had caused her death, that person most likely still had access to patients, probably worked there, and it was up to her to find them.

It *was* going to be fine.

She'd have Emma to come home to.

⁂

The first time they'd met was during one of Jayce's undercover assignments. Emma never had any illusions that there wouldn't be others at some point. She was okay with it in theory.

Since Jayce seemed to have doubts, Emma couldn't afford to let hers show. The problem was she'd seen up close and personal how dangerous these assignments could get, and she knew she wouldn't get a good night's sleep until Jayce was back home. That wasn't what she told her though.

"I'll be fine." She poured another glass of wine for each of them and turned off the stove. Dinner was ready to be served. They had tonight until Jayce would leave early in the morning, adopting the role of a troubled woman better served by therapy than a women's prison according to the courts. "In a couple of weeks, you'll have what you need, or they'll pull you out if there's nothing new to learn, right?"

"Yeah, something like that." Jayce took a sip and sighed deeply. "I'm sorry. I know you took care of yourself long before we met. I don't like the timing of this. Chomsky could have sent anyone."

Emma had many thoughts on this. Maybe she'd taken care of herself for so long in a hostile environment that she appreciated having someone by her side who didn't smother her, or let her down continually, the way Maxine had. Emma was embarrassed to think that she hadn't been the only one, but that was a conversation for another time.

"Maybe she didn't want to send just anyone, because you did a great job last time."

Jayce gave her a long look, slightly amused, and it occurred to Emma that the job wasn't all she was thinking about.

"Right. Even with all the distractions, and I've had lots of them."

That time seemed like another world in the relative peace they'd found afterwards. While Emma would never regret that her time in the halfway house ultimately brought them together, she could understand that Jayce wasn't too happy about the situation. She had her own demons to battle, and her undercover persona came dangerously close to them.

"Will you be okay?"

"I'll be careful," Jayce said, which, in Emma's opinion, was not the same. "I'm sorry I can't tell you too many details. I want to get it over with and come back to the regular job."

"I understand. Maybe I can distract you a bit more later." She managed to keep her tone casual, but she'd conveyed the meaning anyway.

"I can't wait," Jayce said, leaning in for a kiss that made Emma want to skip dinner. They didn't have any time to waste after all.

They ate the meal mostly in companionable silence, each of them busy with their own thoughts. After seven already. A few hours from now, Jayce would leave. She was right, Emma had been taking care of herself for a long time, because she had to. It wasn't for a lack of capability that she needed to be close to Jayce. This relationship was the most special thing that ever happened in her life. She needed to hold on to it any way she could. Jayce would understand.

For dessert, she served a warm cherry pie with ice cream.

Jayce sighed. "You know, you're making it a lot harder to leave."

That might not be such a bad thing, Emma thought. "Because of dessert?"

"Yeah, that too."

She held Jayce's gaze, smiling. "When you're back, we can do this more often. Until then...I hope you'll miss me a little."

"You have no idea."

Emma didn't object though she could certainly imagine based on her own state of mind, the intense longing she felt even now when they were still together. If she could have that reassurance, maybe those two weeks wouldn't be so bad after all, especially if...she didn't want to think about that, not right now.

"I miss you already," she confessed. "I had some more plans for tonight though...unless you're tired, I know tomorrow's an earlier start, and it's even earlier since you're staying here, so if you..."

"Emma. It's all right." Jayce leaned close to kiss her, bringing Emma's nervous ramblings to a halt. "Let's just do the dishes first. I don't want to leave you with all this."

"I'm sorry," Emma said, self-conscious and a bit annoyed with herself. "Everything is going so well, I guess that is freaking me out a little—but the money will come, and you'll be back in two weeks, and life is going back to normal." She shook her head with a wry laugh. "I've been waiting years for this moment. Now that it's here, I sometimes still have trouble believing it."

"That's completely normal after everything you've been through. I understand."

That was the best part, Jayce truly understood. While her story differed greatly from Emma's, she also had to adjust to a new normal. It took time. Meanwhile, they had each other.

Emma ran a hot bath for the two of them. The space was too small for candles, but the bathroom light had a dimmer, the soft glow creating a warm relaxed atmosphere. For so long, she had managed to keep her guard up while getting naked with someone. Jayce had found a way under her skin, and Emma didn't mind. When they couldn't keep their hands to themselves any longer, they retreated to the bedroom, hair still damp and dripping. It didn't matter. There was an urgency, too hard to resist, like when they'd spend the night together in the halfway house not knowing what would or could come out of it. It was different this time. There was a future for the two of them.

Emma didn't want to lose a moment until the daunting goodbye, but at some point, she had fallen asleep, gently coaxed to wakefulness by Jayce's whisper.

"Hey. Emma. It's time."

Emma bolted upright in bed, fully aware. The curtains were closed, but not all the way. It was still pitch dark outside.

She held back all the first thoughts that came to mind, like, *not yet*, and *do you really have to go*? They were grown-ups. They had made it through worse. She got out of bed. Jayce was fully dressed, holding a coffee mug. The smell of coffee this early in the morning nearly made Emma gag, but she forced herself to ignore the sensation.

"Two weeks."

"It might be three," Jayce reminded her, "but not more than that. It's not that big of a place."

"Okay. Don't worry. I'm not going anywhere meanwhile."

"I'm counting on it. You should go back to bed. The coffee will still be good when you need it." Jayce set the cup on the counter. "I have to go now. I love you."

Leaning into her embrace, Emma wanted cherish the feeling, believe that everything would be all right, and brush aside the superstitious notion that instead, something terrible might happen. It wasn't easy. In the past years, she'd had her share of terrible—not now. Everything had changed, hadn't it?

❦

Emma's heart was hammering as the secretary addressed her.

"Ms. Curtis? You can go in now."

She might be making a big mistake, but there was no way she could back out now short of fleeing from the office. Come to think of it, big mistake was a relative term compared to others in her past. She had made it this far. The alternative was to spend those weeks by herself, wondering, worrying. If this worked out, she might gain new prospects in many ways.

If.

She shook hands with the director and the head nurse, glad her hand didn't tremble, and took a seat in the visitor's chair. The director was tall, broad-shouldered, wearing a dark suit, definitely not someone who spent all of his time behind a desk juggling numbers. Emma had found in her research that he was a psychiatrist who had gone into administration recently. The nurse was equally tall, and Emma already felt crowded. She crossed her legs, wringing her hands in her lap, glad that the huge oak desk kept the other two occupants from seeing it.

"Welcome, Ms. Curtis," the director said. "We're glad you're interested in the nurse's aide's position. We just have a few questions regarding your resumé."

Emma had let the pen hover over that particular question for a long time and then decided to be truthful. She couldn't change her past and everything that was rather ugly in it—that's why she was working even harder on the future. If she had lied, it would have come out anyway, even if the lawsuit was hardly high profile.

"I understand that, and I'm glad you're giving me a chance to explain. I filed a lawsuit against the city and was granted restoration."

"We're aware of that," the nurse said to Emma's surprise, her tone slightly impatient. "You said you worked in finances before, and now you're in retail. What got you interested in the field, psychiatry specifically?"

The bad press your institution has gotten lately. The fact that the woman I'm in love with might be in the middle of something dangerous going on inside, and I can't stand to be apart from her. Emma assumed that the truth wouldn't help her case.

"I studied psychology as an undergrad. It was something I was always interested in, and I read a lot when I was in...I looked at all the options that are available to me now, and I think becoming a nurse's aide is a good way to start. I plan to go back to school at some point."

In fact, the part-time position she'd found on the clinic's website would allow her to still work at Kitty's greeting card store and avoid a final decision for now. It wouldn't be easy. Kitty was the first employer who had given her a chance after prison and the halfway house. Emma felt that she owed her.

"You're aware that you'll be dealing with patients who have committed crimes, and they're here as part of their sentence or to fulfill conditions for parole? It's not your usual textbook situation."

"I'm aware of that," Emma said. "I think that my experience will help with that."

"Actually, I agree with that," the director said, the nurse's reaction a slight frown that changed into a terse smile. "We'll give it a try."

"When can I start?"

"Alina can show you around, then tomorrow your probation time will start."

"Wonderful. Thank you so much. I appreciate you giving me this chance."

Emma felt more excited about the opportunity than she'd thought, even with all the complications it might bring. Jayce wouldn't be too thrilled, but she would understand that Emma needed some sort of reassurance.

She wasn't scared of dealing with women who might have a criminal past. Some would try to manipulate the staff while others would simply mind their own business. Some were scared out of their mind, finding themselves in a bad place without truly understanding how they'd gotten there. She had seen all of it before, and this time, she'd be going home at the end of every day. She'd be okay. She hoped Jayce would be too.

It was odd to think that a few days ago she hadn't even known this opportunity existed. The story Emma had told wasn't a complete lie. With some money available to her, she had options, other than to keep working at *Kitty's Greeting Cards & Stationary*. She could go back to school, earn a higher pay grade, and build a new career.

Working for Kitty was fairly safe and predictable, except when a co-worker had tried to set her up, but she was long gone. Kitty's business was going well. For now, Emma didn't have to worry about the job. She still was extremely grateful for the opportunity, but lately, she had begun to wonder if she should challenge herself more. There were avenues that were still open to her at her age, but the window might close in her face sometime soon. This temporary job would give her the chance to look into a different field she'd been interested in a long time ago. While she might not be able to see Jayce or talk to her, she'd know she was close.

It wasn't the most rational approach, but to Emma, it felt right. Two weeks were too damn long.

She hadn't told Kitty the whole truth yet, just asked for a half day which Kitty had eagerly granted her. Everyone in Jayce's life had been so kind and helpful, Emma didn't want to disappoint any of them. She'd just work harder.

Alina showed her the infirmary and introduced her to Tess, another nurse she'd be working with. So far, so good. Her role would be an assisting one, but she had more responsibility at the greeting card store.

Tess also did a class in health education as she was studying to become a therapist. She seemed open and easy enough to work with. So far, Emma's plan was working.

Now she had to go and ask Kitty for more hours off. She'd work as much as she could, but she wouldn't be able to keep her hours from overlapping. What she wanted to do in the future, Emma wasn't completely sure of.

On her way out, she caught a glimpse of patients standing in the yard, talking, a couple of women smoking. Jayce was nowhere to be seen. It was probably better that way. Emma didn't want to be a distraction once more.

She was an adult. She'd survive a day, and a few more, without her lover?

Emma boarded the bus that would bring her to the city. She sank into the worn seat with a sigh. This would not be easy, but when had her life ever been?

Jogging the last steps from the bus stop, she made it to the store just at the time she'd promised. Kitty was behind the counter, shaking her head at Emma's breathless greeting.

"How did you know I was replaced by my evil twin who'd fire you if you were one minute late? Emma, come on."

"I'm sorry. I didn't mean you would...anyway. Can I talk to you later?"

The bell over the entrance rang, indicating another customer.

"Sure, but why don't you come over to dinner tonight? I have some news for you too." Since she sounded this cheery, it couldn't be bad news. While Emma appreciated having a space of her own, she didn't care much for being in it alone under the circumstances, so it was easy to make a decision.

"I'd love to," she said and then turned to the customer, a woman in her thirties who was looking for wedding anniversary cards. For the next few hours, life felt almost normal, at least for what had been normal and encouraging in the past weeks. She didn't think about her new part time occupation, or why she had taken it in the first place, telling herself this might be a stepping stone towards a future career.

Finally, Kitty closed the store. They finished the books for the day, and Emma swept the floor. It wasn't in her job description, but she and the other employees shared chores like this with Kitty.

She wondered how Jayce's day had gone.

❧

Jayce couldn't help flinch when the door fell shut behind her, too many memories coming at her all at once. She had worked undercover in a prison before, and the halfway house. In the latter case, Emma had been a welcome distraction. In here, there was a high level of reflection expected from patients, which inevitably took her back to a time when her whole life could have spiraled out of control.

J. C. Turner was a blend of her undercover personae. Some aspects remained the same. In order to make it believable, she went for what had been the most painful and depressing episode, when she'd been struggling to get back on her feet after the accident. Usually, it got her an opening.

Dr. Simmons, who was conducting the interview, listened with interest. Unlike the director, he was not in the know, and to him, the woman in the worn clothes, a haphazard braid hanging over her shoulder, was a patient like any other.

"We were running out of money, so a friend and I went to a pharmacy to get some. I got caught."

"Is that the only thing you regret?" he asked. "I mean, by get some, you meant breaking into the pharmacy, and threatening the pharmacist who was still there, with a gun."

"Well, since you're asking, I'm not happy to be here. Chick who killed herself? I suppose she must have had a reason."

"Unfortunately, but you don't have to worry about that. Your story is a completely different one. If you're successful here, you could look at a much shorter sentence...I believe that's an incentive?"

"I want to get clean. The gun wasn't even mine, and yes, that was a stupid idea."

"How did you get into this in the first place? There's little information on that in your file."

Jayce shrugged. "I was trying to go back to school, working two jobs at the same time."

"A lot of people do that."

She'd made up her mind about him before he'd said that. Even if Simmons hadn't killed anyone, he was not a pleasant person, talking to her with an air of disdain. Yes, her character had made bad choices, but he was also a psychiatrist and should be able to understand the grip of addiction. Part of her emotional reaction to the man was not an act, but it didn't matter. She was here to find out who had killed the woman whose death was still assumed to be a suicide in this institution.

"Yeah, well, you can see it didn't work out for me. Hanging around all those younger kids, they used all kinds of stuff, staying up all night to study, then something else to counter the effect so they could sleep, not to mention the drinking."

"You've had blackouts, memory gaps?"

"Why does it matter?"

"Humor me, Ms. Turner. I'm trying to get the whole picture, see where you're coming from."

"I don't think I did, no."

"You went to those parties often? That's where you met the friend who let you down?"

"You could say that." Her hand went up to play with her braid. J. C. was not a patient person.

"Whose fault do you think it is that you're here now?"

Jayce scoffed at the question. "You don't think I know you're trying to trick me? It's his fault. And mine. He got the better deal, that's all."

"You think a chance at turning your life around is not a good deal?"

"It's the only deal I could get. Let's leave it at that."

During their conversation, Jayce had studied the office. It was unlikely that he or anyone would hide anything compromising at work, but if there was an opportunity to take a look sometime soon, she would take it. For now, she'd spend time finding out what theories the staff and patients had about the suspicious death and try to get a better image of Gillian Thorne's life in the past weeks. There had already been an incident where a male patient had attacked Dr. Simmons in the men's facility, the building next door. He had claimed to have done it in self-defense, though he never clarified what he had to defend himself against. Then, Gillian Thorne's apparent suicide within one month.

Jayce already knew that she couldn't have had access to the drugs that had killed her unless someone had helped her or forced her to take them. It wasn't something a patient could have planned and executed by herself, so her focus would be on the staff. And Dr. Simmons, already accused of wrongdoing by a patient, was high on that list.

Even though the doors were locked behind them, there were common areas most of them had access to, based on their conduct in the facility. Jayce planned to stay under the radar as best as she could, get to know the other patients, find out what the talk about Thorne was, and who was scared the most.

There was a firm structure, a lot more rigid than in the halfway house where inhabitants were expected to actively work towards their reintegration—not that this was a vacation. There were therapy sessions, group and individual, different approaches, educational classes about substance abuse, meetings with the social worker and the parole officer for those who were approaching their release.

After having gotten out of bed around 4:00 a.m., Jayce was tired, craving a coffee in the afternoon. It wasn't likely she'd get one anytime soon, not the real kind anyway.

When it was time for a break, she studied the therapist who was nervously shuffling her papers on her desk, before she joined the other patients in the yard. Jayce was aware of the glances sent her way, curious, appraising, the same as in any context like this. There were certain rules behind locked doors, and the silent questions were all about whether or not she'd be a threat to the existing power structures. These women had been given second chances, but many of them had violent offenses on their records. Like J. C. She stood leaning against the fence, pretending not to pay attention. A tall blonde standing with a group of four came over to her. Jayce was aware of the other women watching them curiously.

"Hey. I saw you in class earlier. You're new?"

"Yeah. I got here today. Not the worst place."

"Where did you come from?"

"Women's facility in Morgan County."

The woman whistled. "You're lucky then. Who did you sleep with? Normally you don't get out of Morgan so easily. Unless…"

Jayce shrugged. "I had a good lawyer. I'm J. C."

"Eileen. Want a tip? Watch out for Simmons. He's a creep."

"How so?"

"You'll find out. Enjoy your stay, J.C." She went back to her group. One of the women, a brunette, looked irritated with Eileen. Jayce realized in a heartbeat why she looked familiar. Not someone she wanted to meet, but she didn't think it would affect her assignment in any way, other that she was still angry at her. No distractions—the sooner she could get out of here, the better.

Jayce wasn't looking forward to the class about medication abuse either.

⁂

"So, we haven't had a vacation in…" Kitty sent a questioning look toward Daniel, obviously trying to come up with a number. "Forever. We'd like to book a getaway, and I'm thinking you could take care of the store for a couple of weeks. Don't worry, I'll pay you accordingly. I assume you will want to put some of the money from the lawsuit away? Am I too nosy?"

"No, it's not that. I'm sorry, you're right, I don't plan on spending it. That is…a great offer."

Kitty's good news presented a new dilemma, something Emma hadn't considered.

"I've been talking too much." Kitty laughed. "I know there's something you wanted to ask, so I better let you get a word in now."

"That's okay." Emma paused, wondering what Kitty and Daniel would think about her plans, and if they'd consider them unforgivably selfish—or crazy. "I didn't expect this. I'm glad you trust me with the store, but I…I kind of took on another part time job. I was hoping I could still work at the store?"

"Really?" Kitty sounded more surprised than offended. "That's okay, I'm sure we can work something out. What kind of job?"

"As a nurse's aide. I figured that I could use some of the money from the settlement to go back to school." Emma blushed hotly for no good reason. She had a right to take her future into her own hands, didn't she? Except she might not have considered this job at all if it hadn't been for Jayce's assignment.

"Weren't you in finances before?" Daniel asked.

"Yes, but...I don't know. They were pretty nice to me at the hospital when I explained my situation, but I'm not sure if I could do the same work as before. I'd feel like people would still not trust me. It seems like a better idea to go into a whole different direction."

"If that's what you want, sure," Kitty said. "You have to remember though that there are different options. You already have an education. I want to expand and open another store sometime soon, hence the vacation. If we don't do it now, we won't get the chance for some time to come. I'm sure you could manage this one—if you want, that is."

It sounded logical. In fact, compared to this, her own idea looked even crazier. Emma wished she could talk this over with Jayce.

Kitty and Daniel shared a smile.

"I know," she said, "now is probably not the best time for you to make a decision. In fact, Daniel won't be able to get away before Jayce is back at work, so you have that much time. Is that okay with you?"

Only months ago, Emma had hidden from the world best she could. Now she had love, friends, and a cat that wasn't entirely indifferent—could life get any better? It sure would in a couple of weeks.

"Thank you so much," she said. "I had no idea, but...this is good news indeed. I promise I'll think about it."

❦

Jayce saw the therapist again, heading towards the exit, apparently happy to leave the place. Dr. Elizabeth Tanner. All employees had been questioned before, but Tanner might be hiding something. She wouldn't confide in a patient, but one of the patients could probably tell more about her relationship with Thorne. Tomorrow, Jayce would see her for individual therapy.

Heading back to her room after dinner, Jayce realized that Eileen's was right across from hers. That was convenient too. She wanted to hear more about Simmons.

Then there was Maxine Brown. Jayce had to approach her like any other patient, regard her story with the same emotional distance she'd apply to the other women. This one was a tough case. She couldn't see past the fact that Emma's ex was responsible for the sharp and disturbing U-turn in her life. For the sake of the case, she had to. At least, Emma was far from this place—the thought was consoling.

It didn't mean Jayce had a restful night. In a place like this, it was never completely silent. She thought she heard someone crying, but that might be from a dream she'd slipped into. She and Emma had stayed over at each other's places so often lately that she was starting to have trouble sleeping alone.

Her appointment with Tanner. J. C.'s story varied slightly wherever she went, but key elements remained. Some of them were reminders of a place she never wanted to return to.

When she accepted the assignment in the halfway house, Jayce had something to prove. That was over. These days, there was a lot more at stake.

She fell asleep with plans to ask Tanner a few subtle questions, and carefully insert herself into Eileen's group. Her approach yesterday, for all the group to see, was significant. To the women here, she had some authority.

There were nurses Alina and Tess. She might wait a day or so, then ask for something to help her sleep and test how much the staff was going by the book.

Before her appointment, she passed through the day room, wondering if she had time for a coffee—even being decaf, the smell was tempting—when she saw Maxine standing by the machine. In the relatively short time Maxine had spent here, her conduct had to have been outstanding if she was already allowed privileges. That was curious, especially after her sister Deirdre had tried to trick Emma into a dangerous scheme not long ago.

It's too damn hard to avoid these people.

"Hey there." Maxine spoke to her before she could back away, and, to Jayce's surprise, gave a smile. "It's not half bad. You get used to the stuff quickly."

"I'm not so sure about that."

Maxine laughed. "You probably figured out already that it doesn't get much better around here, but I got a cigarette if you like. Come find me after your session."

"Sure. I won't say no to that. Thanks...I didn't get your name?"

"I'm Maxine."

"Nice to meet you," Jayce said before walking away. This might be a good opportunity to check and see if she was upholding her part of the deal. Yes, the fact that she had recanted her statement and admitted Emma never knew about the gun Maxine had brought that day, had helped. She'd told the truth too damn late, after Emma already served a prison sentence and was sent to the halfway house. If Maxine had any agenda here, Jayce's assignment might give her a chance to find out.

Minutes later, she sat in Tanner's office, further establishing her persona. After answering some of the introductory questions, Jayce ventured into more hazardous territory.

"Is it true that a woman killed herself in here? I wonder why she did it."

Elizabeth Tanner looked up from her notes, visibly startled.

"Do you have suicidal thoughts sometimes?"

If Jayce wasn't careful, the conversation could go down an entirely different road.

"No. I want to do whatever it takes to get out of here as soon as possible. Just curious, that's all. These things don't happen out of nowhere, do they?"

"I'm sorry, I can't discuss another patient with you. Given your goals, it would make sense to focus on you in the time we have, don't you think?"

"I suppose. I'm a little freaked out by the idea that something might have happened to her in here—that made her do it."

"I can assure you we take security very seriously, for the staff and the patients. If you see or hear something that concerns you, you should tell one of us right away, but you don't have to worry. This is a safe place." The notepad trembled slightly in her hands.

"You really think so?"

"I do, but it's important for you to work on a detailed plan of what you need to achieve. After all, there's a reason why you're here."

"...and not in a prison, you mean? I'm sure you read all about the stupid stunt at the pharmacy. Someone got hurt. That was a nasty wake up call."

"I can imagine. How are you doing at the moment?"

Jayce shrugged, starting to play with the loose braid again.

"I didn't mean to kill anyone. I try not to think about it."

In fact, that was the easy part. Jayce never had to shoot to kill anyone, in fact she'd hardly ever had to draw her weapon. The part where her story merged with J. C.'s...that was a different ball game.

"It's hard to ignore. Your verdict would have been a different one if no one got hurt."

"I'm aware of that, okay?"

Jayce noticed the slight quiver to Tanner's voice, her eyes welling up. What was she feeling guilty about? If she still thought Gillian Thorne had taken her own life, then she might feel responsible for not seeing the signs. Maybe there hadn't been any signs and someone else had instead decided to get rid of a witness. The truth might help ease her mind too.

"You started to abuse prescription meds after your accident?"

"That's right. It was tough before, keeping up with the college kids. They always had something on hand. After the accident, the doctor prescribed some pills, but I ran out faster than I should have. I tried different pharmacies, alternatives, begged the doctor...at some point none of that worked, but I was still in pain. I was unemployed at the time, and I couldn't seem to catch a break. It all went pretty much downhill from there."

It could have. The memory was still chilling, making her shudder. Emma wasn't the only one who was lucky to have gotten second chances.

"You haven't had access to any drugs in a while. How are you feeling?"

"Restless. Tired," Jayce said which was the truth, but hardly related to the past anymore. "I'm doing okay, but I'm also scared of what comes afterward. Getting a job and all that shit."

"You already know it won't be easy, but taking responsibility is an important first step. You won't get around that." Dr. Tanner sighed, absentminded for a moment. "Make sure you don't miss your classes. They have some important practical information for you. We'll see how it goes. If you can manage to uphold structure, that will make it easier for you when it's time to think about a job."

"I'll do that. Thanks, Doctor."

"You're welcome."

The timing was perfect. She could have that cigarette with Maxine and test her a little, while asking about Tanner. Afterwards, she'd find the nurse to ask her for some sleep medication. Everything was going according to plan so far.

When Emma's alarm rang, it wasn't much later than the time Jayce had left the morning before. Elvis gave her an accusatory look before she curled up again in the middle of the bed.

"Yeah, I know, sorry," Emma mumbled. "This will be over soon, I promise." She wanted to go to the store before starting her shift at the ward, in order to prepare some orders for Kitty. She was already feeling guilty even though Kitty and Daniel had been nothing but supportive. Could she do it? Any of it? Manage the store while Kitty opened a new one, or get another degree in a new field?

The past few weeks had been stressful, but also filled with hopes and dreams, about her new future, with Jayce, with new possibilities for a career. Now that she had to make a decision, she was nervous, about making mistakes, taking the wrong path again.

She waited in the cool morning air for the first bus, then walked the ten minutes to the store where she worked quickly, finishing the paperwork before daylight arrived. If Kitty was okay with that, she could even bring some work home. It wasn't like she had a lot to do there at the moment. Anything to keep her mind off the fact that Jayce might be in close quarters with a murderer—behind locked doors.

At the ward, Tess showed her the computer system and told her about her work as a psychiatric nurse, encouraging Emma to take notes.

"We have a multi-dimensional approach here that is pretty unique," she said. "You know I'm studying to become a therapist as well, so I go to their meetings when time allows. There's a class I have developed with Dr. Tanner. You'll help me do my job, so it's important for you to know your way around."

"I can do that," Emma said.

"Good. For the class this morning, I give this information material to all participants. I'd like you to make copies for everyone and check who's present later." She laughed. "I promise it will get a little more exciting than that."

"Oh, I'm okay with that. I imagine every day is different."

"You could say that." A shadow crossed her face, so quickly Emma thought she might have imagined it.

"Do you plan to train to be a nurse?" Tess asked.

"I'm not sure yet," Emma said honestly which prompted a curious look from the nurse. They had to be about the same age, and maybe it was surprising that she hadn't figured out her choices yet. She didn't care to go into detail and continued her notes. She had imagined the work would be interesting. Emma almost forgot about the true reason why she had sought out a job at this specific institution, but she soon got a reminder.

Tess's class was about the dynamics of addiction and how to break the cycle. Thinking back to prison and later, the halfway house, Emma found she had a somewhat jaded opinion on the subject, but maybe this program was really unique. Some would make it out, either way. At least the staff seemed to care and see the complexity of each case—most of them anyway.

The classroom filled slowly, and Emma stood behind Tess, experiencing a bit of stage fright now that her idea had become real.

She was both excited and nervous to see Jayce walk into the room, do a double take and then slump into a chair as if bored. Even though she anticipated that Jayce would not be too happy with her decision, Emma couldn't help being fascinated by the change in her stance, her mannerisms, the clothes. She seemed like a completely different person. It had been easier to reconcile her identity at the halfway house with the woman she had come to know.

While Tess began the class, she started to distribute the materials. Jayce shot her an incredulous look when she passed her by, but didn't say anything. Emma hoped that she'd have a minute to explain. Regardless, she wouldn't take it personally. She knew Jayce had to keep in character, do her job. Emma would do hers.

She went through the list of names, checking the boxes when the door opened again, and she had to physically take a step backwards, distance herself from the woman walking inside, and the memories.

Yes, there was one more empty desk and an extra set of class materials.

They belonged to Maxine. Emma's first impulse was to run, to admit that she was in over her head. All of this was true, yet she stayed and tried to keep the emotion out of her expression. This was not a coincidence. She knew Maxine had asked to be transferred in exchange for adjusting her statement in Emma's favor. She could have taken a moment to check the patients' list.

The class began, and Emma had to compose herself. She couldn't help feeling like she was watching the scene from the outside. She couldn't afford to acknowledge Maxine's surprised smile, or Jayce's tense posture. The two of them being in the same room made Emma uncomfortable. She had made a choice though. It was this, or be on her own for two, maybe three long weeks.

Then it was finally over. Jayce was one of the first ones to leave the class. Much as she wanted to, Emma couldn't run after her. She helped Tess gather the materials and pretended not to notice that Maxine was lingering.

"Do you have any questions, Ms. Brown?" Tess asked her.

"No, thanks. See you next time."

She sauntered out of the room, and Emma looked after her dejectedly, wondering if she'd taken on too much. Managing the greeting card store looked like such a better choice at this point—if only she had known.

They returned to the infirmary afterwards. Emma had a hard time concentrating on her assigned task, stocking the recently ordered drugs into the locked cabinets. Now, in a safer distance from Maxine, she thought about Jayce's undercover persona, slightly familiar and yet different from the one she'd met in the halfway house. It was a bit strange, yet, Emma had to admit, and thrilling at the same time. This time, one could say that she was undercover too.

A sharp rap to the office door made her spin around. She could see Tess getting up from her desk to let Jayce—J.C.—in.

"Ms. Turner, what can I do for you?"

Emma locked the cabinet and inched closer to the open door.

"I can't sleep," Jayce said. "I want you to give me something."

"I'm afraid it's not that easy. I have to clear it with Dr. Simmons, and even then, there are other options. You could talk to…"

"I don't want to talk to anyone. I need to sleep, okay?"

Emma flinched but had to admire Jayce's talent for precision. She was raising her voice enough to get on Tess's radar, but not enough for the nurse to call security right there and then.

She went into the office, earning irritated looks from both women.

"Fresh air helps me. I leave the window open most nights."

"Great idea. You realize that the windows in our rooms don't open?"

Emma felt her face turn beet red. "I'm sorry."

"Yeah, well, that's not helping my problem. Isn't there anything you can give me? Please! I'm about to go crazy."

"I'll take a look. Like I said, I'll have to clear it with Dr. Simmons first. Wait here." Exasperated, Tess got up to go to the other room, opening a small window of opportunity.

Jayce summed up the situation in a way that left no room to argue.

"What the hell were you thinking? You can't be in this place. Whatever this is, you have to quit right now."

"I'll be okay," Emma said. "I'm working as a nurse's aide, and after that, who knows..."

"No, no, no. You're going home."

"Come on. Yes, I was a bit startled to see Maxine, but I swear, I can handle it. I want to be here."

"You can't!" Jayce's frustration came across clearly even though she couldn't raise her voice at this moment. "This is not about Maxine. There's likely a murderer in here, and I don't want you to be anywhere near him or her. Do you understand that?"

Emma understood just fine, but before she could answer, Tess returned.

"Dr. Simmons is out for today. I'm really sorry."

"Yeah, I got that. Have a nice day, Ms. Curtis."

"What was that all about?" Tess asked with a frown.

"I'm not sure," Emma confessed, "but not sleeping makes me grumpy too."

Tess sighed. "They try any way they can. You know Turner's file? She was hooked on prescription meds, took part in the armed robbery of a pharmacy. Believe me, Dr. Simmons will have none of this."

"What can we do? Are there other classes maybe..." Emma had to remind herself that she was empathizing with a problem that was most likely made up, but she couldn't help it. In the halfway house, and before that, in prison, she'd had trouble sleeping, and little access to resources which could help solve the problem.

"There's only so much funding we get," Tess said. "This is not the worst problem we or they are facing."

"I just thought...never mind."

"Okay. Let's go back to work."

⁂

Jayce hated being this harsh with Emma, but she only had a couple of minutes or so to make her point. It was important that she did. Maxine Brown was only a minor distraction, maybe a help even, but to think of Emma in this place...Jayce knew that she would probably be fine if she stayed under the radar. Whoever had killed Gillian Thorne was unlikely to go after employees next, but she didn't want to take the chance.

There was always time to apologize.

She had heard rumors that some of the nurses were quick to give out medication. That either wasn't true for Tess, or she'd been hesitant with Emma around.

"Hey. You don't look too happy. Had to sit through some boring class?" Eileen's presence jolted her out of her thoughts.

"Something like that," she mumbled. Jayce hoped she hadn't crossed a line making Emma feel like she needed to prove anything. Jayce needed her out of here. She followed Eileen into the canteen. Maxine wasn't too far behind. She didn't mention Emma which was a relief. Jayce had too much on her mind as it was.

"You've been here for a couple of days only, but you're asking a lot of questions," Eileen remarked.

"Why not? I want to get a feel for the place. Someone killing themselves a few weeks before they send me here, I'm a bit freaked out by that. Seems like Tanner is too."

"I'd be careful," Eileen said.

That was definitely a conversation worth following. "Yeah? Why is that?"

"The last girl who wanted to know all about Gillian ended up medicated out of her wits. Simmons signed off on it."

"He seems like a creep, but do you think he has anything to hide? You mentioned—"

"J. C., a word of advice. Eat your meals. Go to your classes, do your work, bide your time. Make sure you don't sit too close to him, that's all."

That didn't come as much of a surprise, but it might be connected to the incident with a male patient, and Thorne's murder. She had to find out if Tanner knew anything.

She had to make a phone call. Jayce knew she couldn't go through official channels. She had something to report, so there was nothing wrong with a personal request along with the information.

After the doors were locked, she took the small cell phone out of its hiding place only the director knew about. He was supposed to warn her in case there were any raids. For now, it was her tentative link to the outside world.

Daniel picked up on the first ring.

"I can't speak for long. I know Simmons doesn't have a record, but I want you to dig a little deeper, see if anything with regard to sexual harassment comes up. I want to know if Dr. Tanner or anyone else ever filed a complaint that someone might have erased—and tell Emma to get the hell out of here."

"Here? By that you mean what exactly? Kitty saw her earlier today. She's fine. How are you?"

"I'm not kidding. Convince her."

"What a minute, Jayce, I have no idea what you're talking about."

It occurred to her that this made sense. Emma had planned it all by herself. Of course, she'd told neither Kitty nor Daniel.

"She took a job as a nurse's aide, here in this place. I need you to make sure she reconsiders that idea. It's bad. I'm relying on you. It's not like I can do much about it from here."

"Wow," he said.

"That's all?" Jayce asked incredulously.

"She told us about the job. We had no idea where exactly it was. I'll talk to her, okay? It's not like I can make her quit, but I think she'll understand."

"Okay. Good. I'll call you in two days. Let me know what you have then."

"Will do. Be careful."

"I know what I'm doing," she said, disconnected the call and hid the phone again. Afterwards, she lay awake for a long time. No matter how righteous she knew her reaction had been, she still felt bad. Emma was working hard on building a life after serving a prison sentence while innocent. She wanted to support her, and at the same time acknowledge that Emma knew how to take care of herself.

Most of all, Jayce wanted these weeks to be over so she could go home to her. She still had a murderer to find.

Emma had another sleepless night with Elvis curled up at her feet, then on the pillow next to hers, just as restless as her human. She jumped, her heart instantly racing when the doorbell rang. While Elvis was off to hide, she resisted the impulse, put on a robe instead and went to open the door. She nearly fainted when she saw who it was. That could only mean bad news, couldn't it?

"Emma, relax. Nothing happened," Daniel said, reaching for her shoulders. "I wanted to talk to you. I'm sorry it's so early, but I wanted to catch you before your shift."

"Well, you did. It's okay, I wasn't sleeping. Do you want coffee? I have to get going anyway."

"That would be nice. Thank you."

"No problem. What is this about?" While they were friendly, Daniel had never visited her at home, nor had there been a reason for it.

"It's about Jayce." He held up a hand when Emma spun around from the counter. "She told me about your new job. It's not a good place to be right now. You don't have to do more hours in the store if you don't want to, but there are other options. The money from the lawsuit came through, didn't it?"

"It's not about any of that. Wait a minute, I thought she couldn't contact anyone during that time?"

"It's for emergencies and information that we need to follow up on. Emma, there might be a predator among the staff or the patients. We don't know yet. It's dangerous, and it makes Jayce's job harder. Thanks," Daniel said when she put a cup of coffee in front of him. "Why did you do it in the first place? Are you really interested in psychiatry?"

Emma poured a cup for herself and sat across from him. "Actually, I am—and I'd like to keep working there, at least for a little while longer. Don't worry, I won't let Kitty down. I appreciate what she offered me. It's just bad timing."

"That it is indeed. Look, I understand. You wanted to be close."

Emma rested her head in her hands, hoping he wouldn't take her words as confirmation. Spoken out loud, it sounded needy and dependent. She didn't want anyone to see her that way.

"I get it. I worry too. The best way to help is to stay out of it. Let Kitty help you prep for our vacation, and I promise you'll be so busy time will fly."

"Have you done the same thing before? These undercover assignments?"

"Some. Not many," he said.

"When you're locked in somewhere, time doesn't fly. It creeps. Granted, in my case I wasn't sure how soon I was going to get out, and it wasn't three weeks, but it's not quick or easy. I need to do this. For both of us."

"No, you don't. You need to give yourself a break, and let Jayce do the job she's trained for. I can promise you I'll badger you some more on this, because if I don't, she'll be on my case once this is over."

Emma couldn't help chuckling. "You're scared?"

"Quit that job, and don't stress about anything else. It will be fine. Thanks for the coffee." Daniel put down the cup and got up. "I need to go. Give me a call when it's done?"

"Sure," she mumbled, not at all sure when—or if—she was going to make that call.

꩜

"What am I going to do?" she asked Elvis who sat on the chair next to her, eyes closed, not much interested in Emma's one-way conversation. "Yeah, it's too early for me too." She yawned. "Jayce is already mad at me, and now Daniel's on my case too. Maybe it was a bad idea. Maybe I should stop." Would that mean giving up?

Emma had liked her job, from before everything went downhill, but there wasn't a chance in hell to go back to it. Even with her record cleared, she couldn't imagine anybody in that field would want to hire her now. She'd been so grateful for the chance Kitty had given her, though at first she had been worried there might not be enough hours in it to pay the bills. Now Kitty wanted to expand. Could that be a sign? "They might be right. I should concentrate on other things."

Elvis snored softly, making Emma laugh. "Yeah, you're a real help. I have to go now."

Ironically, she had never quit a job before. The financial broker had fired her, of course, as soon as they became aware of her arrest. She had tried hard not to disappoint others, but that hadn't always turned out so well for her. For the first time in years, she was back to having financial security, for some time to come anyway. She had to do the smart thing.

Alina greeted her when she entered the nurse's station.

"Hey, Emma. I'm afraid it might be a bit chaotic today. Tess is out sick, and Rena had an emergency at home. Can you stay for the night shift today?"

There was a choice in this, walk out now and take Kitty up on her offer—or...

"Yes, sure, that's no problem." One day wouldn't make that much of a difference, and she could take care of this when Tess returned. She might not even see Jayce all day. To be honest, knowing they were in the same building did not do all that much to ease her mind.

"Okay, let's go. We have to go see a patient with Dr. Simmons. He said to come find him in his office."

Emma straightened her shoulders, willing to make her last hours in her new, but short-lived career count.

"Heather Reilly, has been with us for a couple of months. She had a meltdown in a therapy session with Dr. Simmons, the day before you came, had to be restrained, but she's slowly doing better."

"Okay." Emma imagined that the patient's meltdown was related to the death of Gillian Thorne. She remembered that whenever something happened at the prison, there was a ripple effect that was hard to get away from. She suppressed a sigh. Those experiences were lingering too closely, and that was exactly why her idea wasn't a good one. She should have known.

One of the other therapists, Dr. Tanner, storming out of Dr. Simmons' office and slamming the door, startled her out of her thoughts. Everyone was on edge here, she realized. It wasn't just her, because of Jayce, because of Maxine.

Alina didn't comment but knocked on the door. Simmons' answer was oddly cheerful.

"Come on in, ladies. I have to grab this file...and we can go. We have a new colleague, I see."

"Ms. Curtis. She started as an aide," Alina explained.

"Great. There's no shortage of work around here. How do you like it so far, Ms. Curtis?"

"It's been a great experience, really interesting." Emma blushed as she remembered this experience was supposed to end soon. "Alina told me about the patient."

"Yes, she's doing better now that we've adjusted her medication."

Heather was fully clothed, sitting on her bed when they came in. Emma noticed her vacant gaze.

"Good morning, Heather. How are you feeling today?" Simmons said in the same cheerful tone he had used earlier when Alina introduced Emma. It didn't seem appropriate.

Heather shrugged. "Okay, I guess."

"Have you been sleeping?"

There were always pauses before her answers, as if she either wasn't sure or not entirely present. Emma had questions of her own, wondering if there was anything she could do not only to be close to Jayce, but actually help. She was also wondering if this was really a job she could see herself doing in the future—or if she wanted to.

Some might say selling greeting cards and stationary didn't exactly mean going up the career ladder. What if she enjoyed the work, loved the interactions with people who mostly had something to celebrate? If anything, these three weeks were giving her a lot to think about.

Dr. Simmons said something to Alina, and Emma caught the gaze Heather was giving him, making her flinch. The young woman was afraid. If Emma made this her last shift like she'd promised, she wanted to find out why. There were certain contexts that made bullying and intimidation easier. She had seen her fair share of it. She'd do what she could to help stop it.

✦

During a short lunch break, Emma found the time to call Kitty and tell her she wouldn't be available this afternoon.

"I'm so sorry," she said, anxious to hear whether or not Daniel had told his wife about their conversation.

"That's fine. Emma, I understand that we can't make these decisions for you, but I'm worried. You're not trained for this. Jayce is."

So he had.

"They asked me to do an extra shift today, because we're short-staffed. After that..."

"You're going to quit?" Kitty asked hopefully.

Why did everyone feel so great about it? Emma thought, irritated with her friend. She wanted to work, prove herself on the job market again. Maybe the clinic wasn't the best choice, not at this moment, but Emma didn't give up easily. If she had, she might still be in prison, with no hope of ever clearing her name.

"Yes," she said to cut the conversation short. "I'll be back at work tomorrow—if you'll still have me."

"Of course, don't be silly. Are you free for dinner on Saturday? Ray and Tanya will the there too."

Emma felt more like spending the weekend hiding under a blanket, but she was aware enough to realize that this was a sign she should definitely go out.

"Yes, thank you. I'll see you tomorrow."

She had a few minutes left, but Alina hadn't been kidding about the workload. Emma was on her way back to the office, when someone gripped her hand and the next moment, she was pulled into what looked like a utility closet. It could have been disturbing if she hadn't been in Jayce's arms a heartbeat later.

"Hey. I'm sorry I went off on you like I did," she whispered. "Why are you still here?"

If there was a contradiction somewhere in there, Jayce didn't seem to notice. Emma didn't care, all her worries vanishing in the distance.

"I was asked to stay for another shift, but I swear, I won't do anything dangerous."

"Not good enough."

"Just this one shift." Truth be told, Emma didn't even mind the argument, as they were having it in close quarters. "I feel bad enough about leaving so quickly. I don't think that's going to be good for my résumé."

"I'm sorry, but I swear, we'll find a solution. Stay away from Simmons in the meantime."

"I saw him earlier. We went to visit a patient with him. You don't think...?"

"I don't know yet," Jayce said. "I get a certain unpleasant vibe. I asked Daniel for more information, but he hasn't gotten back to me yet. I want you to be careful, with him especially, as long you're still here."

"As long as you do the same..."

"Sure. Now let's go back to work."

"Wait a moment." Emma leaned in for a kiss that soon became a lot deeper and more passionate than either of them had intended. She couldn't bring herself to let go.

"It's all right. I hear Daniel and Kitty will have plenty of work for you. The time will go by fast."

It sounded logical. There was no reason to fear otherwise, yet Emma couldn't help it.

"You said when this is over…"

"I'll talk to Chomsky," Jayce promised. "We'll both find a better way of how to do this. Now go."

"You're not still mad at me?" Emma had to ask.

"I'm not, I swear. I just need to know you're safe."

"Okay. I…I'll see you."

Funny how it was exactly the same thing they were most concerned about.

Eileen wasn't in the class. Jayce sat at her desk, closer to Maxine. In reality, she despised the woman for what she'd done to Emma, but J.C. didn't mind socializing and curious questions.

"So, about earlier, what did Eileen mean?"

"This is probably not a good idea. Ask her."

"I would, but she's not here. So? You seem to know a lot about what goes on in this place." Maxine leaned a little towards her, obviously welcoming the flattery. "About the girl who was asking too many questions?"

"I don't know what happened," Maxine said. "I swear. I can tell you this, though, no one likes Simmons. Heather wasn't exactly friends with Gillian, but she freaked out when she heard about her. She kept saying she was murdered, and that one of us would be next."

"Where is she now?"

"I told her that something was going to happen to her if she didn't calm the hell down, but she didn't listen. I hear they had her restrained. I haven't seen her since."

"That seems a bit extreme," Jayce said, wondering if Simmons had signed off on this, and if he had a habit of doing so.

"Well, you gotta be careful with the crazies, right? Especially when most of us are here because we're lucky enough some judge thought they'd be better at handling us than prison."

"Do you think someone killed Gillian?"

"I mostly keep what I think to myself, and I'd advice you to do the same. Look, it's not like they're planning to let any of us out anytime soon, so you can just as well try to stay out of trouble."

"Where is Eileen?"

Maxine shrugged. "See? I don't know anything."

"Maybe that's not a good strategy when you could get killed."

"Hey." There was a sudden unexpected anger in her voice. "What do you want from me? We are friendly to strangers, but you need to keep your mouth shut."

"Or what?" Jayce asked mildly.

"Or you'll wish they'd kept you at Morgan. This is not a joke."

"All right, I got it."

Jayce couldn't help thinking that there was fear behind Maxine's tough behavior. She sensed a mood of impending dread with almost everyone she met, and it always seemed to lead back to Dr. Simmons. She had another appointment before dinner.

She had to try and move this forward, but first she wanted to know what had happened with Eileen—and the other girl, Heather, who was confined to her room since her breakdown.

Jayce had to admit that as much as she wanted Emma safe at home, it had been so good to see her. It was also dangerous, making her slip out of her undercover persona. She couldn't afford to let that happen.

Eileen, as she learned later, had spent most of the day at the infirmary sick.

This time, she couldn't talk to Emma as the other nurse, Alina, was around the whole time.

"Can't you just let me know if she's going to be okay? I was worried about her."

"She'll be fine," Alina said.

"Yeah, well, it's about me also. I've been here for a few days, and I can't sleep. Can't you give me something?"

Alina regarded her for a long moment. "My supervisor isn't here today."

"Please, I need something...It's driving me crazy."

Emma dropped her gaze to some forms she was organizing. She looked tense.

"I need you to help me."

Alina sighed. "Okay, okay. I'll be right back." She went into the other room, and, a few seconds later, returned. "Emma, could you please make those copies I asked you about?" Emma was on her feet before Alina had finished the sentence, her back turned to them as she went about her task. Alina handed Jayce a small strip containing two pills. "This should help," she said in a lowered voice, looking behind her to make sure Emma was still busy. "Don't come around asking Tess. I'll see what I can do when I'm here, okay?"

"Okay. Thank you so much."

Jayce put the pills into the pocket of her jeans.

"Like I told you," Alina said, "I need to clear these things with my supervisor. I'm sorry, Ms. Turner. Try tomorrow?"

"Yeah, sure. Thanks anyway."

Emma had finished her task and laid the copies on Alina's desk, giving Jayce an apologetic look.

Jayce left to deliberately arrive five minutes late to her appointment. When she knocked on the door, Simmons opened it to her with a smile somewhere between jovial and thoughtful.

"You're late, Ms. Turner."

"Sorry. I got held up asking about another patient. I was worried about her."

"Come on in, sit. You've been making friends?"

"I thought I was supposed to socialize," she said, uncomfortable when he didn't sit down, but instead stood at the door, outside her line of vision. Her chair didn't swivel, so she had to crane her neck. "What's this, your version of the couch?"

"Don't worry. This is to assess how well you're adjusting to your new environment. Are you?"

"I guess. I have trouble sleeping. The nurse wouldn't give me anything, said she had to clear it with you. I hope you're going to say yes."

"You are still worried about Gillian? It's all right to be curious, but you should use your time here to focus on yourself." He had taken a step closer.

"I'm trying, okay?"

"And you think some sleeping pills will help you? After you have just gotten rid of your problem with prescription drugs?"

"I am not sleeping!" Jayce knew she was convincing. At some point in her life, this had been more than a role she was playing.

"I'm sorry about that, but you need other ways to learn to relax. What are your goals? What is it you want to do when you get out of here?"

"That's more an 'if' than a 'when' at this point." Emma had faced these same questions. They had something in common, Jayce reflected. Of course, Emma's situation hadn't been a job, a choice. There was no reason to feel trapped.

"Don't be silly. You're intelligent. If you use your time wisely, you do have some options. There are people who can help you. I can help you."

His hand on her shoulder made her cringe. "How?"

"In various ways. My evaluations and reports of our sessions can make a difference for you—if you're willing to work with me. Have you ever tried relaxation?"

"Not that I can think of. You're going to teach me?"

"If you want to be successful, J.C., you need to learn to trust other people. Yes, we can work on that together."

He kept his hand in place as if it was the most natural thing to do, and not creepy, crossing every line in the book.

"I'm interested," Jayce said. She wanted to know if he had made similar promises to other patients—like Gillian or Heather.

"That's good, very good." Finally, he broke the contact and went to sit in his chair.

"I want you to close your eyes and try to relax."

Relax? Nothing was easier in an environment where everyone seemed to have something to hide.

Emma had made some more copies, though not all for Alina. She'd been shadowing the nurse, handing out medication, helping to take care of a patient who claimed she had tripped on a threshold, and completed more paperwork. Between shifts, she had a coffee in the break room, planning her next steps. She needed to find a way to get the copies that were burning the pocket of her coat right now, to Jayce. She'd certainly be interested in the initial reports on Heather and Eileen who had shown symptoms of a bad hangover, but insisted it had to be food poisoning.

The door opened and Dr. Tanner walked in, looking dismayed to realize she was not alone. With a minimal greeting, she went past Emma and to the vending machine, groaning in frustration when she realized it was almost empty.

"There's not enough sugar around here," she muttered.

"I only had coffee," Emma said, eliciting a chuckle from the other woman.

"Sorry. I didn't mean you. I'm Dr. Tanner. You're the new aide?"

"Yes." Only until the next morning, but Tanner didn't need to know that.

"Well, good for you. Watch your back, though, it's a bit wild around here lately."

She was gone before Emma could answer to that. "As if I didn't know." She decided to try her luck now and answer questions later, if necessary. Against all reason, she had to smile, remember slipping into Jayce's room in the halfway house, their first night together. There would be no time for any of this tonight, but maybe her findings could help. Eileen apparently was intoxicated though she denied it. How could she have access? Emma assumed that like she'd seen it in prison and the halfway house, there were gaps in security, someone finding something to exploit in a person. Money talked in this kind of environment.

It was too late to give the documents to Jayce now. She'd do it in the morning...before turning in her resignation.

Jayce summed up the situation in her head. First, a psychiatrist who liked to get hands on with his patients, relying on his power to intimidate them into silence. He hadn't been very subtle when telling her he could make or break her future with one report.

Second, a nurse who was giving out drugs without any reservations, asking no questions. This was far from murder, but Gillian Thorne might have found out something, maybe even blackmailed the person in question. In any case there was a lot going on the director probably had no idea about. She hoped he wouldn't cover up for a sleaze like Simmons.

She looked at the strip with the two pills, well aware of what this could mean to some of the patients. Some of them were already on medication, which could create a dangerous mix. Jayce hid them together with the cell phone. At another time, she would have been tempted, but J. C. was a façade, and she had overcome her own demons.

No news from Daniel either. Jayce wasn't sure if she should be relieved, or even more worried. It could mean that Simmons was that good at covering his tracks. Another odd and disturbing coincidence was that so far, Maxine had been most helpful. She hadn't been here for very long though. She had cut a deal after coming clean about the events that led to Emma's, and eventually her own arrest.

Jayce let her thoughts wander for a moment, to the days when she hadn't been able to see a way out, when her own career and life had been in jeopardy. She could have ended up in a place like this. The concept was extremely disconcerting.

Only hours ago, she had been worried about letting too much of her real life seep into the person she had to be for this assignment. Now, the past was catching up. The lines were starting to get blurry.

The next morning, she went back to the infirmary, hoping to talk to Alina once more. Tess was back instead, so she lingered outside the door. A few minutes later, Emma came outside, whispering as she passed her by.

"You have a moment to join me in that closet again?"

Why was she still here?

Emma kept walking, then slowed her steps for Jayce to catch up with her.

"Please, don't be mad. I have something for you. I think it's important."

They somehow managed to get behind the door once more.

"I thought you were going to quit."

"I will. Today, or tomorrow, depending on whether you want me to find out more..."

"Hey, wait a second. I'd like you to be safe at home. What is this?" Jayce asked, unfolding the two sheets of paper Emma gave her.

"I'm not sure what exactly this means. One patient was drunk yesterday though she swears she doesn't have any booze, and a search turned up nothing. That, and the doctors here seem very generous with drugs."

"Like Alina?"

"She gave you something?" Emma asked.

Jayce nodded.

"I think some of the doctors are overdosing the patients, especially Simmons. Maybe he doesn't want to deal with any questions or resistance."

"That fits some of the stories I've heard," Jayce said. "Thank you. This does help, but don't get the wrong idea. I don't want you to take any risks. We still don't know what exactly happened with Thorne."

"I'll be careful," Emma promised.

"No, that's enough. I'd really like you to quit, but I get that this is difficult. Find a good moment to leave, and until then, just do your job, okay? Don't talk to me unless it's necessary for what you are here—an aide."

Emma didn't look too happy about it. "Okay. I need to go back."

"Just a second." Jayce pulled her close for a kiss, before they parted. She would better thank Emma once they were both out of here. Those documents were pointing her in all the right directions, and maybe it wouldn't be too long until she'd be home after all.

❦

Jayce caught Alina when she started her night shift. "I wanted to thank you," she said. "For the first time in forever, I slept like a baby."

"Good for you. Now leave me alone."

"Wait a minute. Only two? I need more." Stopping in front of the office, Alina unlocked the door with her key card. "Keep your voice down, will you? Wait here."

She let Jayce in a few minutes later.

"You'll get me some more? Can you also get me some booze like you did for Eileen?"

Jayce almost expected Alina to flip her the bird. Instead, the nurse gave her a long calculating look. "You have money?"

"I can get some."

"Come back when you have it. I'm no charity."

"Please, just a couple more pills. It's too long!"

Alina gave a sigh before she opened a drawer and took out another strip of the same pills. Oddly enough, Jayce remembered that after the accident, stress would increase the pain she'd thought long overcome, leading her to overmedicate. Another time, another person. She had a job to do.

"Thank you."

"Those were the last ones," Alina warned her. "You want anything else, I want to see some green."

"I'll take care of it. Good night."

The other woman snorted. Jayce barely kept herself from smiling. This was something specific she could give to Daniel, and she already had an idea as to where and when.

Already at the door, she turned around and said, "I need to ask you another favor. I swear I'll pay you whatever you want. I have some money I keep in my room."

She had caught Alina's interest.

Alina counted the bills and nodded before she shoved them into the pocket of her scrubs.

"Okay, this is how it's going to work. You stay silent, no matter what happens, you'll let me do the talking. I don't expect us to meet anyone, but you never know. When you're done with whatever it is you want to do outside, I'll pick you up a block from the front door at five a.m., so I can sneak you back in. You're not there, all hell is going to break loose and it's not going to end well for you, understood?"

"Perfectly," Jayce said wryly though she had mixed emotions about what the nurse's monologue meant. She was letting out potentially dangerous patients, trusting they would come back just like that. Apparently, some had, because Alina had a system from the looks of it. What if Maxine was using her services as well? She couldn't think about it now. Stick to the plan. Get that information to Daniel.

"Okay. Let's go."

As instructed, Jayce kept her head down as they walked along the corridors, through metal doors and past deactivated cameras and motion detectors. At the front entrance, Alina repeated her dire warning.

"Remember, you have it good here, don't you? Lay low, enjoy your pills. You give me trouble, one of your friends in here is going to pay for it."

"I get it." Jayce wondered if this kind of blackmail scenario worked with most patients, or if Alina had a different one for each of the ones she let out at various times. "I'll see you in the morning."

She breathed a sigh of relief walking away from the building, the cool night air feeling amazing after being cooped up inside for days. It hadn't been that long, but long enough for Jayce to miss walking a few steps without being watched and potentially held back. For a moment, she entertained the fantasy of not going back in, discarding it before it could cloud her judgment. She had something interesting to give to Daniel, but much of it was still hearsay and circumstantial. She needed more. At this point, it would be too easy for Simmons and Tanner to cover their tracks.

Jayce crossed the street, hunching her shoulders against the chill as she passed a row of now closed shops. The neon sign at the end of the street signified a bar still open. She had a few hours to get everything done that needed to be done.

She called Daniel who answered his phone on the second ring.

"I need you to meet me," she said, foregoing the greeting. "I'm at the bar at the end of Columbus, the Black Swan."

Daniel didn't ask. "I'll be there in fifteen. You need backup?"

"No. Don't call anyone yet. It's just information. Everything is good." That was a bit of an exaggeration, but time was of importance. She couldn't afford him wasting any on being worried about her.

"Okay. I'll see you."

As the hands of her watch crept closer to midnight, Jayce imagined what she might or might not do after meeting Daniel.

She could hang out at an all-night diner until it was time to meet Alina, but there was a risk of getting seen by any staff having a meal before or after their shift. If she was honest, she had made up her mind already.

Daniel arrived a few minutes later, looking as tired as she felt.

"There's obviously a lot going on here, but what's new is that Dr. Tanner seems to know more than we thought. She and Simmons are in a relationship, and he plans to give her his job once he takes over. Which would be a bad idea, because he's already signing off on drugging patients more than necessary."

"You have proof?"

Jayce handed him the folded papers. "Some of the reports, before, and after. He is increasing the doses of everybody who asks too many questions, about their treatment, about Thorne, or the fact that he has a really hard time keeping his hands to himself."

The disgust showed on Daniel's face. "This is enough to nail him?"

"For falsifying the reports, yes. A few of the patients might testify against him, but we need Tanner, and something more solid on the murder. Now that we know where it's all going, it shouldn't take more than a day or two. I think Tanner is ready to crack."

"Okay, good, I'll pass it on. How did you get here?"

"A nurse who's increasing her salary by making little arrangements with patients. A little trip on the outside, drugs, booze, whatever you can pay for."

"Wow, this place is nuts."

"No argument from me. I'll get you Tanner, then we can wrap this up."

"What about Emma?" Daniel asked.

"What about her?"

"Despite our best efforts, she did not stop working there."

"Once the place is all cleaned up, it wouldn't be so bad, but I hope she'll change her mind. It's not like she has anything to prove. We'll talk about this, but you should go now."

"You're going back to the clinic?"

"Yes," she lied. It wasn't the best solution, but he'd probably try to dissuade her, and she was already feeling guilty for what she was going to do. Alina, however, didn't expect her until five a.m. "I'll see you in a couple of days."

"All right. Keep your head down."

She watched him leave the bar before she got up and followed. When the taillights of his car disappeared in the distance, Jayce called a cab.

⁂

Emma jolted upright in her bed when the doorbell rang. The experiences of the past few years had formed expectations of bad news to come at the drop of a hat. No matter how hard she worked to counter this automatic reaction, it was still easily triggered—especially by a call or someone standing at her door after midnight.

She nearly cried with relief when she realized who her late-night visitor was.

"Is it over?"

Jayce shook her head. "Not yet. I have approximately four hours before I need to go back. You think I could stay here for a bit?"

It wasn't until then Emma realized she hadn't moved since she opened the door with a pounding heart. Her heart was still pounding.

"Yes. Of course. Come on in. What happened? No, let me rephrase that. I'm so happy you're here."

"Me too," Jayce whispered as she pulled her close.

"Are you okay? Would you like something to eat? Drink? Do you need money?"

"Can I just be with you for a little while?"

"Of course. Come with me." Emma took Jayce's hand and led her to the bedroom, where Elvis, feeling insulted by the interruption of her sleep, had curled up on a chair.

Emma felt no longer like being trapped in a dark disturbing dream as she had when the bell rang. Everything was fine. It was going to be even better once this assignment was over, but until that was the case, they had a few hours together.

Jayce's longing look at the unmade bed told her everything she needed to know. Answers could wait. Emma remembered very well how sleep in a place behind metal doors and barbed wire was never restful.

"I can set the alarm," she said. "It's not long, but if you'd like to..."

Jayce gave her a grateful smile. "I wasn't sure what exactly was on my mind when I came here. I had different scenarios...but sleep sounds really good if you don't mind."

"That's okay. I understand."

Jayce stripped down to her underwear, and they lay under the covers in each other's embrace.

"Not that I'm complaining, but how is this possible? Unless I'm still dreaming."

Jayce laughed softly. "You're not, and you'd have every right to complain. You're working two jobs, and I keep you from sleeping."

"I'd rather be awake with you than sleep alone," Emma said, and they were both silent for a moment.

"It's Alina. Not only is she selling drugs, but she lets patients out sometimes, as it seems. She saw me talking to Eileen a few times, so she said she'd make her life hell if I didn't come back."

Emma thought back to her time in prison. She had never been in a position to make deals like this, but she had heard of others who did, little favors for money or sex. The pull of the past was still strong, except that now, she wasn't scared for herself.

"You didn't come just for me," she reasoned.

"No. I met Daniel earlier. I needed to see you though."

There was an urgency in her voice that was hard to miss. Emma leaned in to kiss Jayce, softly at first, then more passionately when she met no resistance. Maybe they weren't going to sleep after all. In a few days, they could resume their relationship and go back to making their own choices, but for now, their time was limited. There was no time to waste.

Nevertheless, she didn't want to make this the rushed encounter they had once to resort to, because someone could walk in on them at any time. It was more than a quick time-out from Jayce's assignment. It was meant to be an idea of the future, when they would have more time together, when they could truly be themselves. Slowly, they undressed each other, every brush of fingertips melting away the tension.

Emma hadn't known how frightened she'd been, always waiting for the other shoe to drop, until she managed to let go in the arms of someone she trusted. She could do the same for Jayce right now. It might be a choice, a job, but the danger was real. They both knew that. Emma wanted to do whatever she could to make them both forget for a while. She could tell she was succeeding.

Fortunately, they had remembered to set the alarm. It woke them precisely at 4:00 a.m. Emma felt a bit disoriented, but she, too, got up and put on some clothes. "I could make you a coffee," she offered.

"No, thank you. I need to go. Alina will throw a fit if I'm not there on time."

"What if I drive you?"

"No way. What if she's early and recognizes your car? You are too involved as it is. This won't go on for much longer."

Jayce was a lot more distant and business like, but Emma understood that too. She'd gone to bed with Jayce and woke up with J. C. Of course, she'd known what she was in for, but it was still strange to witness. Elvis made an unhappy sound and yawned.

"You should go back to bed," Jayce suggested. "I think she'd approve."

"I don't think I'll be able to sleep now."

Jayce stepped into her personal place, cupping her face in her hands. "Thank you," she whispered.

"It was my pleasure. Totally."

"More to come."

They embraced one more time, then she was gone, leaving Emma to wonder if this good new life would ever feel completely real.

A couple of days at the most. Jayce would focus on getting Tanner on her side. There was no doubt Simmons had used his younger colleague, and she had to convince her that he wouldn't hesitate to take her down with him. All she could do now was to save herself. It sounded good in theory. Jayce hoped everything would go according to plan.

She was tired of these surroundings. She couldn't wait to leave and go back to a more normal schedule, and relationship with Emma. Last night had been amazing as usual, but mostly, she had needed the connection to anchor herself in reality. J. C. was confronted with a multitude of old temptations Jayce had overcome. She knew she had, but she also knew that within the confines of this other persona, crossing lines would be easy.

Alina waited for her at the place they had agreed on. She didn't say a word, just reached over to open the car door and drove, barely giving Jayce time to fasten her seatbelt. A few more minutes of awkward silence, and they arrived at their destination. Yawning, Jayce thought that maybe Alina wasn't a morning person. She had let an alleged criminal with mental issues out for the night, but that didn't seem to bother her much.

"You can go to breakfast," Alina told her. "Keep your mouth shut and get back to me when you have more money."

"Sure. Thanks."

Politeness got her no reaction, so Jayce shrugged and went inside her room to get ready for breakfast. She had a session with Dr. Tanner later. She needed to prepare her words well.

"I thought you weren't going to show up. People here have a habit of disappearing. First Heather, then Eileen."

Maxine chuckled when she didn't answer. "Got up on the wrong side of the bed? I saw you with Alina. So, you figured out how to get some of that special treatment, huh?"

Jayce sat up straighter. It would be bad enough if Alina provided Maxine and others with drugs. She didn't want to imagine her out at night.

"I have no idea what you're talking about," she said. She had to stay on track. Strangely enough, Maxine Brown had been helpful to her assignment and followed the rules more than many of the staff did.

"Oh, come on, everyone knows that with a little money, Alina can do things for you. Gillian was hanging out at the infirmary all the time."

"Gillian."

"Yeah, didn't I mention that? Of course, in your case it could be that you have the hots for that cute aide. Believe it or not, she's my ex."

"You're kidding me."

"I swear, it's true! It's partly because of her that I'm in this place, so I have no idea what business she has being here, and I don't want to know. She seems to have a thing for bad girls though, so—"

"Stop." After less than a couple of hours of sleep, the last thing Jayce wanted was to have this conversation.

"I knew it. Well, you have my blessing. She's one of those girls who blushes and gets all flustered, but she'll—"

"I said, stop it!" Jayce got up and walked away from the table under the watchful eyes of the guards.

"Is there a problem?" one of them asked.

"No. I just lost my appetite. Can I go?" The woman stepped aside without further questions.

To her dismay, Jayce realized Maxine was following her.

"Don't be mad. I'm your friend, okay? Friends don't rat out each other...and I promise I won't tell anyone that she went down on you in the utility closet. It would be too bad if she lost that job too..."

Maxine stopped talking, but not until she found herself with her back against the wall in the hallway. She laughed, a tad frantically.

"You are delusional!" It took every bit of self-restraint Jayce had left not to yell in her face. "Leave her alone."

The next moment she felt someone pull her back.

"It's okay," she said. "We're good."

Maxine rubbed her arms. "What the hell? She's crazy. I was just talking, and she attacked me."

"That's not true. She..." Too late, Jayce realized that she couldn't repeat anything she and Maxine had said. It would expose Emma, and it would expose Alina earlier than she'd planned. "I have an appointment with Dr. Tanner."

"She said she was going to kill me," Maxine added for effect.

"I can take the appointment," a jovial Dr. Simmons said behind them. "Ms. Brown, please go back to your meal. Ms. Turner, I need you to calm down. Now."

"That's okay. I am calm. Where is Dr. Tanner?"

"I think we can sort this out among ourselves."

Jayce had known for a while that she couldn't trust the psychiatrist, but even so she couldn't believe the orders he gave the guards.

Damn. Staying on track would be harder than she'd imagined.

"You don't have to do this." It was a futile attempt, she knew, but she had to try anyway. Jayce knew that any mention of Simmons being dirty would only serve to convince the guards and the nurse hurrying after them that she was in fact delusional, and he was doing the right thing.

Restraints. Meds. The treatment for patients who asked too many questions. Jayce gave up resistance as they dragged her into the room, hoping she could do some damage control.

"I'm sorry, okay? I didn't sleep well. I am calm now."

In fact, she was just the opposite. This was an unacceptable, potentially dangerous detour from the plan.

"Well, then you will appreciate being given some time to relax and rest. You and I will talk later, and don't worry about Dr. Tanner. I'll take over your treatment, Ms. Turner."

"This is not necessary! I'll go back to my room."

He leaned over her with a smile. "It's a little too late for that now. I'll go have a look at your chart, and we can adjust your meds appropriately."

"I don't need—"

"Don't worry, we'll keep your addiction in mind," he said. "This is not going to make anything worse. I'll see you in a few. You can go," Tanner addressed the guards and nurse. "I'll take it from here."

There was no objection from anyone. In fact, this could have been a scene that had played out many times before. Jayce was afraid it had.

She couldn't believe the kind of power he had, to order treatment that seemed to be something out of a psych ward from a hundred years ago. Then again, her research had revealed that this wasn't as uncommon these days as one might think. What was even worse, Simmons wasn't just over-zealous, he was a criminal with many means to cover up his crimes. Jayce pondered whether or not to confront him. It might rattle him. It might get her killed. She yanked at the restraints, frustrated with that one slip that had put her into this predicament, then realized there might be a camera. No, confrontation wasn't a good idea until she had her hands free again.

Minutes passed by, and she wondered if he'd been held up. Daniel was waiting for news from her—so was Emma. Neither of them would suspect anything yet. Jayce flinched when the door opened, but it wasn't Simmons. Dr. Tanner walked in instead.

It was now or never.

"I can help you," Jayce said, "but you need to be honest with me."

Tanner gave her a wry smile. "Excuse me, but it doesn't look like you'd be of much help to anybody right now. Sorry."

"I know you didn't want Gillian to die. Now's the time to talk to the police."

"You are showing paranoid tendencies. Dr. Simmons was right about you."

"He harassed her and drugged her for no reason. That's why she killed herself, and you know it. If you turn yourself in, you'll get a reduced sentence. It only gets worse the longer you wait."

Tanner produced a syringe with a clear fluid. "There's no proof for any of this."

"Oh, believe me, there is. The other women will talk."

"Maybe, but who's going to believe them? I'm sorry, Ms. Turner. I promise this won't hurt."

The door opened again, and Simmons walked in. "Elizabeth, what are you doing here? Get out now."

She dropped the syringe and followed his order without thought. Jayce couldn't help being both impressed and appalled at the influence Simmons wielded. She cringed when he brushed a hand over her hair.

"Now, isn't it time that we talked?"

❧

Emma couldn't believe Alina who calmly ate her sandwich as if nothing had happened. She saw her colleague in a whole new light now, as well as this institution. The suicide, a megalomaniac psychiatrist, and a nurse with a side business—and Maxine...Seeing everything that was going on here would only make her final decision easier. Her life had been crazy enough in the recent past. She didn't need any more of it. After the co-worker who had accused her of stealing was gone from the store, the atmosphere had improved a great deal. Now that Jayce's assignment was coming to an end, she was able to see more clearly. The job Kitty had offered her was no longer a temporary solution. She could become manager whenever she wanted to.

How crazy had she been to even think about leaving?

Emma was jolted out of her thoughts when Tess came into the room and mentioned Jayce's name.

"...under observation. Simmons is with her right now."

"What did you say?"

Tess gave her a surprised look. "That happens sometimes. They go from being all friendly and polite to wanting to strangle you. She's going to have some time to cool down."

Emma had been around long enough to know what it meant, and it made her anxious. There was no doubt someone had bent the truth. Jayce was always careful. Had Simmons found out? In that case, what would he do? She jumped to her feet and left the room, heading for Simmons' office. Emma knocked. No answer.

Tanner was next, and Emma found her at her desk, nervously playing with a pencil.

"What do you want?" she snapped.

"Excuse me. I wanted to ask about Ms. Turner. Is she going to be in class later today?"

"Why do you have to know that? It's not like there's a passing grade."

Emma shrank back from the venom in the woman's voice. She had dealt with menacing individuals before, one of which was her ex, but this place scared her. It was almost impossible to tell who was on the right side.

"No...but I heard there was an incident, and we wondered if we should wait for her or...?"

"I don't think she'll be attending today, or tomorrow, if you must know. Is that all? I'm working here."

"Can you tell me what happened?"

"I don't think that's necessary for you to know. Speak to Dr. Simmons if you must. If you'll excuse me now?"

"Sure. Thank you."

Emma closed the door behind her, feeling overwhelmed. What to do first? She wanted to see Jayce, make sure she was okay, but there was something she needed to do before. She hid in the locker room with her cell phone, praying that no one would pay attention to her. She had an advantage—no one knew about her connection with Jayce yet, but she needed to act fast. Other women had been drugged senseless, and worse. With trembling hands, she unlocked her phone and called Daniel. A woman answered at his desk. To her relief, Emma realized she'd met her before. Tanya.

"This is Emma Curtis. Is Daniel around? I need to talk to him."

"He's not here right now. Can I take a message?"

"It's about Jayce. I think she's in danger."

"What? Emma, where are you?"

Emma refrained from cursing. She couldn't tell the whole story at the moment.

"At the clinic. I work here. Daniel knows about it, but you must do something. I'm scared for her."

"I can tell him, but you know that he can't barge in..."

"You have to. Her life is in danger. I think Dr. Simmons might have found out..."

She broke off when the door opened and the man in question walked in.

"Ms. Curtis, I hear you were looking for me?"

"Emma, are you still there?" Tanya asked. Emma disconnected the call quickly.

"Dr. Simmons. I'm sorry, there was a misunderstanding. I wanted to check in with Dr. Tanner if Ms. Turner was going to attend the class today. I understand that won't be the case. I'm sorry if I interrupted your work."

"That's fine, but shouldn't you be in that class?"

"Oh, yes, of course. I'm sorry."

He didn't move from where he stood in the doorway, leaving her little space to squeeze outside of the room.

"A word of advice. If you want to make it here, don't get too attached to one particular patient."

"I'm not. I really need to get to that class now."

Emma hurried to make space between them, but when she'd made it around the corner, she stopped and waited to see where he was going.

How could she have ever thought that this stunt here would lead to a career choice? She should have known that it would likely come to this point where everything was on the line. Emma hoped Tanya would do the right thing.

She followed Simmons at a distance, not sure what she could do from here. She was certain of one thing though: She couldn't leave.

❦

"You said we were going to talk. Why don't we do that?"

"I'm sorry, J. C., but maybe I don't see the point in that. You have caused quite a bit of trouble since you arrived, as everyone said you would, and I guess now it's time to face the consequences."

Jayce could easily see through his boasting, though that didn't make her any less uncomfortable. He had likely never planned for Gillian to die, much as he didn't plan to kill Heather or Eileen. That didn't mean he couldn't do harm, to all of them.

"Is that what happened with Gillian?"

"See, talk like that is what makes me think you suffer from serious delusions. Elizabeth might be a little quick, but she didn't have the wrong idea. Why don't we make you more comfortable?"

"No, thanks, Dr. Simmons. What you said about consequences—I agree. It's about time."

"I have other patients. The more you fight it..."

He jumped when Jayce slipped out of the restraints and got to her feet.

"I'm a police officer. We're aware of the circumstances that led to Gillian Thorne's suicide, and your overuse of drugs on patients. Maybe you're even in on Alina's little business, I don't know yet, but I'm sure she's willing to tell us in order to save herself."

"You're not going to get out of here," he hissed, brandishing the syringe that Tanner had filled earlier.

"I think I will. We have another colleague undercover, and they already called for backup. You're going away for a long time. Adding murder to that list would not be smart."

Without warning, he hit her, the force behind the slap making her stagger. Then again, it wasn't much of a surprise from a man like him. He was now desperate, and more dangerous.

"I really thought you'd be smarter," she said.

***

The clinic was under lockdown. Every patient had to stay in their room while the police were in the house. Jayce had made her arrest, though she looked relieved now that her colleagues had arrived. Emma felt relieved too, and a little lost. She shuddered as she watched one of the officers put a syringe into a small plastic bag with gloved hands, and then her stomach churned as she remembered the last time she'd been at a crime scene.

Jayce, as if sensing her inner turmoil, came over to her in quick strides. It wasn't until then Emma saw the discoloration on the side of her face.

"You're hurt!"

Jayce reached up to touch her cheek and winced.

"Nothing dramatic. You look a little pale though. Let's get out of here for a moment? Tanya?"

Tanya followed the two of them into the break room. It occurred to Emma that she didn't even know if Alina had been arrested as well, or how Jayce had managed to use the leather restraints in lieu of cuffs. She felt a little dizzy though. After the phone call, she had found out what room Jayce was in, but the door was secure, and she didn't have authorization. What if she had been too late?

"Emma. It's all good. You did good."

She blinked, becoming aware of the coffee Tanya had set in front of her. Jayce's hands were on her shoulders.

"Oh God," she said.

"Are you going to be sick?"

"No. No, I don't think so. Did I mess anything up?"

"You didn't," Tanya promised. "This was the perfect moment to put a stop to it."

"I was lucky," Jayce added. "Tanner had a moment of conscience. You helped too. Thank you."

She took a sip of Emma's coffee. "I'll take this if you don't mind. I think it's going to be a while before I can go home."

"You need to go to the hospital?" Tanya asked.

Jayce shook her head. "I want to get a head start. The paperwork will take a while."

"Oh, come on, you don't think Chomsky expects your report tonight?"

"You never know."

"Okay then. You guys have a good night. Emma, I'll see you for dinner at Kitty and Daniel's tomorrow?"

"Sure."

After Tanya had left, Jayce used the moment to pull Emma into a quick embrace.

"You feel better now?"

"I think so. Sorry about that."

"No need to be sorry. I'd like to ask you a favor though."

"Anything," Emma whispered, wishing they could stay like this a moment longer, knowing it wasn't possible.

"You think you could make me dinner tonight? I could make it to around six. Just something simple. We could hang out a bit, just..."

"Be together," Emma finished. "I'd love that. Are you really okay?"

"I promise. I love you."

Those words would see her through until the end of the day.

⁂

Jayce breathed a sigh of relief when she stepped out of the elevator and found the hallway mostly empty, save for a couple of uniformed officers who didn't even look at her as she headed for her unit. Writing her report would allow her to disengage, shed her undercover persona for good and return to her life.

It always worked like that. She'd experienced it before. The last time, she hadn't been sure, but now Emma was waiting for her. Home. Just a few words to put the recent events into perspective separated her from that beautiful notion.

She felt bone-weary. A long hot shower would do wonders.

Jayce sat down at her computer and pulled up the form, starting to type. She usually kept her reports to the point. It was hard to keep her thoughts from straying. She was no psychiatrist, but it would be hard to miss Simmons' superiority complex, his idea that he was above the law, because of his profession and status, because he was a man. The memory made her shudder. Gillian Thorne's death, in his opinion, had been an unfortunate, but at the same time acceptable turn of events. A casualty. She tried to focus on the page in front of her. This wasn't about her interpretation, but the facts.

"You could have waited with that until tomorrow." Chomsky's tone was half scolding, half sympathetic.

"I know. I wanted to get it done."

"How are you doing?"

"I'm fine."

"Finney."

Jayce turned her chair around to face her supervisor. "I mean it—and I would get out of here even sooner if no one interrupted me."

Lieutenant Chomsky laughed. "Not very subtle. I'd like to see you in my office for a moment."

"That's not going to make me leave sooner."

"Humor me, please?"

Jayce saw no choice but to follow Chomsky into the privacy of her office, not sure she was up for this conversation yet, whatever it would be.

"Would you like a coffee?"

"Sure, why not? I could use something pleasant. Look, Lieutenant, I'm sorry. I didn't know Emma was going to take that job."

"That's not what I meant to talk about. It was her decision, and besides, I'm glad she contacted your partner. It made things easier, but you know that already. Good job, detective. I know this wasn't easy for you."

Jayce shrugged. "It was a job. Since we're here, there's something I wanted to talk to you about as well. I was hoping in the future that there might be...others who get the chance. I'm not going to let you down if you really need me, but—that's where I stand."

"I'm aware," Chomsky said. "I'll definitely take that into consideration the next time an occasion like this arises. So, how are you?"

"You're not being subtle either."

"That wasn't my intention. You can come back for the report tomorrow, but this, I want to know."

"I'd like to finish my report. I'll be back at work on Monday. Don't worry. I am fine."

"All right then. I won't keep you from it any longer. I'll see you Monday."

Jayce wasn't able to make her getaway in time. Ray and Tanya arrived the moment she turned off her computer, and Daniel only a couple of minutes after them. She had no choice but to stay for more shoulder patting and congratulations, getting more antsy with each passing minute. The presence of her friends, usually welcome, felt crowding to her. She couldn't wait to go home to her apartment where Emma would find the right words and be silent if Jayce needed her to.

"What a creep," Tanya said, shaking her head. "I can't believe they covered for him for so long. No one deserves this."

"I agree, but I think I really deserve my weekend now. See you guys tomorrow night."

"You're not coming with us for a drink?" Ray asked, disappointed. "I thought we had something to celebrate. Why don't you call Emma and have her come?"

"No. Thanks."

"Drinks are on us," Tanya offered.

"Another time. My couch and Netflix are waiting for me."

"And Emma, I hope?"

"None of your business, but yes. Have a good evening. Bye."

She caught Daniel's concerned gaze, but at least he wouldn't prod. A few minutes later, Jayce sat in her car, leaning back into her seat with a deep breath, glad she had finished her paperwork.

Words could go a long way to contain reality. Containment mattered.

She drove home, forcing the events of the past days out of her mind best she could, focusing entirely on the traffic. When she opened the door to her apartment, the scents coming from the kitchen made her smile, and realize how hungry she was. It was time to let someone else prove themselves. She had done her share.

"Hey. You're home."

Emma laid the spatula aside and came to greet her with a kiss, holding on for a moment. Keep it together, Jayce reminded herself. She didn't want Emma to get the wrong impression, or to ruin her plans for the evening.

"Yes, and dinner's on the stove. That's amazing. Thank you."

"It was the least I could do." Emma smiled, but her gaze was haunted. "Sit. I plan to spoil you for the next two days."

"That sounds great. Let me take a quick shower and change though. I can't wait to get out of these clothes."

"Sure. I'll keep it warm, and we can eat whenever you're ready. You'd like a beer?"

"You thought of everything." Jayce wanted to say how much she appreciated Emma's contribution, but all of a sudden having a moment to herself became urgent. She hadn't lied to Chomsky. She'd be okay. She needed a bit of time to cleanse her mind of all the could-have-been's, then she would go back and give Emma all her attention. "You're going to stay over?"

"If you want me to?"

"I do. I'll hurry."

In the bathroom, Jayce stripped down and stepped into the shower stall, sighing in relief when the warm water came down on her body. It was a first step, if nothing else. Forward. She wasn't going to be drawn back into the past, not by anything that happened. The tears came anyway.

Emma understood more than anyone that Jayce needed her own rituals. It wasn't something they had talked about beforehand. It certainly made sense to Emma, who knew what it was like having to adjust to a different reality. Safer, yes, but with memories that carried a weight.

She wanted to give Jayce the time and space she needed, if it was this evening, this weekend, or however long it might take.

She also knew what it was like to cry alone, because there was no one who cared, or they were too busy taking care of themselves. It had felt terrible at the time. She wouldn't wish it on anyone. Dinner was on low heat, the beer she'd bought earlier this week, chilling in the fridge.

Emma knocked on the door carefully and then went inside the bathroom. Without hesitation, she went into the stall with Jayce and wrapped her arms around her.

"I know this was bad, but you're not alone," she whispered.

Jayce leaned into her. "I don't know where this came from. We've both been through worse."

"It adds up."

"Yeah. Sucks, doesn't it? Wait. You're still wearing clothes."

Emma looked down at herself. "I guess so. I didn't want to waste another moment."

Jayce laughed, wiping her face with her hand. "I suppose this was kind of urgent. Thank you. For everything. I swear I'll make it up to you, but right now, I'm starving. The food wasn't the greatest."

"It hardly ever is in places where they lock the door behind you. Come. Let's put on some clothes and eat. I want you to know this is okay."

"I know."

To Emma's relief, dinner wasn't awkward or uncomfortable in any way, their reassurances for each other more than an exchange of words, their connection deeper than ever before. If it was up to her, she'd prefer if Jayce never went into that kind of situation again, but Emma was able to identify her own better and worse choices as well. Meddling with Jayce's job could have gone either way. She was glad it had been helpful, this time.

"Have you decided yet whether you want to stay on with the clinic? They have lots of changes coming and probably need the staff."

"Kitty would like me to run the store while she and Daniel are on vacation. Since she's planning to open another one, that could become a permanent position."

"Wow," Jayce said. "That sounds like I was gone for months. It's a great idea. Congratulations. I imagine that makes it harder for you to choose though."

"Not really." On the table, she laid her hand over Jayce's. "It's true, I am interested in psychiatry, but I love working in the store too. It would come with a pay raise. When I applied for the clinic..." It made her self-conscious to say it out loud, but then again, it was the truth after all. "I wanted to be close to you. I was so afraid for you."

"I know. It's over now."

"Thank God. Even seeing Maxine wasn't so bad in comparison. I think all this time, I made her more powerful in my mind. She can't mess with my life anymore. I am grateful she told the truth, even though it was more for her than for me."

"That sounds accurate. I got the impression that pretty much everything she does is more for her than for anyone else," Jayce said dryly. "I really don't feel like doing dishes tonight. How about we have another beer and watch some mindless TV?"

"I'd love that, but let's have dessert first."

"I'd love to have you around all the time." They both got up, Emma to retrieve the vanilla mousse with raspberries from the fridge, Jayce, to wrap her arms around her and kiss her neck.

"I'm afraid this is store-bought," Emma confessed, aware of the breathless tone of her voice.

"That's not what I'm talking about."

"Let's take it one day at a time. I'm not going anywhere, not unless you want me to."

"You promise?"

"Yes. I do."

As they sat on the couch, comfortably entwined, Emma had to admit she'd given the question some thought. Having her own apartment was important to her, or at least it had been in the beginning, after leaving the halfway house. Independence, a space of her own, it mattered—it mattered even with Jayce in her life, because as much as she loved her, she couldn't ignore their individual histories that had brought them together. Life was good the way it was. Maybe something was about to change, and that might not be a bad thing. When they were both ready, they would return to this conversation.

The thoughts came back to her later that night, with Jayce sleeping next to her, and the realization sinking in that aside from the assignment, they had been spending more nights together than apart. Regardless of her need for space, the closeness made Emma feel safe, and maybe it was something she could give to Jayce as well, especially now.

Was this a sign as to where they could, or even should, go from here? For a moment, she allowed herself to daydream, Jayce doing her work without having to slip into the life of a made-up stranger, herself, managing the store. Moving in with someone hadn't worked so well for her the last time, but that was Maxine, in another life.

Maybe waiting for the right moment was overrated. She would talk to Jayce this weekend, get a feel for where she stood on the subject. They could even find a new place together.

Emma didn't ever want to put off something this important when her life was finally in the present, when she knew she was already home.

A dinner at Daniel and Kitty's was always relaxed and cozy, even with cops at the table who couldn't resist a little shop talk. There was a time when Emma had been hesitant about meeting Jayce's colleagues, wondering how they would react to her past. Daniel, Tanya and Ray had made her comfortable even before Maxine decided to change her statement and thus opened the door for Emma to clear her name. That was something she would never forget.

"I was going to ask you about your decision tonight," Kitty said to her, "but I'm afraid you and Jayce might need that vacation first."

"That's a wonderful thought." Emma had been so used to longing for things she couldn't do or have that she'd almost forgotten about the money in her bank account. She wasn't going to spend it frivolously, but a small trip was well within in the budget.

"Oh, damn, now I gave you the idea," Kitty joked. "Look, I'm really sorry. I never meant to put pressure on you. Of course it's your decision, and if you want to pursue another career, that's up to you."

"I know, and thank you. I don't think I will. I understand not every place will be as crazy as this one, but...There was pretty much one reason why I applied."

"And she did a great job. Maybe you'd like to try for the academy?"

"No, thanks." Emma laughed at Jayce's suggestion. "I'm around cops all the time as it is. I'd like to stay with the store. I don't know what I was thinking. I love the work."

"I'm so glad." Kitty reached for the wine bottle and poured each of them another glass. "Here's to the new store manager—and the cruise my husband has been promising me forever."

"I see I can't get out of that now. Then we have to do it, I guess."

Glasses clinked together, and amidst all the happiness, Emma couldn't help remembering last night's musings. Was it too early? What if she missed that window? What if—the scariest thought of all—she had misinterpreted all the signs?

"Jayce, can I talk to you for a moment?"

Jayce didn't hesitate, obviously sensing that whatever Emma had on her mind, couldn't wait any longer. They retreated to a farther corner of the room, next to the big window.

"I understand I didn't do everything right," Emma began. "I mean, it turned out all right, and I'm glad I was there to call them, but...I should have talked to you, and I shouldn't have been so dependent."

"Come on. It's all good. I know I gave you a hard time about it, but I was glad you were there. That gave me the idea for a good bluff, and it worked. Kind of."

"I know. I want you to know what I'm telling you next, is something I have thought about for a while, and it's not another rash decision, because I'm scared, or anything..."

"Emma. Will you tell me what's going on?" Jayce sounded equally concerned and amused.

"I love cooking for you every once in a while. I'd like to do it more often, and that would be easier if we actually lived together. If you want to. If it's okay that Elvis will be there too, and I..."

Jayce interrupted her ramblings with a kiss which was as good an answer as any words could be.

"Yes," she said. "Yes, I think that's a great idea."

CLOSE
QUARTERS

During those long nights in prison, Emma had often dreamed about the beautiful things she would surround herself with once she got out. At the time, most of these things seemed forever unattainable, but dreaming and envisioning her future had kept her sane.

All of it and more had come true, she realized with excitement when she stepped into the sunlit kitchen that morning, the scent of fresh coffee tempting her from her sleep.

"Hey. You're awake."

Jayce, still dressed in a tank top and PJ bottoms, pulled her into a close embrace. The affectionate greeting was soon interrupted by the insistent meows directed at them. Elvis the cat sat on one of the chairs, demanding attention.

Jayce sighed. "Come on, I fed you already. Now it's the moms' turn." She had set the table for a leisurely breakfast, including two glasses of champagne.

"That's beautiful, but I can't drink. I need to work later." Emma didn't mind. The cozy scene was every bit a reminder that she didn't have to fantasize about the ideal life any longer. She had it.

"It's in a few hours. We never really celebrated your promotion."

"I thought we did." Emma couldn't help but smile, amused that Jayce actually blushed at her words.

"There's more than one way to do that, right? Come, sit. You must be hungry after all that earlier...celebrating."

It was Emma's turn to blush. She had finally arrived at a place where she knew that whatever good had come into her life, she deserved it. She had paid her dues in advance to be able to live a quieter life now, with the woman she loved, a job she enjoyed going to every day. Elvis jumped from her chair to Emma's lap where she curled up, purring happily.

She caught Jayce's affectionate gaze on her. Moments like this, she could easily cry from sheer happiness, but of course she wouldn't. That would be ridiculous.

"There's a new girl at the store today," she said. "My first training assignment."

"You'll do great. Kitty is lucky to have you."

"I think I'm the lucky one...if it wasn't for you, I could have never made it this far."

"I don't know about that. You're one of the most resourceful people I know...but let's not get gloomy. You earned this. I'm proud of you."

"I'm happy."

It meant everything, coming from Jayce who had seen her own share of professional and private challenges—but she was right. For a long time after her release, Emma had been ducking, waiting for the other shoe to drop. What she'd learned in those days was that it did anyway—and the best that she could do was to be ready, to surround herself with as much good as possible.

Now, after winning the lawsuit against the city, and being promoted manager in Kitty's greeting card store, her financial future was more secure that it had been in a long time. She was living with Jayce now, and she had found good friends. Whatever happened from here, she was able to deal with it.

"I don't have that much time, but maybe you'd like to come in the shower with me?" she suggested.

"I'd love to." Jayce's tone was warm, suggestive. It reminded Emma of a time when they hadn't known each other that well, when their association could have been dangerous for one another, and the space around them had been rather claustrophobic. They had once made love on the small single bed in the halfway house. All of this had changed.

Life was beautiful.

When Emma arrived at the store, sixteen-year-old Keisha was standing by the front door, looking eager to start her shift. She was going to work on the weekends mostly. Emma had shown her around already after her interview. Today, she would shadow Emma. Besides the usual work, they would also finish the decorations for the upcoming Pride celebrations.

"You can start here," she told Keisha, handing her a box with colourful cards displaying best wishes to the brides and grooms that needed to go on the shelf. "We have a bigger selection this year, so we give it a little more space."

"It's great that you do that," Keisha said. "I have to tell my moms to come here. They're already married, but you have some cool stuff here."

"True. And you can always use your employee pricing. Oh, if someone comes in, just push that box out of the way a little. Give them some time to look around and ask if you can help them. I'll be over there."

"Okay. Thanks."

If that was at all possible, Emma was even giddier than earlier this morning, and she had to remind herself to remain professional in front of her younger trainee. It made her happy and hopeful that there was a younger generation growing up, rejecting the stereotypes that their parents still had to live with. It was more than her personal micro-cosmos changing to the better.

She settled behind the counter to do some paperwork while Keisha continued to work on the display.

Sure enough, a few minutes later the first customer arrived, walking past the marriage display—LGBTQ and otherwise. Keisha proved to have excellent timing, giving the middle-aged woman some space before she approached her, friendly, professionally.

"May I help you?"

"Yes, please. You have cards for...condolences?" From her vantage point, Emma could see the woman's eyes well up, while Keisha's face fell until she caught herself a second later.

"Yes, of course. They're over here. Let me know if you need anything else."

"Thank you." The woman chose quickly and went to pay at the cash register.

"I'm sorry," Emma said to Keisha when she was gone. "I promise you the happy occasions are the majority."

"That's okay. It just caught me off guard. My Grandma died two months ago."

"I'm sorry about that—" The ring of the bell above the door interrupted Emma, and a young mother walked in with a baby and a toddler in a stroller. Keisha jumped to open the door for her, and the customer in search of a children's birthday card immediately struck a conversation.

Emma was happy to see Keisha interact with customers, quickly developing a sense for who needed assistance, and who just wanted to browse the display, maybe buying something, maybe coming back later.

When she had finished her papers, she went into the small kitchen to make some coffee and put cookies on a plate. She wasn't sure if the teenager liked coffee, but she'd give it a try. After her own late breakfast, she hadn't brought anything for lunch. She'd meet with Jayce, Kitty and her husband Daniel for dinner.

She was about to ask Keisha if she wanted to take a few minutes, but the young employee was currently engaged in a conversation with two elderly women who were admiring the marriage display. Keisha seemed in awe of them.

"Emma, meet Mildred and Carol," she said, smiling brightly. "Their grandsons are getting married next month."

"That's great, congratulations. Are you finding everything you need?"

Mildred laughed. "Dear, I'm finding a lot more than I need. Your stationary paper is so beautiful, it makes me want to write letters again."

"And she just learned texting," Carol chimed in. "I'd like you two to take a look. Which one of these cards do you think two young handsome gentlemen would like?" She held up a choice of three.

"I think this is—" The sound of a police siren close by made Emma flinch. She saw that Keisha had jumped too. Mildred and Carol were patiently waiting her to finish her sentence, which suggested they might not be hearing that well.

"It depends. Are they into sports? If you're not sure, I'd go with something like this." She pointed at the card displaying a cake with two groom cake toppers. "You can always go more neutral..."

"No," Carol said. "This is probably the only gay wedding I get to attend, and we want to make sure they know we're very happy for them. They found love. You can't beat that, can you?"

Emma wholeheartedly agreed. "You're right. Go with the cake, then. I'm sure they'll appreciate it."

"Thank you so much, dear. I know that's not your job, but could you recommend a good place for the wedding cake?" Mildred inquired. "My grandson's parents are going to pay for it, but they're so busy, I'm afraid they might forget to make a reservation early enough."

The siren sounded again, closer this time. Casting a look past Mildred, out of the store window, she could see the squad car on the other side of the street, with the siren now turned off. She wondered what was going on, and if Jayce knew. She had the weekend off—Emma hoped it would stay that way.

"There's an excellent bakery only a block from here. It's called..."

"I know," Keisha said. "Precious Cupcake."

"That's right. You could ask—"

The doorbell sounded again as the front door was yanked open. Late twenties, all dressed in black, the man who had walked in wasn't the usual clientele for Kitty's store. Even more, shockingly, out of place, was the gun in his hand.

"Stay where you are. Hands up!" he yelled. "Who's in charge here?"

Emma didn't hesitate, not because she felt particularly brave. She was just reacting.

"I am," she said, trying to keep her voice firm and calm. She had been threatened before. She'd been scared, and come out alive, and she would again, along with everyone in the store. Never mind the bizarre situation of someone about to rob a store for greeting cards and stationary. They had some expensive pens on display, but she doubted the man was much of an expert.

Never mind her shaking hands.

"There's not a lot of money in the register, but you can take what's there. Nobody will remember your face. Right?" She turned to the other women behind her who nodded, the fear visible in their faces. Emma wondered if she was showing hers so clearly, hoping it wasn't the case.

"No one is going anywhere," he said menacingly. "Get on the floor. Not you," he pointed his gun at Emma again. "You come over here."

For a brief moment, her body didn't obey, her feet refusing to move.

"She can't," Keisha said desperately, pointing to Mildred. "She just had a hip replacement."

"Keisha, get her the chair then. That's okay with you, right? She's not going to do anything."

"All right, just the chair. Hurry up."

"You," he said to Emma. "Close the blinds and lock the door."

Her heart was beating so loudly she could barely hear him over the rush of blood in her ears, but she managed to follow his order. He pushed one of the displays to cover the door, the light in the store all of a sudden dim. Emma forced herself to take deep breaths. No one was panicking. There was still a chance to turn this around.

"See? We're doing everything you say. Excuse me if that sounds strange, but what are you doing here? We're not a bank. I took this week's cash there on Friday, so there's not much of it. Can you tell me your name?"

"None of your business," he hissed, looking around frantically. Next, he took aim at the security camera and pulled the trigger. Emma wasn't sure if the scream had come from her or someone else as pieces of glass and plastic came falling down.

⁓

Jayce was on her way to meet Kitty, her partner's wife, who had convinced her to come along shopping. It wasn't her favorite pastime, but they hadn't spent some time together in a while. They'd pick up Emma at the end of the shift and meet Daniel at the restaurant. Daniel was spending the morning fishing with a few buddies from the department, including their colleagues Ray and Tanya. Jayce wasn't into fishing much, but she preferred the outdoors to the closed mall. Then again, she might find something nice for Emma.

"Thanks for coming along even if you didn't want to," Kitty said good-naturedly. "I'll buy you a coffee. It's cute, but it's too long for Emma." She pointed at the skirt Jayce was holding. "Try something over there. It's more her style."

Jayce took the subtle scolding in stride. "I don't know what I'd do without you."

Kitty laughed. "You're doing fine, you know that, right? Emma is so in love with you. She doesn't mind that you have no fashion sense."

"Come on, that's harsh."

"It's the truth, but I love you anyway. I'm going to try some things, and then we'll find something for her."

Fortunately, by the time Kitty decided what to buy, Jayce had already found a dress she approved of.

"You're getting better at this. Let's get that coffee now."

They were about to sit down with their cups when Jayce's cell phone rang.

"Oh no, on a weekend?"

"Why do you think it has to be work?"

Kitty's gaze spoke volumes—from experience. After all, her husband was a detective too.

Jayce was surprised to find her supervisor, Lieutenant Chomsky, on the phone. She could count the occasions that the woman had called her privately on the weekend, on one hand.

"Detective Finney. I wanted to talk to you before you hear this from anyone else. There has been a hold-up at the convenience store on Walker." She spoke fast, not giving Jayce enough time to come up with all the worst-case scenarios, given the proximity to... "The two perps fled on foot, one of them holed up in the greeting card store."

"I'll be there in ten minutes," Jayce said, the image chilling her.

Emma.

"Do we know anything about what's going on inside? Did he take hostages?"

"I'm afraid so. There's a tactical team in place. I'll let you know more when you're here."

"Wait, I have the owner of the store with me." She saw Kitty's eyes widen. "I'll bring her with me. She can give you an idea of the layout—"

"That would be helpful," Chomsky said. "Get here as soon as you can."

"Is there anything you're not telling me? You know it's my partner in there..."

"I understand that. We know very little at this point. I see you in a few minutes."

"What happened?" Kitty asked.

Jayce was used to reacting to rapidly changing situations, even when it was personal. At this moment, she had trouble moving or even relating the events to Kitty. This was different from the mean girls in the halfway house, or Emma's unexpected undercover stunt at the psychiatric ward. It was her, the new girl, maybe a few customers, and a man with a gun who was obviously desperate, knowing he wasn't going anywhere.

"It's bad," she said.

She had to get herself together. For a brief moment, she considered letting Kitty drive, but she needed to be as fast and efficient as possible right now.

"You can come with me and describe the layout of the store to the cops on the scene, then I'll drop you off at home."

"Wait. Jayce. Emma is my friend. There is no way I'm going to sit at home and wait for news. I want to be there. I'm sure there's a yellow tape that tells me how far I can go. Oh God."

There was no time to argue, so Jayce accepted. "All right. But whatever happens, you stay in the car. Keep the doors locked. It looks like one of them is still on the run."

"I'll do whatever you say."

Twelve minutes later, they were at the scene.

Jayce reminded Kitty of her promise and went in search of Lieutenant Chomsky. The storefront was dark, the blinds lowered. There were a few windows in the back, the kitchen, and the apartment above the store that came with a small loft. As far as she knew, there was a connecting door between the apartment and the store...She was brutally jolted out of her thoughts when she heard the words *shots fired*, and a moment later, Chomsky appeared next to her.

"What else didn't you tell me?"

After the initial panic reaction, an odd kind of calm had settled over their group. Emma wasn't sure how to interpret it. Hope? Resignation? She had faced too many seemingly insurmountable obstacles to give up now. The beautiful life she'd found, it was worth fighting for, and fight, she would.

"Excuse me," she said to the man who was pacing in front of the store window, shielded from outside view by the blinds. Keisha was looking up at her, then quickly averted her gaze. Mildred and Carol were quiet.

"Since it looks like we're going to be here for a while," Emma continued, "why don't you tell me your name? I'm Emma. I was promoted to manager a few weeks ago."

"It's not your lucky day," he said, and she shivered.

"Maybe we can keep it from getting worse for all of us?"

"You have no idea what you're talking about." He had turned to her though, listening.

"Really? Then why don't you tell me why you came here in the first place? You weren't going to rob the store. Nobody robs a greeting card store. What do you want?"

"What's it to you?"

"Hey, you're the one who's spoiling the day for me, and Keisha, Mildred and Carol as well. It's Keisha's first day, now I'm afraid she's not going to come back after this experience. Mildred and Carol were picking out a wedding card for their grandsons, and—" Emma broke off her sentence, unsure if she was going in the right direction. What if the man was a homophobe? At best, he didn't care, but she thought she had to get somewhere...Knowing someone's name, getting a glimpse of their story, that made it harder to kill them, right? In an ideal world, anyway.

"Why don't you shut up?"

She cringed when he made a quick movement, but he was reaching for his cell phone. "Damn, what is taking you so long?"

"Someone's coming to get you? They won't get in here," Emma said. "The police will have already surrounded the place. If you give yourself up now—"

"Could you stop the hell talking? I'm not going back to prison. I'm not."

Emma was silent for a moment. That, she could understand, even though their circumstances had been vastly different. She didn't know what she'd do if there was ever the danger. For sure, she wouldn't pick up a gun and threaten to hurt anyone else. As much as she hated the entitlement of someone who thought he could, she had to keep trying. For all of them.

Everyone in the room jumped when the phone rang. It wasn't his cell phone, but the store. It rang another time...and once more.

"Should I answer?" Emma asked. "They probably heard the gunshot and want to know if everyone is okay. We are, right? I could tell them."

"You don't go near that phone!"

It didn't stop ringing, the sound getting on all their nerves.

Finally, he went to pick up.

"What I want?" He gave an angry laugh. "I tell you what I want. Two million dollars, and a car, with a full tank. You don't follow me. Otherwise, this is going to end badly."

Emma listened intently, to the words and their meaning. He hadn't threatened to kill anyone. If he wasn't saying it out loud, that could only be good for them, right? Did it mean that he didn't want anyone to get hurt? Did it mean anything?

She was still standing, shaking, but he hadn't ordered her down on the floor with the others. Maybe she was fooling herself into thinking she could form some sort of connection with him, and he'd shoot her first...She blinked back the tears, reminding herself that there were three other women here with her, depending on her to keep calm. She could do this.

"Hey, you. Emma," he said. "Somebody wants to talk to you."

She picked up the phone in trembling hands.

"This is Emma."

"Ms. Curtis, can you tell us what the situation is? Is anyone hurt?"

Someone took the phone from her, and the next moment, her knees nearly buckled when she heard Jayce's voice. "Emma, are you okay?"

The tears kept coming, beyond her control. Emma knew that he was going to yank the phone from her any moment. She couldn't afford to waste time.

"We're okay," she said shakily. "There's four of us here, me, Keisha, two elderly ladies." She could have sworn Mildred scoffed a little at that description. Emma didn't feel very creative at the moment, and if that was an ageist comment, she'd apologize for it later. She assumed the police would want to know if there was anyone in the store who might help or hinder their efforts in arresting the hostage taker.

"And...the guy. He shot the camera, not any of us. He hasn't hurt anyone, and I trust that he won't."

"His name is Tim Marsden," Jayce supplied. "He and his brother tried to rob the convenience store across the street, the owner activated the alarm, and they bailed. His brother Joe is still at large, but he didn't get any money."

"Wrap it up," Marsden warned. Emma clutched the phone tighter, all of a sudden terrified of losing this lifeline to the outside, her reality outside of this nightmare.

"Emma, listen to me. We'll get you out of there in no time. I promise."

"I love you," she whispered before Tim Marsden took the phone from her. She should have done something with all that information, tried to get through to him, used everything she had.

All she could think of was the owner of a convenience store lying on the ground in a pool of blood. Maxine, her unpredictable ex, had run after shooting a man for fifteen bucks worth of junk food. No matter how far she got, she could never escape that memory.

⁂

"Okay, what are we going to do? There's a little balcony on the side to get into the apartment, from there we get into the store..."

"Finney. Hold it right there. You're not going anywhere, and by the way, this wasn't what we agreed on."

"I had to talk to her." Jayce knew she had overstepped a line, but the moment she realized it was Emma on the phone, she couldn't help herself. Nobody was hurt, which was good. She didn't want to wait until that changed. Marsden had to know that this was the end of the line.

"Yeah." The lieutenant sighed. "Now you have to let your colleagues do their job. Captain Reid is a friend of mine. I would trust him with my life."

Jayce did trust Chomsky's judgment, too, unhappy as she was to be on the sidelines. Emma had risked her life and career to save her, when Jayce's undercover assignment at the psychiatric ward took an unexpected turn into danger. She needed to do more for her.

"I know what you're thinking, but they got it covered," Chomsky said. "Knowing that you're here will help her more than anything, and you'll be there for her once she gets out."

"Of course."

There was no question.

⁂

"Emma. Emma, are you all right?" Keisha's frightened voice cut through the fog, drawing her mind back to the present which wasn't much better. Her skin felt cold and clammy. The air in the room seemed to be a lot stuffier than before, but damn it, if a sixteen-year-old and two nice older women could keep it together, so should Emma.

She had felt helpless before. She had made it through.

"Tim," she said. "Your name is Tim."

"So? Why do you care?"

"Do you really think this is going to work out? That they'll give you two million dollars?"

"Emma, dear, maybe you shouldn't ask that question," Carol said.

"Why not? I mean, what comes after that, a life of being on the run? My ex tried to rob a store once. She got caught within the next hour."

"She was stupid then."

Emma didn't think she'd ever feel the impulse to defend Maxine in any way, but his words almost did it. "Not exactly stupid, but she didn't think it through. They caught your brother."

She hoped that when the police called the next time, it would be true.

"You're lying."

Anything else would have been too easy.

"No, I'm not. Joe it is, right? I'm sure he's worried about you. My ex didn't care much about what happened to me, but I bet Joe's different."

"You robbed the place?" he asked incredulously.

"She did. I went to prison."

There was a gasp that hadn't come from Tim Marsden. Emma was aware of his quizzical gaze. "Believe me, it wasn't great, but it's better than being dead. I got a chance at turning my life around…"

"…and see what you got out of it."

"Maybe that's not so bad after all. Maybe I can help you."

He laughed but sounded uncertain. "How are you going to help me?"

The cocky front of the guy who had demanded two million dollars and a getaway car, was cracking. Was that a good thing? If he felt cornered, he might snap.

"First of all, show them your goodwill by letting some of the hostages go. I'm responsible for the store. I'll stay here with you. Let the others go."

"No!"

"The police outside are less likely to shoot at you if they understand that you're not going to hurt anyone. Believe me, I know what I'm talking about."

He parted the blinds quickly to take a look outside, the small sliver of sunlight filling Emma with longing. She wanted to get out of here, now. She was almost certain that she could convince him to make that happen…but she had to think of the others first.

"All right. The old ladies can go."

"I resemble that remark," Carol mumbled.

Mildred painstakingly got to her feet, casting a glance towards Keisha who still lay facedown on the floor. "I don't know if that would be right. She is so young, she has so much ahead of her…"

"It's either you two or no one," he warned. "You," he said to Emma. "Open the door. Don't try anything, don't run away, or I'll shoot them."

"I understand. You can trust me. No one's going to get shot."

She made sure not to make any sudden movements as she picked up the keys from the counter and slowly opened the door.

"I'm so sorry," Carol said, tears glistening in her eyes. Mildred looked scared, her eyes fixed on the gun as they made their way to the door, appearing older than they had when they'd walked in searching for a charming greeting card.

"We'll be okay," Emma said firmly. "Keisha and I will be okay, and Tim will be too. If you see Jayce out there, please tell her. This is important. Please tell her it's going to be fine."

"Now go," Marsden snapped. Then they were outside, and he shoved the door shut. "Lock again. Hurry up!"

Emma did as told. She noticed Keisha was shaking.

"Why don't you let her get up for a while? She's not going to try anything, I promise."

"It's okay," Keisha said, her voice small. "I'm okay here."

"You heard her."

"That was a good decision, Tim. I'm sure the police will appreciate it. They will reconsider your demands for sure."

"They better." He frowned. "Hey, what's back there?"

"The kitchen," Emma said quickly. "There's not much, but if you like, the coffee should still be warm, and there are cookies. Keisha, I didn't even know if you like coffee." Her voice wavered on the last words, as her mind went back to a moment shortly before their world turned upside down. If she had opened the store later, or not at all today...There was no point in this. She had to deal with this situation now. Emma really wanted to hear Jayce's voice again, carry her through it for another hour maybe.

"You two, get up and go into the kitchen. Lower the blinds. If you try to get a knife, I'll shoot you. Get me a coffee," Tim Marsden said. The phone rang once more. With the phone in one hand, and the gun in the other, he directed them to the kitchen.

Providing a car and pretending they'd let Marsden get away in it, wasn't a problem. No one was going to invest two million dollars, and he had to know that. Captain Reid was now in charge, and Jayce resented him, if only for that. Rationally, she knew there was a reason why she shouldn't be involved in any of the action that was about to go down soon. There were other hostages to consider.

All she could think about was Emma, trapped once more through no fault of her own. It wasn't fair. When they first met, and during the time in the psych ward, Jayce had to be careful not to blow her cover. She had a job to do. There was no distraction for her now, nothing to stop her mind from imagining the worst. Marsden had let two of the hostages go. That could mean a lot of things, one of them that he didn't want to be slowed down by the older ones when staging his getaway. On the other hand, maybe he was ready to give up.

"Detective Finney."

She saw one of Reid's men headed her way, an older woman who struggled to keep up with his long strides, with him.

"This is Carol Patton. She wants to talk to you before we get her to the hospital."

"Ms. Patton," she said, shaking the woman's hand.

"Call me Carol, and I don't know what they're talking about. I don't need a doctor." Jayce saw the amused smile on the man's face before she directed her attention back to Ms. Patton. "I have a message for you from the lovely lady who's the manager. She said to tell you everything will be fine."

Jayce hadn't expected the words, or the rush of emotion they brought with them, that made her barely able to speak.

"Thank you so much, Carol. That means a lot." It meant everything. "You should go to the hospital though, so they can make sure you're all right."

She got a shrug for an answer. "I guess. They're taking Mildred too. Did we at least help a little bit?"

"Yes, Ma'am," the SWAT team member assured her. "You've helped a lot, but now it's time to leave."

"Ma'am. Why don't you try to make me feel older? I'll go, under one condition. You have to let me know once this is over, and everyone's safe."

"I will," Jayce promised.

Everything will be fine.

If only she could believe it. She saw a dark blue SUV pulling up in front of the store, the vehicle Marsden had requested, two men in SWAT gear getting out. Marsden had shown himself to be willing, this was Reid's answer. Something was going to happen, and soon.

⁂

The building was surrounded. She had seen the flash of black in the bushes that framed the backyard.

There was no way Marsden could get outside without risking a shootout, Emma realized as she briskly pulled the curtains shut. In a bizarre twist, Marsden was still training the gun on them, but he had put cups on the table, serving them coffee. He helped himself from the plate of cookies.

"You must be hungry," he said. "Eat. They're actually good."

"My boss made them," Emma said. She was aware of Keisha's uncertain glance. She sat at the table, afraid to move. Emma was afraid too, but she still wanted to convey the idea that their situation wasn't helpless. If Tim could be lured into a sense of security, he might even lay the gun aside. Not that she could imagine...She'd do whatever she had to, in order to save Keisha and herself.

Her stomach rebelled at the idea of food, but she picked up one of the cookies and took a sip of her coffee. It was still hot, and slightly bitter.

"Are you going to tell me what went wrong? I don't think you were planning to come here for coffee and cookies."

"No." He laughed. "Maybe Joe was as stupid as your ex. I mean, robbing a store that has a few hundred in cash lying around? How far can you get with that?"

"Not very far, I imagine. They brought your car."

"I won't move until they show me the money. I know it—they're going to try all kinds of tricks."

"Yeah. They do that on TV. I'm not sure how much of that technology the local police have on their hands."

At this point, she was desperate enough to say whatever, but surprisingly, it seemed to work on Marsden.

"Joe's been watching these shows forever. I guess he was studying."

"So, it was his idea?"

"They can't listen in on us, can they?" He seemed unsure.

"I don't believe they can."

"Then yes, it was all his stupid idea. I would have never gone with him if he didn't need the money so bad. And now the idiot got himself caught."

"What does he need the money for?" Keisha asked. Emma gave her a smile she hoped looked reassuring.

"He and his girlfriend were going to get evicted. She's pregnant. When I get out of here with the money, I might be able to help them, though he certainly doesn't deserve it."

"Yes, family is important. I'm sure Keisha's moms are worried about her too. What if you let her go too? Wherever you're going after this, you don't really need her. One hostage is enough to give you leverage."

"You know everything, don't you, Miss Manager? No. The girl stays here, and so do you. You really went to prison?" he asked Emma. "Tell me more about it. Maybe you can help me indeed."

⁕

Time was ticking by excruciatingly slowly. Kitty was no longer in the car, but Reid and Chomsky had brought her to the command center where she had provided them with as much information on the building as she could.

Jayce was listening in on another call Reid made with the hostage taker.

"Look, you made the right call letting the women go. You saw we have your car here. The money will take a little longer as you can imagine, but we're working on it. Once it's here, we need something else from you though. We'll let you go, but you need to let the other women go first."

He waited a moment, then shook his head in frustration. His tone, however, didn't reflect it when he spoke again. "We'll keep up our part of the deal if you keep up yours. Nobody gets hurt, nobody is going to follow you."

Jayce had her doubts. If this guy had ever watched an episode of *Law & Order*, he knew that there were sharpshooters in position. She too, hoped desperately that any gunfire could be avoided. Emma was too close to all of it.

To stand back, to let others take charge, pained her. The only reason Jayce could do it was because she knew any interfering would put Emma in more danger. The team working the scene was experienced. They would handle the situation.

If only the idiot inside realized that his best chances were in giving himself up. She didn't want him dead. She didn't want

Emma to see him get shot and die, relive the traumatic situation that had led to her arrest and prison sentence.

"Let me talk to him," she said. "Please." Jayce wouldn't take the phone from him like she had with Chomsky, but she wasn't above playing her supervisor's friendship with Reid.

He handed the phone to her with a warning glance.

"Mr. Marsden. It's Jayce Finney. As Captain Reid told you, we're working on getting the money here. We need to be sure that the women in there with you are still okay. Let me speak to Ms. Curtis, please?"

Odd, to talk to this man about Emma the way one would handle a business call, politely, no emotions. She didn't want him to die. Jayce wouldn't mind if he got hurt a little. A moment later, those thoughts vanished.

"Emma! How are you holding up?"

"Barely," Emma admitted. "But it's okay," she added quickly. "We're doing okay in here. Tim isn't happy that Joe got himself caught, but he agrees that it was all a bad idea. He wanted to help—"

"Enough," Jayce heard Marsden's voice. "They don't need to know that."

"I think it would be good if they did," Emma said softly.

"That's not for you to decide. Give me the phone, now!"

Apparently, Emma did so without protest.

Jayce had a moment of inappropriate thoughts regarding what she would have liked to say or do to him for snapping at Emma.

"Tim," she said quietly, "it's been going well for you so far, despite everything. You haven't hurt anyone. We know that you don't have a record, so that's good. If you try to get away with the money, all kinds of things could happen, none of them good for you."

She saw Reid waving at her, knowing she had to be careful. "We all want the best possible outcome here, right?"

"That's right," he said. "Get me my money, let me go, and everything will be fine."

He hung up on her.

Before Reid could reprimand her for interfering with the call, Lieutenant Chomsky came heading their way.

"Finney, I'd like you to come with me. We got Joe Marsden."

Captain Reid didn't comment, but Jayce sensed he was glad to see her leave. She didn't mind. She might not be able to get to Tim Marsden at the moment, but his brother would help them. She was going to convince him.

Reid obviously had the same thought.

"If he has anything sensible to say to his brother, get him in here."

Chomsky nodded, and they headed over to the area where the older Marsden was held in a squad car, two officers with him.

He flinched when Jayce yanked the door on his side open.

"Okay, just to bring you up to speed. Tim is in that store over there with two hostages, and he says he won't let them go unless we give him two million dollars and let him get away. I hope you have something to say to that, and it better be good."

"Two million dollars?" He shook his head. "Man, that's crazy!"

"Robbing the convenience store was his idea, then?"

"No...yes...we kind of came up with it together. I had to pay my rent, or we were going to be out on the street with the baby! We never talked about that kind of money!"

As if that made any difference now.

"We're going to call him again, and you're going to talk to him. Make sure he knows giving himself up is the best alternative."

Joe's eyes widened. "You're not going to shoot my little brother? He was so nervous the whole time..."

Jayce cringed of the idea of Marsden, with the gun on him, nervous. She couldn't afford that image in her head.

"If he lets the hostages go, it's not going to come to that. You made him help you with this really stupid idea, I hope you can convince him to do the smart thing."

"I'm not sure he would listen to me."

"And why is that?"

Joe Marsden sighed. "It's my fault. I ran...I thought he would catch up with me, but instead he went into that store across the street. I let him down."

Jayce couldn't believe his ignorance. She was not alone. A crying woman, accompanied by an officer, came towards them as quickly as she could in her heavily pregnant state.

"Joe, you're an idiot! What the hell did you get yourself into?"

The young officer had underestimated her anger, not reacting quickly enough as the woman leaned inside and slapped Marsden. Only then, she pulled her back gently.

"Ms. Bryant. That's not helping."

"That's right," Joe said. "I'm not the one holed up in there with hostages. He's gone off the deep end."

Jayce couldn't stand it any longer. She spun around and walked away a few steps from the ridiculous scene, none of it bringing them any closer to a solution. Why hadn't Reid sent in a team already? The brothers were not experienced at this, but Tim wasn't helping himself either. Going in was becoming the most likely option, and the layout of the building suggested this as well.

She couldn't wait anymore.

"Jayce, I know it's tough," Chomsky said behind her. "But it makes sense to try at least. He let the other women go. Let's wear him down a little, get his brother to talk to him. This can still end peacefully."

"It's not peaceful for Emma in there."

"She's holding up."

"Yes, but for how much longer? How much bad luck can one person have?"

Chomsky was silent. Jayce hadn't expected an answer.

"I'm sorry. You don't have to worry about me. If Reid is as good as you say they'll have her out of there soon." If she said it out loud, maybe that would make it true.

Tim Marsden had ordered them back to the front of the store. Emma wished she hadn't talked and nervously drunk that much coffee, because she needed the restroom. Soon. He glanced out between the blinds again. There was some movement, a man shoving a suitcase onto the front passenger seat.

How could any of this work in real life? Emma wondered. They wouldn't give him all that money, let alone let him get away with it. But he wouldn't know until he got into the car and checked...He had to know that there was no way out?

"You told me the truth about prison? You robbed a store with your ex, killed someone and everyone in there left you alone?"

She shuddered at the memory. "I didn't kill him. I tried to save him, but it was too late."

"That wasn't the question," he grumbled.

"You can get through it if you keep your head down. Look, I know what they've been saying to you on the phone. The sooner you take responsibility, the better for you. You'll get a lawyer, and you tell him or her about your brother's situation. You were desperate. You didn't know what to do."

"It can't be that easy." He shook his head.

"I didn't say it was easy. I said you can get through it."

"I don't want to die!" Keisha started sobbing, startling both Emma and Tim Marsden.

"Stop that," he said gruffly. "No one's going to die. You do as I say, and you'll be fine."

She wasn't consoled, crying even harder. Emma wanted to cry too, but she couldn't let herself, not yet.

"Would you shut up! I'm not taking you. You'll stay right here, until the cops get you."

It wasn't until she saw Keisha's fearful expression that his words truly registered with Emma.

"No," she said, her voice shaky. "You don't have to do that."

"The moment I walk past that door, they're going to take me out. No one will take the risk if you're with me. You were right—one person is all it takes. The girl can stay here."

"Emma, I'm so sorry!"

"It's not your fault, Keisha. We'll be okay. Tim just needs a moment to think this through, right?"

Why would he listen, if he hadn't thought any of this through?

He went around the counter, careful to keep an eye on Emma and Keisha, and picked up a roll of packing cord.

"Sit in the chair," he told Keisha, and to Emma, "Tie her hands behind her back. Not too tight, just so she won't run away. I promise I'll let you go if everything is okay with the money, and they're not following me."

He'd said *if*.

"Do it!"

Her task wasn't easy, as Keisha was shaking as hard as she was, but finally Emma managed a few haphazard knots, not tight enough to leave bruises.

"Don't worry," she whispered. "They'll get you out soon."

As of now, her own fate was still unsure.

She caught Marsden's look on her, and it made her shiver.

"Hey, I'm sorry, Emma," he said. "I need to be sure they're not screwing me over. Open the door."

The keys fell from her hands the first time. After she picked them up, it took her a few attempts until she managed to fit the right key into the lock and turn it.

What would happen once they were outside? If he felt cornered, would he pull the trigger?

"Don't freak out on me now," he warned. "You've been doing okay so far. Don't let me down."

Then he pushed the door open, his grip on her arm painful as he kept her in front of him. Had the police sent sharpshooters onto the roof? The image of the street, the area taped off, blurred in front of Emma's eyes as her memory forced her back to that other time. The store owner had bled to death under her hands as she tried to stop the bleeding. She couldn't go through that again, not ever.

"It's just a few steps. We're almost there," he said. "Open the door, check that suitcase. Now!" He pushed her slightly, and that moment, a shot rang out. Emma screamed until her breath ran out, and then she sank against the side of the vehicle, not sure if her feet were going to hold her up any longer. She didn't dare look, her vision starting to grey out even though she hadn't been the one who got shot. All of a sudden, she was surrounded by uniformed officers, and then she felt a warm hand enclosing hers.

"Emma. It's over."

She let herself fall into Jayce's embrace, wishing she never had to emerge from it.

For Emma's sake, Jayce didn't let her anger show—at Tim Marsden, for unnecessarily creating this scene. He'd been carried away to an ambulance, and she hoped he would make it. Things could have been so much easier if he hadn't tried to get to the vehicle.

Her emotions weren't all that important now. She gave a nod to the young officer who had brought a wet towel, so Emma could clean herself up before she'd bring her to the hospital for a quick check up.

"It's okay. I'm okay," Emma said tiredly, shuddering at the sight of the white towel turning pink. "Don't I have to give my statement or something?"

Jayce thought it was heartbreaking that the idea still made her uncomfortable. Emma had made friends within Jayce's own circle, but it was hard to forget that speaking to the police had once ended in a false conviction for her.

"I can meet you at the hospital," the officer suggested. "A few minutes won't make a difference."

"Just wait a second...Keisha!"

The new employee was on her way to her mothers, who were waiting for her in a safe zone outside the perimeter. She made a detour to Emma, and the two of them hugged.

"You were very brave," Emma said. "I'm sorry you had such a horrible first day."

Keisha shook her head. "You saved all of us. Thank you."

Emma tried to laugh, though it didn't sound very convincing. "All I did was talk his ear off. Eventually he would have given up."

Now that the danger was gone, Kitty, who was familiar with many of the cops still on the scene, had made it past the yellow tape.

"Emma, Keisha, I'm so happy you two are okay. Keisha, I spoke to your moms. They're waiting for you."

Keisha gave her a grateful smile before she left, and Kitty shook her head.

"What a day. I'd understand it if you two preferred to be left alone, but frankly, I would love it if you could still come to dinner. We could order in, come down from all of this…"

"I don't think—" Jayce began.

"That would be great," Emma interrupted her. "Really, I'm fine. And we still need to eat."

"Okay then," Jayce agreed. "Hospital, home, then we'll come over."

"You do that." Kitty sent a regretful look towards the store. "Not that it's the most important thing right now, but I assume it's messy in there. Emma, I hope you'll want to come back."

Emma managed a smile. "After you promoted me? I sure will. Wait, that came out wrong. I'll be happy to come back. We can clean up tomorrow and open on Monday? I mean this is not an ongoing crime scene. We move on."

Jayce laid an arm around her shoulders, feeling her trembling. "We will, but let's see a doctor now."

❧

The images lingered with Emma the way a nightmare lingered, intrusive and unwanted. She had sometimes woken in a cold sweat thinking she was still in her prison cell, or on the cold floor of that convenience store, trying to save the man's live without success. The nightmares had been most prevalent in the halfway house, then less frequent when she moved into her small apartment. In the short time she'd been living with Jayce, they had almost stopped.

The doctor who saw her didn't find anything wrong with her except a slightly elevated blood pressure.

"No kidding," she couldn't help but say.

When they were in the hallway, about to leave, she asked Jayce about Marsden.

"He's going to make it," Jayce answered curtly. "He's lucky."

"Lucky?" Emma remembered having the man's blood all over her about an hour ago.

"Yes, because from the moment he held that gun to your head, things could have gone either way."

Jayce looked alarmed at her own words. "I'm sorry," she said. "It's been a long day. Are you sure you want to go to Kitty and Daniel's for dinner?"

"Yes. I need to shower and change, but right now, I really need a bathroom."

"Are we okay?" Jayce asked softly.

In the middle of the hallway, Emma leaned into her. "Yes, of course. I'm not going to pretend it never happened. I just want to spend the evening like we originally planned. Because we can."

"You're right. We can. That's a good thing."

Emma wondered if there was a hint of doubt to Jayce's voice. She couldn't worry about that now. She needed to take one step after the other.

In the bathroom, she splashed cold water on her face before joining Jayce again. There was blood on her blouse. Bad decisions always got somebody hurt, but she, they'd been lucky once again. Sometime soon, she'd feel like it.

❦

Jayce had to admit that spending some time with their friends wasn't the worst idea. Daniel had made it back into town earlier after Kitty had called him to update him on the latest events.

Now they were sharing a few beers and comfort takeout food, and Emma seemed to be holding up. After the initial shock of having a gun fired so close to her, she was improving. Jayce was grateful for that, because she couldn't seem to relax for a moment, her mind still occupied with useless *what if's*. If she had come to the store with Emma, stayed...but why would she have? It was Emma's work. She was proud to train her first employee. Jayce couldn't always be around and try to protect her. She hated that fact, no matter how many challenging and sometimes dangerous situations Emma had mastered without her. Listening to Emma relate the events to the officer, Jayce had been proud too. Emma had handled herself well, engaged Marsden, appealed to his conscience. Too bad he'd been stupid enough to risk his life and hers. For that, Jayce was unwilling to forgive him.

"How are you doing?" Kitty asked when Jayce followed her into the kitchen to help bring coffee and dessert into the dining room. "I wasn't even close," she continued, "and I was feeling horrible the whole time. I can't imagine what Emma must be going through. I keep wondering what if I had been there instead..."

"Kitty, don't. There's no point. Everyone came out okay, that's what matters."

Kitty's look said she still had doubts.

Jayce hadn't been close either, and maybe, that was her problem. Even though she knew the people in charge had made the right call, it made her feel like a coward.

Emma sat on the couch with Elvis curled up in her lap. She'd drawn out the moment as long as possible, kept the TV on to avoid any questions. She was terrified of lying down and closing her eyes, knowing her subconscious hadn't caught up to what she knew: The danger was past. She was safe.

Jayce kept her company, but at some point, past one a.m., she turned off the TV. Emma flinched at the sudden silence.

"I think it's time to get some rest," Jayce said softly. "It's been a long day, and you promised Kitty that we'd help with the clean up tomorrow."

"I know. It's not going to be that long."

Then Emma remembered the shot taking out the camera, and the glass on the floor. Kitty would have to replace her security system. The irrational thought sprang to mind that she might blame Emma for it. This was always lingering underneath her more understandable fears. Whenever dealing with the police, she was wary, anxious, wondering if something she'd say might make them distrust her.

With Jayce being a cop, and most of her friends, it could be a precarious situation sometimes.

"Let's go to bed anyway?"

Emma found she had no more excuse to stall.

She could manage as long as they were lying together in the dark, Jayce's arms around her. She was afraid of falling asleep. The first nights in prison had been the worst, when her mind was still struggling with the realization that everything was real, from the moment Maxine pulled the trigger, to Emma's conviction.

"I'm sorry it took so long," Jayce whispered, tightening her hold. Emma could imagine what was going through her head.

"They were trying to avoid anyone getting shot. I understand that."

"Yeah."

Jayce's tone revealed that she wasn't completely convinced. After all, someone did get shot. Emma turned to her, reaching for her hand.

"I'll be honest. I'm terrified of falling asleep right now, but I know that when I wake up, nothing will have changed. We'll still be here together, and that's the most important thing right. No one died. There was nothing you could have done."

"I know." Jayce kissed her softly, and Emma could feel the tears warm on her face—or maybe those were her own. "I'm sorry."

"Don't be. I knew I was going to make it out, that we all were. Some days, in prison, or even in the halfway house, I wasn't so sure. It makes one hell of a difference to know what's waiting on the outside. Tomorrow, we'll clean up. We live. That's all we can do."

"You're right," Jayce said.

Emma fell asleep holding her close, and to her surprise, there were no nightmares.

⁂

"It doesn't look all that bad in here. We could reopen on Tuesday, if you're up to it?" Kitty suggested. "I'll try to get someone from the security company on the phone to replace the camera...all else is just cleaning up." She shuddered. "I'll take care of the sidewalk if you can straighten up things inside."

"Are you sure?" Jayce asked.

Kitty cast a quick glance at Emma who was standing in front of the display of wedding cards, lost in thought.

"Yes, I'm sure. If you put things back where they were—Emma will tell you—it will be all good."

"We can do that."

Emma spun around. "Yes, sure. That display belongs over here. The chair goes in the back. If Kitty can get the camera installed, we could still open on Monday."

Jayce laid a hand on her shoulder. "I don't think it would be so bad to take a day. I could take Monday off, too, and we take it easy."

"Yeah, maybe. There are dishes in the kitchen."

The sight struck Jayce as odd—the plate with the chocolate chip cookies, the three cups of coffee, the pot still on the table. She was torn. She hated to let Kitty clean up the blood off the concrete by herself. She didn't want to leave Emma alone either, even with the mundane task of doing dishes. She opened the cabinet under the sink and took out a bottle of dishwashing detergent.

"We can do this quick, sweep up the glass and then we're almost done."

For some reason, she was the most anxious to leave the store. It was irrational, Jayce knew. Emma would come back to work. Nothing else would happen in here.

Emma picked up the plate and put the remaining cookies in the trash, gathered plate and cups to put them into the sink Jayce had filled with water.

"Thanks. I still don't know if Keisha actually likes coffee. Well, maybe she won't anymore. I hope she's not too freaked out."

"What about you? Are you okay being here?"

Emma shrugged. "How many robbers can be stupid enough to come to a greeting card store? I hope Marsden was the exception."

"Yeah, me too. Come on, let's wrap this up. I'll buy us lunch once Kitty is done."

"You're not already hungry? We had breakfast not long ago."

Maybe she needed to stop worrying. Emma had gotten through tough, sometimes dangerous situations without her. Jayce knew she had to give her credit for that.

"You're right. Take the time that you need."

Emma had spoken to Keisha and her moms on the phone, and everyone agreed that Keisha would come back to work the upcoming Saturday. That meant Emma and one of the regular employees would mind the store starting on Tuesday morning. She was fine with that—at least she tried hard to convince herself and Jayce that she was.

Jayce insisted on driving her, and she stayed until Emma had opened the store and settled behind the counter.

"Come on, you need to go to work too. It's all good. Marisa is going to be here in an hour. I'll be fine."

"Okay." Jayce sighed. She couldn't deny Emma was right on all counts. The reprieve was over for all of them.

Tim Marsden wasn't in critical condition any longer. As soon as he was able to leave the hospital, a prison cell was waiting for him. She wondered what was going to happen with Joe and his pregnant girlfriend but decided to draw the line. There was a limit to how much she was going to obsess about other people's lives. Right here and now, she had enough to deal with.

"I'm serious. Go."

They shared a quick kiss before Jayce left for work. Emma cast a glance at the new security camera. For all the good it had done the last time...

Fortunately, she soon had customers coming in, and no time to think of what had happened in here two days ago. It was best to go back to a routine as soon as possible—another lesson she had learned from the times her plans had been harshly interrupted. Sometimes, any routine would do.

When her stomach grumbled, and she checked her watch, it was close to noon. She'd brought a salad and a bread roll with her earlier. Marisa would be here in a few minutes, so she could take her lunch break.

The phone rang, and Emma almost dropped the container holding her salad. Twice, three times...She heard Tim Marsden's angry voice in her head as he told her not to touch the phone. Then, the seconds racing when she was able to hear Jayce's voice, not wanting to let go.

Emma had promised herself to make it out, and she had. That didn't mean she had worked through all of it, and the breathless fear was attacking her all at once. The gunshot. Glass raining from the ceiling. Then another time, when it looked like Marsden was going to pull the trigger, and the cops at the scene weren't going to take that chance. She sank into the chair, her vision blurry with tears.

She had tried so hard to stay strong so the other women wouldn't lose hope, despite the fact that she'd been terrified. Now that there was no one around to make her keep up the pretense, Emma couldn't hold herself together any longer. She picked up her keys and purse, locked the store and left. She couldn't be here, not now.

Emma wasn't sure where to go, but she kept walking.

⁂

Jayce and Daniel had left a witness's house when her cell phone rang.

"Please, don't worry. I'm sure it's okay," Kitty said by way of greeting, achieving the opposite instantly.

"Kitty, what's going on?"

Daniel gave her a questioning look, and she shrugged.

"Marisa was going to join Emma on her shift today. She says when she arrived, the store was closed, and nobody was there."

Jayce closed her eyes for a moment. It had been too quick, too easy, Emma's insistence on going back to the store. She was certain that Emma wouldn't do anything to harm herself or anyone else, but she didn't want her to be alone right now.

"I'll find her," she promised.

"Thank you so much. I know you're at work, but…"

"It's okay. I can take a few hours."

Chomsky would understand. The question was, where would she start?

Her heart ached for Emma who was hiding out somewhere, thinking that she had to work this out all by herself, the way it had been before. Not anymore.

⁓

Emma hadn't made it quite home, emerging out of the fog embarrassed and unsure about what to do next. She had to go back to the store at some point, be responsible, earn her place in society…earn it back. She had worked hard for that goal. At the moment, she didn't think she could face Kitty—or Jayce. She needed to clear her head—wash her face. Right now, she probably didn't look like a responsible member of society.

The café on the corner of the street drew her in. She used the restroom to make herself fairly presentable again, then retreated to a corner booth with a vanilla latte.

Small comforts—she had dreamed of this during the long nights and dreary days at the prison. There had always been an undercurrent of tension, something that told you not to let your guard down…but it was mostly boring. Emma was quiet, she didn't get into any trouble, and so it got better when she was able to work in the prison library, or so she'd thought. At the time, it seemed like a cruel joke, millions of stories, and then her own, being stuck in this place, because someone she'd trusted had made a horrible decision.

These days, she couldn't blame Maxine so much anymore. Those were her own doubts and fears holding her back—and a desperate man with a gun who thought he should be able to change his fate by similarly bad decisions, uncaring who got caught in the crossfire.

She resented him, resented Maxine...and herself for giving them so much weight.

"Do you mind if I sit here with you for a while?"

Emma jumped at the soft-spoken words, but she shook her head.

Jayce sat across from her. "Hey. How are you?"

"Okay. God, I'm so embarrassed. I need to go back to work. So do you, for that matter."

"That's okay. We can both take a moment." Jayce had brought a black coffee with her to the table.

"How did you find me?" Emma asked, eliciting a small smile from her.

"You probably don't want to know. It included inappropriate use of resources...but this was important. I needed to be with you."

Jayce had experienced what it was like to constantly have to keep one's guard up. Still, she was genuine, not afraid to say what she felt.

"What if it never ends?" Emma blurted out. "What if you do one bad thing, and it screws up your life forever, no matter how hard you try?"

"Except you didn't do anything wrong, back then, and now," Jayce said calmly. "In fact, you made sure everyone was safe before thinking about yourself. I can't promise you it will always be easy, but I'll always be here for you. I love you."

"This, when I just managed to stop crying...I love you too. I don't know what happened in there. The phone rang, and I freaked out."

"You were right to go back, but it's also normal that this happens. It will get better."

"Yeah, I know." Emma sighed. She shook her head with a wry laugh. "Is it something about me? I mean, I'm always afraid for you. I, on the other hand, have the safest job in the world, and then this happens. I know I'll get through this. I wish I didn't have to."

Jayce took her hand, holding it in hers. "After the accident, it took me a while to enjoy driving again, not think about it all of the time. Eventually, it happened. You love your work. You'll be comfortable again...and you're right, it sucks having to get there first—but we don't have to do it alone anymore."

Emma held her gaze, grateful for the reminder. It was all that mattered.

Emma went back to the store, apologized to Marisa and Kitty, and resumed her work. Customers came streaming in, a couple whose daughter would turn eighteen next month, a group of girlfriends planning a birthday party for their friend's thirtieth, and two teens wanting a card for their friend who had finally passed his driver's test.

Kitty stayed for another hour before Emma sent her home.

"I am so sorry. I swear I'm not going to freak out again."

Kitty hugged her tightly. "Honey, I'm still freaked out about what happened here. You have every reason."

"Maybe, but now I have work to do. I won't let you down again."

"You did great. Everyone knows. All right, I'll let you get back to it."

Moments after Kitty had left, the door opened again, and Emma was startled to see two familiar faces.

She left her place behind the counter to greet Mildred and Carol.

"It's good to see you. How are you doing?"

"Oh, we're fine." Mildred made a dismissive gesture. "I mean…That was certainly not what we'd planned for a Saturday morning, but he let us go first, thanks to you."

"That's why we're here," Carol said. "We have to thank you so much…"

"That's okay. I did what I thought would make him give up." Emma laughed ruefully. "It didn't work out like I planned either."

"I hear the young man is alive and almost ready to go to court, so that's good," Mildred surmised. "What Carol was trying to say is, we realized that now we have even more to celebrate, and you should be a part of it. We'd like you to come to Jason and Elliott's wedding. They would love to meet you."

"But…are you sure…That part when I said I went to prison, wasn't a lie."

"Oh dear, do you really think that matters? I'm sure there's a reason why you're here, and someone trusted you enough to make you the manager. All of us would be really offended if you didn't come…and of course you may bring your lady friend."

Emma couldn't suppress the smile at the term. She wondered what her lady friend was going to think about the invitation. "Thank you, that's very kind. We'd love to come."

"That's settled then. She was very scared for you," Carol said.

"I know. You're right, we deserve a little celebration, and a wedding sounds just about perfect."

Mildred winked at Carol, both of them obviously happy with themselves.

Emma thought she'd be flinching at the sound of the doorbell or the telephone for a while to come, but that wouldn't stop her from coming to work—from living her life.

When Jayce came home that night, Emma was already there, cooking. It made her feel a bit guilty, since her achievements seldom went beyond ordering in, or picking up takeout on the way. For Emma though, preparing a meal meant something more. She always seemed happy and serene in the process, which eased Jayce's guilt a bit. That, and it smelled delicious.

"Hey," Emma said. "Mildred and Carol came by the store this afternoon."

Jayce moved in close to steal a kiss for a greeting. She remembered Carol Patton who had passed on Emma's message to her.

"What did they say?"

"They invited us to their grandsons' wedding."

"Oh. Okay. That's nice of them."

"I said we'd come."

Emma turned in her embrace, looking up at her with a smile. "You should have seen it. It almost looked like they were secretly plotting."

"Do you want to get married?" Jayce almost regretted her question. It needed context, a ring, deliberation. Emma had faced many changes in the past months, they both had. She should know better.

"I haven't really thought about it," Emma admitted. "I'm happy with the way things are now. You?"

Jayce leaned forward to kiss her softly, relieved that Emma had let her off the hook so easily. After all, it wasn't that she hadn't entertained the idea. It deserved more thought. "I am too. We'll talk about it when the time is right."

"There's something else we could do..." Emma's voice dropped to a whisper, and the next kiss they shared wasn't so chaste. "Dinner will be fine on low heat for a bit."

They were halfway to the bedroom when Jayce remembered she'd never given Emma the dress she'd bought for her, but she assumed that could wait a little while longer. All thoughts vanished in the pleasure of making love in the light of the evening sun.

Later though, when Emma was almost asleep in her arms, she thought of marriage, and that it wasn't hard to imagine at all.

✦

Much to their credit, Jason and Elliott didn't seem to mind that their grandmothers had extended their guest list. They went out of their way, making everyone feel welcome, and thanked Emma once more for her intervention at the store. She and Jayce got to sit at a table with Keisha and her moms who were equally as grateful. Keisha confirmed that she'd come back to work as planned.

Lastly, the setting was giving her a lot to think about. After the grooms' first dance, other couples began to fill the floor, and to Emma's surprise, Jayce asked her to dance.

"I know you're getting a little self-conscious with all the praise, even though you deserve every bit of it," she whispered.

"Yes. Thanks for rescuing me."

"I'll always rescue you. And you look gorgeous, by the way."

There was a lot Jayce hadn't known when she let Kitty help her pick the red dress, bad and good.

She saw Mildred and Carol watching them, sharing a knowing smile. Maybe she and Jayce were that obvious to everyone who took a closer look. Emma didn't mind. They had been inevitable from the moment she'd laid eyes on Jayce in the halfway house. If they'd made it past another dangerous situation to join the celebration of another couple's bond for life—it meant something.

✦

"Detective Finney. Busy, I see."

Jayce quickly minimized the window showing a wide selection of rings. Chomsky's amused smile told her that she hadn't been fast enough.

"I'm sorry about that. What can I do for you?"

"Come to my office for a moment?"

"Sure." It wasn't until they entered the room that Jayce realized her friend and colleague Tanya was already there.

Chomsky looked apologetic. "Finney, I heard what you told me after your assignment in the psychiatric clinic, and I've been trying to accommodate your wishes best I can. Flynn will be primary on this, but she's going to need someone to back her up."

Though Jayce had hoped the situation wouldn't arise so soon, she wasn't surprised it did. She had wanted a slower pace, room to figure out her future with Emma, the next steps. She'd known that in her job, she wouldn't always be able to control those perimeters.

"Tell me about the case," she said.

It looked like her alter ego, J. C. Turner, was going to keep her company for a while longer.

⁂

"I had a conversation with the lieutenant earlier." Jayce had waited until later that night, when the lack of daylight hopefully softened what she had to tell Emma. Considering some of her assignments in the past, this was probably one of the least dangerous ones, but the timing wasn't the best. Then again, the timing was never perfect, and still they had managed to move forward, even against the most difficult odds.

"Let me guess. She couldn't keep her promise." Emma sighed. "Not that it was really a promise. I understand that. It's your job."

That was almost too easy. Emma sensed her hesitation. "Come on. If you had to go on a business trip you couldn't cancel, it would be the same. It's not all about me. Sure, I wish Marsden hadn't chosen Kitty's store of all places." She laughed wryly. "Now that came out wrong. I didn't mean to say I would have wished that on somebody else."

"You were very brave," Jayce said, kissing her softly.

"I'll be okay. How long?"

"I'm not sure yet. Tanya is primary on this. And no, I can't tell you more. I don't want to tempt you."

Emma turned to her with a smile. "It's much too late for that, don't you think?"

"Okay, I'll take that back. I love to tempt you."

"You know I always say yes," Emma teased her. It was impossible to ignore the flash of heat.

"Now that's what I like to hear," Jayce told her, her cheeks heating with all the possible ways she could interpret Emma's words. "I love you."

"I love you too. And I know things have been kind of difficult, but we got a wedding invitation out of it. That was nice of them."

"It was," Jayce agreed. "Speaking of which..."

Emma's eyes widened.

"I know we said we'd postpone this conversation, but maybe the timing is right after all...You told me you'll always say yes, so I was wondering...I'm so sorry, I'm doing this all wrong. I should have a ring or something—"

The next moment, Emma was on top of her, ending Jayce's ramblings with a deep, passionate kiss. "Yes," she whispered. "Of course. What did you think I'd say?"

"Once we have wrapped up this case? Are you okay with that?"

"More than okay. Let me show you."

Jayce resented her boss a lot less than before she'd made her confession.

❦

Emma hadn't lied. She knew that in the long run, she couldn't stand in the way of Jayce's job, no matter how much she worried, and she couldn't always be involved. That didn't stop her from crying bittersweet tears and clutching Elvis a little too close the morning she found Jayce's note.

I can't wait to be back and get the planning started. Don't worry too much. Love, J.

She would worry all right, and she still had chills every time she walked through the store's front door. She felt calmer when Kitty or one of the other employees was around. It would get even better with time.

Emma hated having to be patient once more, but the ultimate reward was waiting for her.

HONEYMOON SUITE

It was Jane Finley, Jayce's newest alias, showing up for her job at the warehouse at 4:00 a.m. sharp. Ten days max, driving goods from one location to another, no questions asked. After a few run-ins with law enforcement, Jane had a hard time finding a job. She could use the money. Discretion was not a problem.

No one would notice, but Jayce had struggled making the transition earlier that morning. On paper, this was supposed to be easy. It was Tanya's case. Her colleague had posed as a buyer and successfully infiltrated a group of counterfeiters awaiting huge amounts of merchandise in the next few days. Even though she had managed to collect a wealth of information, they still needed some important details about those shipments. They needed hard evidence.

Tanya caught a lucky break when one of the drivers got himself arrested for an offense unrelated to the counterfeiters' dealings. She suggested a friend of hers, and her business partners trusted her enough to give "Jane" a try.

Jayce, while happy for her colleague, didn't have the same enthusiastic outlook. She had known that in the long run, an assignment like this would come up. She was good at it, slipping into another persona, making cocky criminals trust her. Too good, maybe. She wanted a different life, a slower pace, now that her relationship with Emma was moving forward. She hated leaving her with just a note, but it seemed like the easiest way for both of them. Once this was over, Jayce would consider a career change if it kept her from having to cozy up to greedy, ruthless people. She had left J.C., a long-time alias, behind. Now Jane. This would be the last time.

She steeled herself and knocked on the metal door.

A man in his mid-thirties opened the door to her. "Finley?"

"That's me."

She stepped inside the warehouse, taking in her surroundings. Tanya stood with one woman and three men. Only one of them was wearing a suit—Roger Winston, one of the mid-level suppliers. He had high ambitions, according to Tanya, and was supposed to lead them to the bigger players in the near future. If all went according to plan with the incoming shipments, a big bust wasn't too far ahead.

"I'm here," she said. "Where am I going?"

The man who had let her in laughed.

"You're not going anywhere by yourself, yet, honey. T over there says we can trust you, but I'd like to see for myself."

Jayce suppressed a wince when he stepped forward and started frisking her, hands lingering in places.

"There I thought you might buy me dinner first. No piece, no wire. I'm not suicidal."

"All right then. Looking good. I'll get Connor in here, and we'll send you on a test run."

"What does that mean?" she asked, frowning, even though she could guess. "I've been driving since I was fourteen. I don't need a babysitter."

"Well, I guess T left out some things. You'll spend a few days with Connor, get familiar with the routes. Don't worry, we'll pay you."

"I hope so," she mumbled.

"Once we think you can handle it, you can go on your own. Please bear with us, but this is last minute, and there can be no mistakes."

"She'll be fine," Tanya said. "We don't have a lot of time."

"Let's get Connor in here, and send them on their way."

Jayce caught Tanya's gaze on her. Everything had worked according to plan. They would have a better picture of the routes and the supply network soon.

***

Connor regarded her with suspicion, something, Jayce learned soon, that had nothing to do with her abrupt addition to the group.

"Another girl? That's all they could do?"

"Really? What body parts do you think I'm driving with?" she asked, exasperated as they walked towards the box truck.

"At the moment, you won't be driving anything. You sit, shut up and listen. When I tell you to do something, you do it. We have the papers. If cops stop us, we have no idea what's in the back."

"I have no idea what's in the back, and I don't care," Jayce assured him as she climbed into the passenger's seat. "My friend told me I could make a few bucks. That's what I'm here for."

"What part of shut up and listen did you not get?"

"Whatever."

For the next fifteen or twenty minutes, they drove in less than companionable silence, leaving Jayce with not much to do other than to contemplate her current situation. She'd pull the routes off of the GPS, so she didn't have to memorize the way. This was...different. She had done a lot of undercover assignments where people were interested in details of her story that she needed to have ready at any moment. It wasn't yet time to relax, but perhaps this could be as easy as she'd hoped, leaving the bigger part and the credit to Tanya while she did her own job. After that, no more. She had a wedding coming up.

"What's funny?" Connor snapped, and she quickly schooled her features into a more neutral expression. She couldn't slip up like that again, allow herself to daydream.

For Jayce, those ten days couldn't be over soon enough. At least, she didn't have to get close to those people. Her discretion and driving skills were all they were interested in.

⁘

Emma had a busy morning at *Kitty's Greeting Cards & Stationary*, but every once in a while, she snuck a glance at the calendar on the wall behind the counter. Ten days. It wasn't that long and yet it seemed like an eternity. It might have to do with the fact that she couldn't wait to start making wedding plans with Jayce. She had been fantasizing about that day a lot ever since the proposal. For a long time, she hadn't even dared hope something like this could ever happen to her—now it was within reach.

Jayce had hinted at some more permanent changes to come after this assignment, adding to Emma's anticipation. When Emma had worked for a financial planner before a series of tragic events turned her life upside down, she couldn't imagine doing anything else.

Prison and the life after had changed that outlook. She had welcomed the opportunity Kitty had given her. Now, after she'd cleared her name and gained some financial stability, she had made herself at home in her new career.

Jayce had worked hard to come back to her job after her accident. Her perspective had changed as well. Emma wanted to be supportive of all her decisions, even though she didn't want to be the sole reason Jayce left a profession she'd once loved. They would have many more conversations once she was back.

Despite her many musings, the workday came to an end. Emma was about to close the store when Kitty, the owner, and wife of Jayce's partner Daniel, knocked on the glass.

"Hey. I thought when you're done here, we could have dinner?" Emma stepped aside to let her in. Their friends could be too obvious at times.

"You're supposed to keep me out of trouble, I assume," she said, amused. None of them had forgotten that when Jayce went undercover at a local psychiatric facility, Emma had gotten herself a part time job at the same hospital, ending up finding crucial evidence.

Jayce certainly hadn't. Emma wasn't going to try and insinuate herself into her work this time. While she worried the same, she understood her own motives better now, and she felt secure and independent enough to make it through ten days. A lot would change after that.

Kitty shrugged.

"Sometimes I like to have dinner with my favorite employee. Besides, it's anyone's guess who needs to be kept out of trouble. Daniel is working late, and I feel like going out."

"I could eat," Emma admitted. "Well, at least you know he'll be coming home tonight."

"Jayce is coming home in a few days," Kitty reminded her.

"I know. So, what did you have in mind?"

Kitty waited until she had gathered her keys and coat.

"It's a new restaurant I've wanted to try for weeks. Since my husband is AWOL, you'll be the first to share the experience." Before Emma had time to react, she must have realized how that sounded. "And that's not how I meant it. I am so glad we met you...and that someone knows what it's like."

They came back to the subject once settled in the booth in the cozy bistro-style restaurant in the city center. It was next to a bookstore where Emma had once hoped to find a job. Over appetizers, Emma shared her dilemma.

"It's not my decision, I know," she said. "But it's getting harder each time, and we've been together for less than a year."

"It's a decision you will make together. I've known Jayce for a long time, and when she says she's tired, she's not kidding. Daniel hasn't even done as many of those jobs, but it took a toll on us at times. It's important to be honest about these subjects."

"Yeah." Emma sighed. "We will talk about all of this soon."

"Well, there are other important things you need to talk about, too. Have you figured out where to hold the wedding?"

"We haven't been able to figure out much other that we want to get married. Something small and private."

"And the honeymoon?"

"I'm not sure we could afford..." Emma became aware of Kitty's patient gaze and shook her head, laughing. "Yes, I know, we could now. I'm still getting used to the idea."

"I'm not saying you should do a trip around the world, but some time away would do both of you good."

"It's true. I'll add it to the ever-growing list."

After the meal, they walked along the main street, deciding to finish the day with a cappuccino at the nearby coffee shop. Kitty went to get their orders, and Emma sat at one of the tables in the back. Nearby, an employee was wiping tables, and when their eyes met, it took Emma a moment to realize they knew each other. The other woman, Caren, was as baffled as she was, but she came over, smiling.

"Emma! It's so great to see you. How are you?"

Kitty arrived at the same moment, regarding the scene with friendly curiosity as she set down the cups.

"Caren, this is Kitty, my boss. Kitty—Caren, an old friend." Emma didn't care for giving Kitty a timeline, and she felt instantly guilty about it. She had done whatever she could to leave the past behind. There was no reason to be worried about what either of these women might think, about her, about the decisions she'd made. Not anymore, right?

She saw Caren's eyebrow rise at the description and couldn't blame her. What was she afraid of?

"Yes. I was just asking how things were, but I guess the answer is pretty good if your boss takes you out for coffee."

Oh, no, Caren was possibly getting the wrong idea altogether.

"I'm good. How long have you been working here?"

"Three months," Caren answered. "How about you come by another time, and we talk some more? I'd love to catch up."

"Yeah, me too. I'll definitely do that."

"Great. Excuse me, but...I need to go back to work now."

"Of course," Kitty answered for a tongue-tied Emma. "Nice to meet you, Caren."

❧

Jayce wasn't going to spend 24/7 with the group, Connor or even Tanya, but she couldn't go home either. They had already demonstrated that they checked their associates thoroughly, so she spent the night in a non-descript one bedroom apartment rented for this purpose.

There was a motel across the street, and a 7-11 on the corner. She had bought some beer, and frozen pizza that was thawing in the microwave while she was going over her notes. She hadn't yet been able to get the data from the GPS, but they had indeed paid her for the first day. Connor was grumpy and silent most of the time, however, he was doing his job and seemed to assume that she'd be able to do hers. He let her drive on the way back.

So far, so good.

She stood at the window and watched the cars down below as she sipped her beer. Jayce was certain that they had someone watching her. For Roger Winston, a multi-million-dollar business was on the line, and he wasn't even all that high up in the hierarchy. They only let her play because she didn't ask questions, and they could get away with paying her a minimum in return. Who would she complain to?

The sound of the microwave alerted her that the pizza was ready. Jane didn't have a care in the world other than getting the job done and earning a few bucks.

Jayce's thoughts were drifting. She missed Emma, not just because of this one day they weren't spending together, but knowing this was only the first of ten—and knowing that the world outside wasn't all that safe.

The pizza was surprisingly good. She put away the notes and settled onto the couch with another beer. Halfway through her meal, the sharp knock on the door interrupted her.

"Who's there?"

Jane didn't carry a gun to her job, not unless her employers told her so. In private, that was another story.

"Can I come in?"

Connor. She didn't think this was a good development. It meant they were even more blatant about watching her than she'd thought.

Jayce went to the door and opened it but left the chain in place.

"What do you want?"

"Just talk."

This was curious. Jayce wasn't sure how much she could learn from him, considering that he, too, wasn't supposed to ask too many questions, but he had been with the organization for a while and might have picked up some things.

"About what?"

He shrugged.

"You can put that away," he said, guessing correctly even though he couldn't see the gun she'd picked up. "We're going to spend a lot of time together in the next few days."

Jayce finally removed the chain and opened the door.

"Funny. Judging from today, I didn't peg you for much of a talker."

He didn't give her any explanation.

"You want a beer?"

"Sure. Thanks."

Jayce went to open another bottle and returned to the living room, handing it to him.

They drank in silence for a moment, until he asked, "Why did you take this job?"

Could they really be this obvious, or did he have a personal agenda? Either way, Jayce was going to find out.

"Why did you? Pays the rent. It's better than waiting tables, and no one tries to grab my ass on a regular basis."

"Aren't there other ways to make money? Your friend seems to have enough of it if she can do business with Roger. Why doesn't she help you out?"

Jayce leaned back against the couch, shaking her head.

"Well, this is her helping me out. We're not that close, and I'm not a charity case. Besides, she didn't always have that kind of money. Worked herself up."

"That something you want to do, too?"

"I'm not thinking that far ahead. I hope the guys can see I'm doing a good job, and they might hire me again."

"Yeah, if there is another job."

"What do you mean?"

Connor looked startled, as if he'd already said too much. The evening was taking a promising turn.

"Hey. You came here to talk, right? I'm not going to tell anyone, especially if there's something I should know. I was told I'd do a few miles, ask no questions, and I get to take the money home. I'm not looking to get arrested."

"That won't be the problem," he said and drank from his bottle. "The cops have no clue. We've been doing this for months, and they are still in the dark."

"Oh. That's a good thing then. What are you worried about?"

"It's probably nothing. Thanks for the beer, Jane." He got up and put the bottle on the table. "See you tomorrow."

"Yeah. Good night."

Closing the door behind him, Jayce smiled. Not as much in the dark as you imagine.

She was optimistic that Connor would be a whole lot more talkative in the next few days—if only to save his own hide.

❧

Kitty and Emma had planned to share a cab, but when the driver pulled into the driveway of Kitty and Daniel's house, the space was still empty.

"I guess since the girls are busy, it's a boys' night out," Kitty said, referring to the fact that both Detective Tanya Flynn and Jayce were away on the job. "Do you want to come in for a nightcap?"

Emma hesitated. So far, she had successfully circumvented every mention of Caren. It wasn't like she was under any obligation to tell Kitty. No matter how caring and understanding her new friends were, something would always separate them. Wouldn't it? In any case, if she was to approach the subject anytime soon, she wasn't sure she could do it sober.

"Just one drink," Kitty coaxed.

"All right. If I don't show up to work on time tomorrow, I'll blame you."

Kitty laughed. "It's Keisha's turn to open anyway." She took a bill out of her wallet to pay the driver, and they went inside where Kitty poured them both a glass of Irish cream liquor over ice.

"It's okay not to get used to this, their job..." she said. "I never did."

"Everything will be fine," Emma declared, unsure who she was trying to convince, Kitty, or herself.

"Of course. And perhaps this is a good time to connect with an old friend. That will take your mind of things. I'm sure she'll be happy for you."

Perhaps that was true. Caren was one of the most generous people Emma had met during the darkest time of her life. She also presented a reminder of that time. It might not be fair, but Emma found it hard to make the separation. Especially now, with *everything* about to happen for her.

She nearly downed the drink in one gulp, prompting a surprised look from Kitty.

"Or maybe I should stop talking, because I don't know if you have any good memories with that woman at all. I'm sorry, Emma."

"No, don't be. It's fine. I met Caren in prison."

It had been a different reality, one in which Emma could only hope to do her time and try to make a living afterwards, stay by herself, stay out of trouble. She hadn't imagined being able to work full-time, manage a business, or even fall in love. The rules had been completely different.

"I figured. But things are better now, for both of you as it seems."

"Am I a bad person for wanting to pretend it never happened?" Emma wondered out loud. "For wanting to pretend I didn't know her?"

"Oh honey, if that's the worst a bad person did, the world would be so much better. I understand wanting to focus on the good. It's important. But if we ignore the rest, it can sneak up on us."

Kitty and Daniel's marriage was a happy one, as far as Emma knew. She was aware that Kitty, like herself, had been in an abusive relationship before. It was important to name things appropriately.

"I was so afraid, all the time," she admitted. "I didn't even realize how much, until it was over."

Kitty wordlessly refilled both of their glasses.

"So, I'm not sure if she and I have good memories. I suppose we do. It wasn't so much about making friends as it was about forgetting reality for a few minutes."

Emma didn't have to go into more details.

"You don't have to catch up if it makes you uncomfortable. You don't owe anything to anybody."

To Emma, it was incredibly liberating to hear those words. She straightened her shoulders, relieved to feel the tension leave her body.

"I might go for a coffee, to see how she's doing. You're right. It doesn't have to be more than that." There was no need to fear the past when the future was looking this bright. Chances were Caren wanted to talk about her present life more than anything they'd shared back in those dark days.

Connor picked her up the next day, 4:00 a.m. once again, and drove them to the warehouse. He had brought coffee. Aware of Jayce's surprised look, he lowered his voice to a whisper. "For the beer."

"All right. Thank you."

It was her turn to move a truckload full of designer shoes, handbags and watches to the location closer to the big sale. Later that day, they would pick up another load at the docks, but for now, their route took them out of the city. The state police had a couple of people on the task force. They weren't going to bust Winston yet. Everyone was focused on the players higher in the hierarchy.

They had about an hour to go. Jayce found the drive surprisingly relaxing. Her latest assignments had all taken place within the context of an institution, where she'd been under observation constantly. At least, in this, there was no doubt as to who the bad guys were. The only question was when she got to arrest them. Even that was becoming clearer.

Connor requested a pit stop, and she parked the truck at the next rest stop, waiting until he was out of sight. Then she quickly pulled the data from the vehicle's GPS and went through the glove compartment. She found a handful of receipts from gas stations, and a note with some numbers and names. Jayce copied them quickly and had barely closed the compartment, when Connor asked, "Looking for something?"

"No. Trying to find a radio station, but no such luck."

"You're going to fall asleep?"

"No way. I'm good."

"You better be. We don't want the cops to stop us."

"Yeah, you're right about that. So, about last night..." He stayed silent, so Jayce continued. "You said the cops weren't the problem."

"If we can wrap this up within the scheduled timeframe, there isn't going to be a problem," he said.

"And what happens if...?"

"We deliver high quality. Some people want in on the cake. Their products aren't as good as ours, but cheaper."

"Then maybe somebody should rat *them* out to the cops. We'd have a clear path," Jayce mused.

He grinned. "That would be something, wouldn't it? Let's make a little detour on the way back. I cleared it with Roger."

⁂

Emma sat on the couch with Elvis, her cat, in her lap. The TV was on, but she didn't pay attention to the flickering images. Her mind was on another movie, from a past time not as far behind as she'd hoped. Kitty had said the past could sneak up on them—perhaps that warning had come too late. The way perception changed over time could add an additional layer of complication.

Before prison, Emma had made choices, not all of them good ones, granted. She'd wanted to meet women who were edgy and confident like Maxine had seemed. She had been prone to repeating mistakes.

When she found herself with Caren, it had been out of fear and loneliness. She'd said yes, but it wouldn't have been that hard for anyone to persuade her. She needed to be with someone she was fairly sure wouldn't hurt her, and Caren had seen that need, perhaps exploited it—except she didn't have many more options either.

Did it matter how Caren remembered the story? Did she want to know?

Emma had broken her dysfunctional patterns with Jayce, even before she got to know the woman behind the undercover persona. What more could she learn?

After her shift at the store, she walked past the coffee shop, then turned around and walked inside.

Caren was behind the counter, putting on her coat.

"Emma, you're here," she said with a warm smile. "Frankly, I wasn't sure you were going to come back."

"The cappuccino was really good," Emma said, making her laugh.

"Well, I'm glad, but let's go somewhere else, okay? I know a great place."

A bit startled, Emma agreed, nonetheless. It didn't mean anything. She didn't have to flatter herself. She had often been aware that few people understood what she'd been through. Jayce had done undercover work in a prison, so she had an idea of the atmosphere, but she'd known it was temporary, for a job.

Caren was probably happy to have found a person she knew understood, because there were things you couldn't share with many people. Jayce wouldn't mind if Emma had dinner with her—even if she had known.

"So...when...?" she started, unsure how to formulate the question.

Caren linked her arm with Emma's. "They let me out last summer. I worked different jobs, but this one is the best so far. I get to be around nice people and sweet stuff all day—that's quite the difference from before."

"Yeah, I can imagine."

"What about you? That was really your boss?"

"Yeah. She's a friend too."

Caren gave her a quizzical sideways look. "How are the benefits?"

"Pretty good, I became manager a while ago..." Emma let her words trail off when she realized Caren wasn't talking about the job at all. "Come on. It's not like that. She's married."

"Doesn't stop all of them. I'm just saying it's easy to take advantage of someone like us, but I'm glad it's not that way. Oh, and here we are."

It was with growing discomfort that Emma realized they were standing in front of an apartment building.

"Caren..."

"There's a bar on the other side of the building. It's not expensive, I promise."

Emma followed her through the gate along a path to a big yard. As promised, there were some businesses located on the other side. A flight of stairs was leading down to a place called *Pink*.

So, Caren didn't invite her to her home. Emma still wasn't sure if she had judged her intentions correctly when they walked down the stairs and into the bar. Caren waved to the bartender and then pointed out a table on the other side of the room.

"Is over there okay for you?"

"Sure. It's fine."

This wasn't what Emma had in mind. She'd expected a half hour or so over a coffee, but she could do one evening, right? Not everyone who had left prison behind was as lucky as she was. There wasn't that much that separated them—only a handful of people, who believed her side of the story, had made all the difference. Caren might have done what she'd been accused of, but she had her own side too, an abusive boyfriend who had forced her to participate in his scheme of drugs and blackmail. Lucky, they both had been.

They sat down, and a moment later, a waitress appeared.

"I'll have a beer," Caren said. "What would you like, Emma? They have cocktails...I think you're more into wine, right?"

"A white wine, please." Emma decided quickly, uncomfortable for reasons she didn't want to address at the moment. She'd been fortunate enough to meet a couple of women who had cautioned her against sharing too much, any sort of information that someone could use against you. It had been quite harmless when one night, she'd told Caren how much she'd give for a glass of wine. The context hadn't been so innocent, and she was surprised that Caren remembered.

"So, tell me what's going on with you," she said.

"I'm doing okay, working, keeping a roof over my head and staying away from bad boys...and girls." Caren winked. "We both know that ends badly. But you seem to have a lot more interesting things to tell. That boss of yours seems like a classy lady. How did you get that gig?"

"She is...and a friend of hers introduced me." My fiancée, actually. "It's great. She opened another store, and so I became manager of the first one. When I first started, I had no idea this would happen."

"Yeah. It's not easy when you have a record."

Their drinks arrived, and Emma took a sip of hers before she said, "I don't, not anymore. I sued the city." Spoken out loud, it still sounded surreal. "They settled."

Caren's eyes widened. "Really? I mean, that's great news. I'm happy for you. You found some folks who helped you."

"I did. How about you?"

It was a precarious dance, this conversation, in this place—only a matter of time before someone touched on more delicate subjects.

"Well, like I said, I'm making better friends. No offense, I always knew you'd go places. Everyone knew you didn't belong there."

"Well, not everyone, apparently, but I know what you mean." How did that glass become empty in such a short time? At this rate she was going to have a problem by the time Jayce returned. At least, Caren considered them friends. That was an acceptable, if euphemistic term.

"I knew it," Caren continued. "I was selfish, too, because I was glad I met you, and that we reconnected." When the waitress came by, she gestured for another round.

"Oh no, I should go home..."

"Anyone waiting for you?"

"Right now, my cat, but—" Emma halted when Caren started laughing. "You haven't changed a bit. I remember you were talking about having a cat. See, it all came true for you. I think it's no coincidence that we're here."

"On this earth?" Emma asked, thinking she definitely didn't need a second glass of wine.

"I missed you so much."

Caren's smile was entirely too happy, alerting Emma that she might have been slow to explain some facts, that in fact she wasn't flattering herself.

"Give me a second? I'll be right back."

"Sure." Emma took another sip, then took out her cell phone and pulled up Jayce's number. Chances were she couldn't answer her private phone at the moment, but Emma couldn't wait. *I love you so much,* she texted. *I miss you, and I can't wait to be married to you.* She was done seconds before Caren returned.

"This is so amazing." She reached out to lay her hand over Emma's, not fazed when Emma retrieved hers.

"Caren, I think I should—"

"Don't worry. I know this is not prison. There is no rush."

"Caren. I am with someone. We're getting married."

"Oh. Really. Where is she now?" She sounded genuinely interested, still putting Emma on the defensive. What had she gotten herself into? A few hours ago, she had thought she could get away with a conversation over coffee. Obviously, that wasn't all Caren had in mind.

"At work. She's a cop."

"Wow. You changed sides so quickly it can make a person's head spin."

Emma shook her head and got to her feet. "I'm sorry, but this was a mistake. I should have told you earlier. Besides, I never changed sides. I always told the truth. That's my side." She had planned to pay, even after the supposed coffee turned into drinks at a bar, but she was so angry she'd changed her mind.

"Emma, please wait! Don't run away like that."

Caren tossed a couple of bills on the table and hurried after her.

"I misunderstood, I'm sorry. I thought we could pick up where we left off, and I didn't realize...I'm sorry."

"It's okay." Emma decided that running away wasn't projecting the mature image she had in mind. "I don't think we could, anyway. I'm not the same person I was then. I don't think you are."

"Oh, believe me, you are exactly the same person," Caren said ruefully. Emma wasn't sure what she meant by that. "Are you happy?"

"I am. Right now, everything is so much better than I could have ever hoped for—even before."

Because the Emma of "before" hadn't known what she wanted, all too eager to be led astray in search of something.

"What if you were single?"

"I am not. I wish you all the best. I really need to go home now."

"To your cat."

"To my cat and future wife. Bye, Caren."

⚬

Connor had directed Jayce to the old harbor where a few of the warehouses were still used. Most of them had been converted to condos, offices, a few bars and restaurants, and a museum.

"What are we doing here?" she asked. They were still on time for the job they were both being paid for, and she wanted to keep it that way. It was better not to raise suspicions with Winston and any higher-ups. At the same time, she was curious about the turf wars Connor had hinted at.

"Don't worry, the boss will be more than happy if we can help take out some of the competition. I'm just going to show you around today. There's a ton of space behind the museum. The people who own these buildings, look the other way, but the ones who use them are not our friends."

"They are in the same business, or...?" Jayce could think of a myriad of other issues. Drugs. Human trafficking.

"Not that either of us knows what is in those boxes, right? But yes, it's the same. Last month, they stole a couple of our containers. We take them out, the boss is going to have a nice reward for us."

"You mean Roger."

Connor laughed. "Sweetie, you have a lot to learn, and you better learn fast. Roger doesn't have much of a say in anything."

"But you know the people who do," Jayce concluded, letting the misplaced endearment slide. This was getting too interesting.

"You bet."

"You're telling me this because...?"

"We'll need a distraction. I'm thinking you'll do a great job."

"At what?"

"Let's go back to the warehouse now. I'll tell you later."

Emma had tried to leave Maxine. More than once. That was back in those days when she still had a job in finances, was bringing in most of the money, and felt like she shouldn't take the brunt every time Maxine had a bad day. Back in those days, she'd told her so. Months went by, and more and more the notion manifested itself that maybe she needed Maxine, that if she left her, she might be alone forever.

Emma had been scared of being alone, more than of Maxine's unpredictability, so she stopped speaking up for herself. She had made another attempt when she found herself in an interrogation room with a homicide detective, but that had gone horribly wrong. She learned to be quiet, not to stand out too much. To acquiesce.

This could be an explanation why she still wasn't home. When Caren called after her, she had hesitated for a few seconds, then turned around. Emma agreed to hear Caren out instead, as if there was anything left to say.

Was there?

"It's been really tough," Caren said. At this point, all pretenses were gone. "No one wanted to hire me at first. Some old friends reached out, said they had a job for me...Well, they're not really friends. You know what I mean. I didn't know how to pay my rent otherwise."

"I'm not judging."

"Maybe I still shouldn't tell you. You're dating a cop now."

"I didn't know she was a cop when we first met. Not that it matters. You're not hanging out with those people anymore, are you?"

"No. I guess we can't have everything." Caren sounded somber.

Emma didn't feel somber. She felt queasy, thinking about how thin that line had been, how easily her story could have been a different one. She had mailed her résumé all over the city. That was before the city agreed to pay her damages for the time lost. Potential employers were cautious and suspicious when they found out what she had done in recent years.

"It's only been a few months. You could meet someone. You will."

"I really wish things were different. I was going to look out for you."

And Caren had, for the time they'd been on the same block. Emma couldn't deny that. Nothing ever came for free, inside those walls, or on the outside.

"I don't think we should meet anymore. We've said everything, haven't we?"

"Your fiancée, does she know? Everything?"

"Yes, she does." That might stretch the truth a bit, but Jayce had gone undercover in a women's prison as well. Even if Emma hadn't told her every little detail, she did know. "Thanks for the wine," she said, getting to her feet, this time in a less rushed fashion. "Good night."

⁕

"You're absolutely sure?"

"We've seen the places. They have shipments of their own coming, and we could get back at them hard. We spoke to T, she agrees. And she might be able to bring in even more buyers if we have the merchandise."

"It's risky, but someone needs to show them who's the boss around here. All right, let's do it."

The man they'd met, Thomas Wayne, gave Jayce a long, considering look. "T's friends come with a lot of potential. I like doing business with them."

"Thanks, sir," she mumbled, and he laughed.

"Get back here tomorrow, and we'll talk about the details. I look forward to teaching those amateurs a lesson... What did you say your name was?"

"Jane Finley." She didn't believe for a second that he didn't already know the moment she was hired. "You do this right, we might have some more use for you in the future."

"Thank you. I'd like that, sir."

The meeting ended, and they went back on their way. "Come on." Connor was in an excellent mood. "I'll buy you a drink."

Jayce had to act a little more low-key, restrain her enthusiasm some, but she, too, had a reason to celebrate. She couldn't believe they'd just walked right into Thomas Wayne's apartment, the businessman pulling the strings behind people like Winston. Tanya had heard talk about him, but even Winston wasn't in regular contact. Connor definitely had ambitions, and those would be a great help once the clean-up started.

"I won't say no to that. This is good, right?"

"You bet it's good. Wayne understands how the business works, better than the guys in bad suits. We play this right, there's a reward in it."

He wanted to go past Winston? This was getting better and better. She had to get in touch with Tanya and Daniel to update them. By the time the big day rolled around, they could likely take down even more of the counterfeiters than originally planned.

The bar Connor chose was somewhat dingy, but not the worst Jayce had seen. They sat at the counter, and he ordered beer and vodka shots for them.

"That's quite the start."

"It's the beginning of something great," he said, picking up his beer glass and clinking it against Jayce's. "Watch me, sweetie. You'll be able to learn a great deal for the future."

She suppressed the laughter in favor of what she hoped was an admiring smile.

"I'm sure I will."

Elvis had decided both of her humans had left her alone for too long. Since Emma was the only one available, the cat greeted her with insistent meowing only to bolt when she tried to pick her up and ignore her for the rest of the evening.

"Thanks for your support," she said out loud. Only two days. She had promised to handle the temporary separation better, and she should. Emma had taken care of herself for most of her adult life—but that wasn't really the point, was it? She needed someone to sort out her conflicting feelings about her past, and the people in it. It wasn't so hard with Maxine, who had used her the whole time, because she'd seen she could get away with it.

Caren had her own traumatic experiences to deal with, but that didn't mean she was innocent in everything. Emma didn't know, or perhaps she didn't care to remember, how easy she'd made it for her. It was hard to place any blame when she'd felt lonely to the bone, at the same time crowded and trapped—like most of the women she'd met.

It was good to remember that in the outside world, she had options, to say no, to be with a person who understood and cherished her.

If only that person was here right now.

Elvis eventually overcame her irritation and joined Emma on the couch, curling up in her lap.

Perhaps, once Jayce was home, it would be time to address some subjects she hadn't dared look at yet—like the fear that one day, she might be thrown back into a life where there were no more choices. That fear had been a lot more present right after her release from prison, but Emma hadn't been able to get rid of it altogether. She wondered if she ever would.

She spent Sunday morning sleeping in, then, not much motivated to make breakfast, Emma went to a café within walking distance from the apartment. She might have overreacted. Or she'd been on a good path, and the man holding hostages in Kitty's store had set her back more than she'd been willing to admit. Emma had done better when she'd been able to create her own undercover assignment, leaving her busy and feeling in control.

Caren hadn't forced her to do anything. She brought unwelcome memories with her all the same. But she was doing all right, too, and Emma didn't owe her anything. That was something she had to remember. After a second coffee, and a third, she left the café. Emma walked past a store for evening and bridal gowns, standing in front of the window for a long time. She was free. Nothing bad would happen.

From here, it wasn't far to the greeting card store, so she dropped by to say hi to Keisha who was working today.

"Oh, hi, Emma. You want a coffee, and a cookie maybe?"

"No, thanks, I just had breakfast."

Keisha had shared those fearful hours during the hostage situation with her, and Emma was glad she had chosen to come back to work in the store, nonetheless. Sometimes it helped knowing a person had gone through the same thing...sometimes it didn't.

The door opened, and Caren walked in, smiling.

"I thought I would find you here. I hoped we could talk and—"

"What the hell do you want from me?" Emma snapped, only becoming aware that she'd raised her voice when a couple of customers sent her curious glances. Keisha looked alarmed, and so did Caren.

"I'm sorry. I meant to apologize. I was wrong to assume..."

"Emma, is everything okay?" Keisha asked.

"Yes. I'm sorry. I haven't slept well in a while. Let's take a walk?" she suggested to Caren.

"Sure."

Once they were outside the door, Caren spoke.

"I know I went at this all wrong. It's not often that I get to see someone who was on the inside with me. My stupid attempt at coming on to you aside, I didn't realize you weren't as happy to see me. I can't blame you."

Emma was silent for a long time as they walked. The conclusions she was drawing from her own behavior, and Caren's, weren't all that comfortable. She was grateful for Keisha's presence in the store—yet, she had trouble dealing with Caren. Granted, their relationship had been a tad more complicated—or maybe not. Maybe the complications were all on Emma's part, because she didn't want anything or anyone to intrude on her new, perfect life.

"I'm sorry, too," she said.

"I said some pretty mean things."

"It hasn't been that much time. I still understand where you're coming from. I'm happy that things are starting to work out for you, I swear."

"I shouldn't have pretended that our situation is the same," Caren said ruefully. "It isn't. You never did what they accused you of, and you did clear your name."

"I knew it, and Maxine knew it, but nothing would have happened if I hadn't met people who believed in me. I'm sorry I overreacted. It's just that sometimes I'm still afraid it could all be taken away."

"Tell me about it. I prefer the uniform that says *Coffee Paradise*," Caren deadpanned, and they both laughed.

"I imagine. The truth is, for a long time I wasn't free even though I was. I went back there in my mind, every day. And lately, I've been trying to ignore it even happened, which, of course, doesn't work either."

"That middle ground is hard to find."

"It sure is."

"I hope you'll come by the coffee shop sometime anyway. For a coffee on the house, and no strings attached, I swear. Bring your fiancée next time."

"I might even do that."

They parted ways, and Emma felt a bit more optimistic, regarding her future plans, regarding her past. It had been good to clear the air.

Just a few more days to wait until life could continue as planned.

⌾

"Change of plans," Roger Winston told them curtly after he'd called Jayce and Connor into the makeshift office behind the warehouse. "The shipment will arrive tomorrow night. T is going to bring in another couple of clients soon, so it will be all hands on deck. No more probation," he said with a quick glance to Jayce. "Finley, you can handle that?"

"Sure."

Jayce was excited that her assignment would potentially end sooner than expected, even though this news could bear complications, given the information she'd received.

She made a couple of solo trips that day, but later joined Connor for a coffee. Even though he had warmed up to her considerably since the first meeting, he didn't seem to care much for company today.

"It's a good sign, right?" she wondered out loud. "If the shipment is early, there's a chance the competition hasn't gotten wind of it, and everything goes down smoothly."

"I don't know about that," he grumbled. "Something about that doesn't sit right with me."

"Why are you saying that? It's in Winston's best interest that we get this done, isn't it?"

"It would make sense. I'm not sure I trust him."

Jayce barely suppressed a smile. When Lieutenant Chomsky and Tanya had briefed her on the situation, they had assured her that she didn't need to play a major role. The backup driver, that was all. It looked like this organization was already so fragmented it wasn't too hard to poke holes in it. Once they'd made arrests, individuals would stumble over their feet to be the first to turn on the others.

"Have you talked to Wayne?" she asked.

"He's not answering his phone. As for now, we go with the orders. I don't like it," he repeated.

"What's the worst that could happen?"

"I'd like some peace and quiet now, okay?"

"Hey, no problem. I'm going home. Big day tomorrow."

Connor didn't answer, and she left, heading for her apartment from where she called Tanya who, miraculously, had a few minutes to talk.

"Talk about cutthroat," Tanya said after hearing Jayce's summary. "Everyone wants to please the boss, and mess with the boss. Connor isn't so wrong. Winston has had a lot of talks with a guy named Shaw. His people have supposedly stolen goods worth hundreds of thousands."

"Wow. So, it could get ugly tomorrow."

"If Winston told his buddies about the shipment, yes, but backup will be in place. From the looks of it, this could be the big takedown."

"God, I wish."

Tanya laughed. "Yeah, I know. You can't wait to get back to the wedding plans."

"I won't deny that. Also, I miss my apartment."

"I can imagine. Good job on making Connor trust you. Usually, it's hard to get more than three words out of him."

"Well, he didn't want to talk much today."

"He has a bit of a crush on you. From what I hear, he hardly ever hangs out with the others."

"Well, yeah. I'll be driving by myself tomorrow."

"Good. As soon as Wayne arrives, we'll get started."

They talked for a few minutes longer before Tanya said, "This is not a good time, Mom. I'll call you back," and ended the call.

Tomorrow night couldn't come soon enough. In the past, developments like this would have been thrilling to her, the opportunity to take down the bad guys...

Even though it was early in the evening, Jayce felt tired. She had known for a while that it was time for a change, and she would have to make that even clearer to the lieutenant. Most of her colleagues loathed having to do a desk job on any occasion. Jayce thought she could do with a bit more safety, and less excitement, and she wasn't ashamed to admit it.

After she'd finished this job.

Around noon, she got a somewhat frantic call from Connor. There was another change of schedule, and now, the deal was going to take place in the late afternoon—with Wayne present. Connor hadn't been able to reach Winston yet, and they had to move fast.

"Slow down, it's okay. We can handle it."

"I'm glad you're this confident," he scoffed. "I tried calling him three times. It's all pretty fucked up."

"I won't argue with you. I'll see you in fifteen minutes."

Jayce thought that Connor was overestimating himself greatly if he expected Winston to be at his beck and call. On the way, she tried to call Tanya but only reached her voicemail. Eventually, she left a message she hoped was cryptic enough to alert her, but no one else. As the major buyer, no one should doubt "T" wanting to be present.

Now, she had to focus on her own task.

❦

It might be a good idea. It might be a terrible one. Emma wasn't yet sure when she stood in front of the house that had been her home for a critical period of her life, where past and present merged. She had called the other employee who was in the store today and told her she'd be in a bit later. Emma was curious and a bit terrified when she walked through that door once more. It was all part of closure, of finding that elusive middle ground.

The door to the office was open, as usual. When she knocked on the door frame, Marley looked up, and, recognizing her, she jumped to her feet.

"Emma! You look fantastic. What brings you here?"

"Something I should have probably done a few months ago. I wanted to say hello."

"Better late than never." Marley walked around her desk to shake her hand, and she closed the door. "This is a really nice surprise. You were gone so abruptly."

"Yes. That was a crazy day."

"They made me leave and put a cop in my office for that day, to be on the safe side. It took some time, but we bounced back from it. It's a safe space again. But tell me about you."

Emma could feel the smile light up her face. Not such a bad idea to come here after all.

"I'm good. I have a job I enjoy—and I'm going to get married." Those were the major, relevant parts of the story.

"That's so great. Who is the lucky guy?"

"Lucky woman. I hope. You probably remember her, Jayce."

"Yes, of course. I'm really happy for you. You worked hard for everything you've achieved."

"Well, I was very lucky. Many people helped me."

"Believe me," Marley said, "there's a lot more to it than luck. I see that every day. I was about to take a break. Would you like to stay for a coffee?"

Emma checked her watch and decided she did. A bit of flattery didn't hurt.

Jayce, Connor, and another couple of drivers had been working non-stop until the last container was unloaded, and they went to the warehouse for their final pay. So far, everything had gone according to plan—for the counterfeiters, anyway. There had been no interference by any of Shaw's people.

Winston was there, Tanya as well, and they were waiting for Wayne who was running late.

"Get him here," Tanya snapped at Winston. "I'm not going through with a deal this big with middlemen."

He bristled at the thinly veiled insult but tried Wayne's number one more time.

At this point, Jayce was worried. Sure, they'd have Winston, Connor, and a few others, but Wayne, possibly Shaw, were the ones that counted. If they could arrest Wayne, he would likely be happy to give them everything he had on Shaw. They needed him to be there.

"I can't reach him," Winston said. He was sweating. "You don't want to be here all night, do you? Let's get started."

"Without me? I'm offended." Thomas Wayne, in the company of his bodyguards and a younger woman, joined them. "I believe we had some scheduling issues, but we're not in that much of a hurry, are we?"

He winked at Jayce, the woman with him giving him an angry look in return.

Then her eyes met Jayce's, and both of them flinched.

"Tom," Terri said, "We should leave. Something's wrong."

"Why are you saying that?"

Jayce saw Tanya's hand go to her gun. She did the same. After the first day, no one had frisked her.

"I want to see the merchandise right now," Tanya said coolly.

"I'm sure we have a few minutes. What are you talking about, honey?"

"That woman? I know her. She's a cop."

All eyes were on Jayce now.

"That's nonsense. She went to prison. I saw her release papers."

"Well, she didn't tell you the whole story. When I met her, she was an undercover cop in a halfway house," Terri insisted.

A shot rang out, and everyone dove for cover—but it hadn't come from anyone who'd come for the deal. Shaw's people had gotten wind of what was about to go down anyway. They were moving in.

Jayce only hoped that the same way true for their backup. She dove behind a crate only to come face to face with Thomas Wayne, who had his gun trained on her.

"The place is surrounded. The best you can do is to turn yourself in," she yelled over the gunfire.

"You're a traitor. You know how we deal with them?" His eyes widened when the stray bullet hit him. He stumbled and fell. More shots. Jayce moved forward to check for a pulse, picking up the gun from the unconscious man. Then her world exploded in pain, and for a moment, she thought it was the car that had crashed into hers...but that was before.

She came to in the ambulance for brief, painful and confusing moments, paramedics talking to her. Emma...Emma was safe, Jayce remembered. *I was shot.* She was tired.

"Stay with us!" the paramedic told her, but awareness was slipping away.

❦

The car crash came back to her every once in a while in dreams, the impact, shattering glass and screeching steel. Darkness...

Jayce had seen her share of dangerous situations. It was part of the job, choices that she'd made. The pursuit was a part of it. None of it could have prepared her for the moment she realized the car barreling down the street wasn't going to stop in time, that its driver was in fact intending a crash.

Gentle hands eased her back to reality every time, but the reprieve was only temporary, until the next dream...

The drug dealer she'd arrested the week before the incident had made bail but violated his conditions. He was so furious when he realized they were after him that he was willing to risk money and life in order to get back at her. He was more severely injured than Jayce.

In the aftermath, progress turned out to be slow. Her partner Daniel, and Kitty, his wife, came to visit her regularly. So did many friends and colleagues.

While Jayce appreciated their support, it only served as a reminder that life went on for everyone while she was trapped in a drastically altered day-to-day reality. Getting back on her feet proved to be harder than she'd imagined. Physical therapy came with lots of pain and frustration, and even a desk job seemed out of reach—until it wasn't.

At that time, Jayce had had no idea about how long the road ahead would be. Going back to work came with mixed emotions. It got her out of the house, which was the good part. She didn't appreciate being stuck behind her desk, unable to join her colleagues out in the field, and it was only part time. Jayce knew she should be grateful for the department and her supervisor assisting her reintegration, but her patience was tested every day.

Daniel, Tanya and Ray were in with the lieutenant, discussing strategy on a case Jayce only knew on paper. Everything had to be by the book. Lieutenant Chomsky wouldn't even let her on a stakeout—not that Jayce was sure she'd be able to handle an all-nighter yet after falling asleep on her couch early most evenings. Even though the work wasn't physical, she came home with pain on most days.

The crash had left the perpetrator in a coma from which he was unlikely to wake up. Jayce couldn't bring herself to feel one way or another about that fact, but she resented him for his senseless actions. He could have been out of jail in a few years, have a do over, and she could have...anything but this.

"Hey. Are you ready to go? I was hoping you might keep me company tonight."

Kitty's cheerful voice jolted her out of her somber musings.

"Tonight?" Jayce was pretty sure she hadn't missed any messages or otherwise planning. She had an idea, though, where this was coming from.

"Yes, if you don't have any other plans. Daniel is going to be here for I don't know how long, and we haven't spent time together in forever. What do you say?"

"I don't know. Frankly, I was planning on a quiet evening at home. I have an early morning tomorrow."

"Well, with the way things are going, I wouldn't mind if you came in later tomorrow," Chomsky, who had come out of her office, remarked. "Take a little time, Detective. That report isn't going anywhere."

"It's not like I'd know how things are going, as I wasn't invited to the meeting."

Chomsky shrugged, ignoring Jayce's harsh tone.

"We aren't keeping any secrets from you, don't worry. Now go."

"I guess if my boss wants me out of here, I should go." She was aware that Kitty had followed the exchange with interest. She waited until Jayce picked up her coat and keys, and they left the station together.

"Everything okay?" Kitty asked when they sat in her car.

"Yeah." Jayce sighed. "I'm sorry about the drama. I'm not used to being on the sidelines."

"It's only temporary, right? I know it's tough for you, but maybe you should try to relax for a bit. You'll be in the thick of it soon enough."

"I guess you're right."

"I always am, remember?" her friend teased. She got serious a moment later. "I know you're not in the condition or the mood to party all night. I was thinking dinner, and I'll drive you home after."

Jayce gave her a quizzical look. "I can't remember us partying all night, ever."

"True. So, dinner it is."

"Daniel told you to look after me."

Kitty looked a little hurt at that. "He's worried about you, but so am I. We just want to know you're okay."

"I will be." Jayce kept her gaze straight ahead, willing to make both of them believe. The notion that she might never return to the career she'd once taken for granted, terrified her, but neither Kitty nor Daniel needed to know that.

"Yes, and I want you to know we'll always be here for you if you need anything. I promise."

To her dismay, Jayce found that Kitty's words made her tear up. She would chalk it up to the pain, or the painkillers, whatever.

"I'm grateful for that. Right now, to be honest, I could use a drink."

The doctor had advised her that she shouldn't combine those pills with alcohol. Jayce was fairly certain that she knew her limits, and she didn't do it often anyway. There was a reason why she hadn't spent much time with friends lately. A beer or two would help take off the edge. Kitty would drive her home. No harm done, right?

It didn't exactly happen that way.

"You should put yourself out there more often," Kitty said when Jayce returned to the table after insisting she'd pay for their beers. "I wish I could pick up women like that."

Jayce laughed, even though she'd had to concentrate hard not to spill any of the beverages. The glasses were heavy, the place more crowded than she remembered. At least the burger and fries they had were still as good as in her memory.

"There is so much wrong with what you just said. First of all, you don't want to pick up women. Second of all, that's not what happened."

"Do you have her number or not?"

"I sure do."

It was something, but she wouldn't call the woman who had chatted her up while waiting for drinks.

"I knew it!" Kitty said, a tad too loudly. "Besides, I made you laugh, so it's all worth it. Are you going to call her?"

"I don't have time to date, not once I'm back on the job."

"You are back on the job."

"Not yet. Not really."

Jayce didn't care for being reminded of the less comforting possibilities. She liked the challenges that came with her normal job, and she liked her apartment. If she couldn't get beyond the part-time gig, both were likely to change. Jayce couldn't fathom any more change at this point. For sure she couldn't imagine anyone looking for a flirt in a bar would want to be burdened with her current problems.

"It's fine. I could use a little flattery. I don't think I'd have the energy for anything else yet." If this was a little TMI for Kitty, she didn't let on.

"I understand. But you should be proud of what you've achieved. Your recovery is going well...and damn, we're all so glad to have you back."

Jayce guiltily remembered the many hours Kitty had spent at her hospital bed.

"Me too. You have no idea."

Kitty had chosen a bar with fairly comfortable seating arrangements, but even so, her back and legs were making themselves known. Jayce hated to be reminded of all the progress she hadn't yet made. She didn't want to cut short the first evening out with a friend she'd had in months.

"I think it's time to call it a night." Kitty, ever observant, had picked up on her fidgeting. "We have to do this again soon."

"Come on, you heard Chomsky. She basically told me to come in late."

"I know, but..."

"You're the one who said I needed to get out. I am out. I'm enjoying myself. One more drink, okay?"

"Are you sure?"

These days, Jayce was sure of few things, but she nodded.

"All right then," Kitty relented.

<hr/>

The evening had gone fairly well. Jayce paid for it in the morning, feeling hung over and in pain the moment she woke up, knowing she'd be late for work. She had planned to fill her new prescription at the end of the week, but realized she would have to run that errand during her lunch break, as there were only two pills left. She hoped she'd make it through the morning.

Daniel was at his desk when she arrived. Jayce was overly aware of the worried glances he kept stealing.

"What?" she snapped.

"I was going to get a coffee. You want one?"

"Sure," she said, mortified at her tone. "Thanks."

A few minutes later, he returned with two paper cups, setting one in front of her.

"I might have to have a talk with my wife about keeping you up all night. You okay?"

"I'm fine." Jayce didn't know how convincing that sounded, but keeping her voice level was all she could do. Fine was a bit of an overstatement. She'd be better once she'd make that run to the pharmacy. She had to admit that one or two of the beers had been too many. Whom did she want to prove anything to?

She hadn't been much of a drinker before the accident. When she was off the pills, soon, there'd be enough time to kick back a few with friends. "Don't say anything to Kitty. I guess I was a bit too enthusiastic about going out for the first time since…" She didn't say it out loud. She didn't have to.

"I get it. It's not ideal right now, but let me tell you, there'll be enough work left once you're up to it."

"I can't wait."

"Meanwhile, would you like to come to dinner Saturday night? You could bring someone if—"

Jayce laughed. "Tell Kitty I was serious. I wasn't going to call her back."

A few hours later she returned, far from having the rest of the week settled. The pharmacist had refused to fill her prescription until she could talk to the doctor, who was off for the day. Unnerved, Jayce had left and gone to another pharmacy where she bought the strongest over-the-counter meds she could find. It wasn't what she'd hoped for, but there was nothing else she could do until she'd talked to Dr. Marten and explained the situation to her. It was important that she returned to a normal life as soon as possible. There was a limit as to how much pain she could tolerate meanwhile. Dr. Marten, a professional herself, had to understand that.

❦

"What are you saying? This is crazy." Jayce shook her head in disbelief. "You know me, my complete medical history. I am not addicted to anything. I need another prescription. This is probably the last one. I might be going back to work full time next month." She halted, aware that this rambling statement wasn't how she'd wanted to explain herself to the physician.

Dr. Marten looked too serious for her liking. Jayce sensed that she wasn't going to give in easily.

"That's good news, but remember we said we were going to phase it out over the past few weeks? Was there any time when you were able to lower the dose? Did anything out of the ordinary happen?"

"I sit at a desk for hours. That's very much out of the ordinary. The weekends are better." Jayce felt her face heat as they were nearing the inevitable conclusion. She still slept a lot on the weekends, her condition not even close to where it had been before the crash. Well, actually not an accident in the truest sense of the word. "Someone tried to murder me and almost succeeded. I'm still in pain."

"What about the pain management classes? Do you practice your exercises regularly?"

For a moment, Jayce stared at her blankly. She didn't want to admit that she'd skipped the last three classes. It wasn't so much that she didn't believe in their worth. Jayce didn't know for sure why she'd let them lapse. Perhaps it was too early to start believing in mind over matter again. Matter, at the moment, demanded all of her attention.

"Look, I'm sorry, I didn't mean to argue with you or tell you how to do your job. It's just that I need to do mine. Help me out, Doc. One more time, and I swear I won't miss any more classes. They have been helpful actually."

"I'm glad to hear that," Dr. Marten said. "Still, I'd like you to start going with a smaller dose and make an appointment with the therapist before you leave. I know it sounds scary, but I promise you this will work. I'll fill your prescription, but I want you to spread them out as much as you can."

Jayce thought of the over-the-counter painkillers in her medicine cabinet. The combination of both might work. Dr. Marten had a point. She'd need a clear head when she went back out in the field. She had survived the car wreck. She could handle this.

⁂

Things had to get worse before they got better, didn't they? If Jayce hadn't been the pragmatic person she was, she might have concluded that someone was stealing the pills right out of her pocket. This couldn't be happening, not when Chomsky was gradually starting to reintegrate her into the tightly knit work group. Jayce was officially back in every meeting. Two long weeks until her return to full-time work. Jayce equally longed for and dreaded that day.

In the women's restroom, she stood leaning against the wall of the stall, staring at the empty bottle of pills, trying to remember where all of them had gone. She had seen the therapist and gone to the classes, but her mind was blank. The pain was just there on the periphery of her conscious, ready to hit her full force anytime soon.

"Jayce, you okay? Chomsky moved up the meeting," she heard Tanya's voice.

"I'll be there. Thanks!" She closed her fingers around the small plastic bottle, thinking that she'd have to find a solution, and soon. Jayce unlocked the door, washed her hands and joined her colleague in their supervisor's office. She hoped the new case would at least distract her for a little while.

It didn't do the trick.

Chomsky asked her to stay behind afterwards.

"What would you think if we delayed your return to full-time, just for another few weeks?"

"Why? I expect the doctor to give me the go-ahead soon, and frankly, I need to get out from behind that desk at some point. It's starting to drive me crazy...no offense," she offered.

"None taken. If the doctor says you're ready, and you think you are, we'll go from there. I want to make sure we don't rush anything. I need you to be 100%."

"I am. I swear."

"Good. This case is turning out to be bigger than we thought, and there might be an opportunity for you soon."

"Thank you. I appreciate your honesty. I assure you, I can handle it."

"That's the best news I've had in a while," the lieutenant said warmly. "Welcome back, Finney. You gave us all quite a scare."

"Not on purpose," Jayce mumbled before she left the office.

⁂

There were better days. She was starting to believe that her old life was within reach. Then came the day where she nearly had an accident on the way to work after a pain-filled and sleepless night. She'd nearly lost count of how many pills she'd taken, begged the pharmacist to help her out.

Even in the dire state she was in, Jayce could sense the young woman's discomfort clearly. Pity. Discomfort was nothing in comparison to what she'd been through in the past few weeks. Who could live like this?

"Look, I have somewhere to be." That wasn't true, but who cared at this point? "Why don't you do your job?"

"Ma'am, this prescription has already been filled. Please talk to your doctor. If you don't leave, I'm afraid I have to call the police."

Jayce left without further argument, a sense of dread and shame piercing the cocoon of medication.

Not much later, she sat at her desk, replaying those scenes in her mind, the uncomfortable truths that came with them. Not only had she almost done something illegal, she had also endangered another person's life. That wasn't what she had signed up for, worked so hard for every day. Protect. Serve. She couldn't even protect herself.

"Detective Finney. A word?"

Jayce braced herself. She rose, resigned to the fact that she had screwed up, badly, and there were steps she'd have to take. There could be dire consequences. She was tired of pretending. She followed Lieutenant Chomsky into her office and accepted the offered seat.

"It's fine. I know what you're going to say."

"No, you don't. But I need to know what we're dealing with here. Are you getting the help you need?"

Jayce wasn't sure how to answer the question. Did she need help? Was she getting any, and did she even know how to ask for it? In any case, confiding in her supervisor could get her in trouble, potentially fired. Maybe that was already on Chomsky's mind, and she was easing her into the dire subject gently.

Breaking down crying would not be an appropriate reaction either, though for a brief, desperate moment, Jayce considered it.

"I'm working hard," she said.

"I can see that, but that's not the question. You're one of the best cops I've ever worked with, and I'd like to continue working with you."

"Thank you. Same here. If that's all—"

In a heartbeat, worries and shame had won over her desire to do the right thing. She couldn't tell Chomsky any of it, could she? There had to be another way.

"Finney, please, cut the bullshit. We're going to need a plan, and I think you know that."

This was perhaps when the true magnitude of her problems registered with her. They weren't going to end so soon.

"Yes. I do. I've been meaning to talk to you."

"I know. It's not an easy thing to do, but I promise you, we will find a solution. As long as you want to stay on the force, and in this department."

There was nothing that Jayce wanted more.

She slept badly, those nights coming back to her time and again, the doubts, the fear that she might never be able to do her job again, go back to her life the way it was before. Eventually, Jayce made peace with the fact that she couldn't turn back time. She beat the odds and convinced a reluctant lieutenant to let her back on a months long undercover assignment, first in a women's prison, then in a halfway house to track the flow of drugs.

The nightmares always followed suit, sometimes of the car crash, something of the abyss of addiction. Jayce refused to let them dictate her life. And sometimes, she dreamed of those gentle hands making everything more bearable.

Present

Emma's hand shook a little as she disconnected the call, her heart beating fast. Kitty would be so thrilled about the chance to sell the exclusive designer collection of pens in her store. It was Emma who had sealed the deal for her, even though her mind was on so many other things these days. Okay, to be fair, her thoughts mostly revolved around imagining the wedding, and praying that Jayce was safe. She tried to tell herself that they'd been through this before, and Jayce knew how to do her job. It was hard to distract herself, even at work. Especially this time.

Now, however, she couldn't stop smiling.

She couldn't wait for Jayce to be back home, to share the good news. Even though their workdays were so different, they were always interested in each other's. Emma's job might not dramatically improve people's lives, but the cards and gift she sold were tied to important occasions. Like weddings...

Today's achievement was important to her for many reasons. She had successfully negotiated the deal without conjuring up the past, wondering if the person on the other end could be aware of her story, or parts of it.

The settlement money had made little difference, but time had. Emma cast a look at her watch, realizing it was five minutes past time to close. There was no customer in the store, so she went to the front door and locked. She had barely turned around when there was a sharp rap against the glass. Spinning around, Emma wondered if she should make an exception, since there wasn't much to do for her at home.

She was happily surprised to see Kitty. That was even better. She could tell her about the news right away. Emma unlocked the door again, blurting out,

"It's great you're coming by. We have something to celebrate! I would have called you later. I got off the phone with—"

"Emma."

Kitty didn't sound happy, and it wasn't until then that Emma realized Daniel was with her. The somber expression on his face sent a chill down her spine. This could only mean one thing.

"No."

"Emma, it's going to be okay," he said, but that wasn't all she heard. Between the lines, there were undertones confirming some of her worst fears. If okay was a state sometime in the future, it meant that Jayce wasn't. For sure, Emma wasn't either.

"No," she said again. Apparently, that was all she was capable of.

Daniel took her by the shoulders and made her face him.

"Jayce's cover got blown. She was shot, but she'll be all right. I'm telling you the truth."

Emma stared at him, struggling to process his words, part of her still wanting to deny that this was reality in the first place.

"How? What happened? Oh God, I need to go to the hospital."

It was starting to sink in, the situation drastically altered from a moment ago.

"I'll drive you," he said, and Kitty nodded.

"I'll close up here and catch up with you later."

Emma made herself move, still caught up in a nightmare of her worst fears as she picked up her purse and keys. *She'll be okay.* For now, that was all she had to hang on to.

"Tell me everything," she said, barely choking back tears.

✺

Emma wondered what Jayce was seeing in those dreams that had her restless, robbing Emma of her sleep too. She had an idea. At least, every time she got up to touch her, Jayce seemed to quiet under her hands, slipping into a more restful sleep. Emma sat back down and continued to watch over the woman she loved, grateful that they both still had a future together, something neither of them could have imagined only a few years ago...

✺

Emma lay in her bed, shivering, unable to get warm. She longed for quiet, around her, and in her mind, but quiet was something this place never offered...

She couldn't stop her overactive imagination, from replaying this afternoon over and over again, from conjuring up worse scenarios that might happen at any time.

Somebody had smuggled a knife inside, and one inmate stabbed another. Emma hadn't seen the incident unfold. She'd seen the blood, lots of it, and even though most of the guards were friendly to her, no one told her about the woman's condition. Emma didn't know her well. She wanted to be sure she'd live....

Her stomach was churning, an older memory overlaying the pictures, and she felt even worse crying for herself, once more reliving the chain of events that had led her to this prison cell.

Emma had potential. She was taking classes and working in the garden, keeping to herself, keeping her hands clean best she could. It would finally pay off. In a few weeks, she'd be able to leave for the halfway house, adjust to life on the outside again, find a job, a place to live, and re-enter society. She'd had an appointment with the probation officer before the stabbing happened.

Caren who had been present, had tried to intervene, and she got hurt too. Not life-threateningly, but she had to go to the infirmary as well.

Emma was scared of what could happen another day. She was scared of what life on the outside would look like for her. She longed for a past when she hadn't been so afraid every single day of her life.

<hr/>

Marley, who was running the halfway house, had shown Emma around. She was friendly, a bit chatty even which Emma found odd given the work she did. After all, the women who came here had a past, conviction, addiction, something that made society reluctant about welcoming them back. Something that required a transitioning period.

Did she?

Emma had wished so hard for this moment to arrive, to go the next step, to be free save for some appointments and curfews to keep for a little while longer. Being there, in that moment, felt strange and a little scary. That wasn't normal, was it? She should be happy, appreciative to have left prison behind, and with it, the dangers of getting caught in a potentially life-threatening fight. Caren was doing fine, but neither of them had ever heard about the woman who had been the original target. They hadn't seen her again. Emma shivered which hadn't gone unnoticed by Marley.

"I'm sorry if it's a little fresh in here. We have just started the heating for the year."

"I'm fine, thank you." Emma managed a smile, relieved when Marley nodded and continued the small tour. Not needing anything helped with staying under the radar. Staying under the radar had helped her survive.

"Here's the kitchen. You will share some responsibilities equally. There's a common room, and a couple that we use for therapy sessions...here. I'm going to show you your room, and then you can settle in before dinner."

"Thank you."

The room was a bit warmer, though not a lot bigger than the cell she had exchanged it for. A single bed against the wall, a door opened to a tiny closet. A dresser served as bedside table, and a chair sat beside it.

"The first day can be a bit overwhelming," Marley commented. "I'll leave you to it now. Take your time. If you need anything, come find me in the office."

"Thanks," Emma mumbled again, overcome with a sudden desire for sleep.

After Marley had left, she put away her clothes, realizing she wasn't going to fill up even this small space. She stepped in front of the narrow window. Clouds formed a background in various shades of dark grey. The rain was coming down hard now. She was barely able to see the other side of the street.

She was finally here.

Emma had made it this far, because she'd been a model prisoner, barely noticeable to anyone, intent on remaining quiet and invisible—not because anyone had believed her story, the truth, that she was completely innocent in any of the charges brought against her.

It was too late for that. She could only hope to build a new life from everything that had been broken. It made her feel ungrateful and guilty, but she cried anyway.

You couldn't have everything in life.

Present

Some sound or other jolted Emma awake, and after a moment of confusion, she realized she was still in the hospital. Jayce was still in a deep, medicated sleep, the light of the full moon casting shadows in the room. Emma shifted, suppressing a pained sound. No one had kept her from staying, but no one had thought of offering her anything more comfortable but the hard chair either.

Not that she wanted to complain, about anything. All that mattered to Emma was that Jayce was in good hands, and that she'd indeed be okay, as Daniel had promised her. She could deal with everything else. She would.

There was still a wedding in their future, and a honeymoon.

In the dark of the room, clinging to hope, Emma started to make plans. As they were taking shape, she was convinced Jayce would like them too, once she was awake. If only she'd been able to tell her right now...

It was a beautiful vision that eventually allowed her to sleep some more.

Jayce was momentarily confused when she woke to see Emma asleep and slumped somewhat painfully in the visitor's chair. She soon realized that those images of other hospital stays and her subsequent struggles belonged in the past. They had come to her in bizarre dreams.

So far, so good.

She was still here. Emma had spent the night here waiting for her to wake up. She longed to know what happened, if Tanya was okay, and about the arrests that had been made. She wanted to have that conversation with Lieutenant Chomsky...but in her current state, it was obviously too much to ask for. This time, however, her sleep was without nightmares.

Emma could truly say she'd never been so grateful in her life as in that moment when Jayce was awake, still exhausted, but happy to see her. All those other experiences, lucky breaks she'd gotten lately, paled in comparison.

Kitty and Daniel had been in and out, both of them insisting that Emma take a few days off. These days, her financial situation actually allowed her to do so. She found it hard to leave the room, if only for a short time to shower and change.

She could see their point when she nearly fell asleep during one of their visits, when she felt like she could let down her guard a little. Besides, she wanted to be there for Jayce when she'd come home. Whatever challenges lay ahead, based on the past, this time, they'd handle them together.

When the day came, Emma was prepared thanks to Kitty's insistence that she'd take a few hours to go home and sleep in the past days. She had also stocked Jayce and Emma's freezer with home-cooked meals. Keisha had come by as well, and, assuring Emma that she was more than happy to work more hours.

Elvis greeted them at the door, happily brushing up against Jayce's legs.

"Someone is happy to see me," she joked.

"I'm so happy you're here," Emma said, and nearly burst into tears. She picked up Elvis, tried to breathe through it, but the tears started falling anyway. "I'm so sorry. Would you like a glass of water? Lie down for a bit?"

"Emma."

"I could get you the comforter if you'd like to watch some TV..."

"I will lie down. And I'd like you to come with me. There's nothing pressing at the moment."

Though still embarrassed, Emma could easily admit that this was the best idea of all. They needed to be close.

There were setbacks as well. Given the nightmares at the hospital, Jayce wasn't surprised to find herself triggered into the darkest episode of her past.

Emma being around made it easier, and then there were moments when, unintentionally, she made it harder. Being in pain, being afraid of going down a dangerous road once more, wasn't a good enough reason to yell at her. That's why she had retreated to the bathroom in the middle of the night, praying this episode would be over soon, tempted to throw all caution in the wind.

But they didn't have anything stronger than Tylenol in the house.

"Talk to me." Emma stood in the doorway. She came into the bathroom and sat next to Jayce on the rim of the tub.

It was Jayce's turn to be on the verge of a breakdown, only because she had so much more to live for now, and still couldn't seem to get it right.

"I know," Emma whispered. "You'll be all right."

Jayce didn't have the energy to snap at her. She was grateful not to be alone. Against all odds, they both had to laugh, when an angrily meowing cat reminded them it was still in the middle of the night.

⁂

And then there were better days, becoming more and more frequent, until they were the rule rather than the exception. Her leave would be coming to an end.

Lieutenant Chomsky had come to visit her as well, but Jayce thought the hospital wasn't a good setting for the conversation they needed to have. Besides, she wanted to make her point clear, looking a bit less worse for wear when the moment came. For the time being, when things were still difficult and in the balance, Jayce was grateful for Emma's steadfast presence, and she didn't mind getting pampered a bit.

However, it took some creative measures to get her out of the house that day. Even at the reminder that only one of them was working at the moments, Emma had doubts.

"Are you sure you'll be okay?"

"The fridge is full of meals that just need to be micro-waved. I'll be fine. Remember we have a wedding and a honeymoon coming up. We're going to have to pay for that."

Emma laughed, obviously happy with the reminder. In the past few days, there hadn't been a lot of time to focus on these subjects.

"I guess I can't argue with that."

"No, you can't. But you could bring some samples for invitations, and we look at them later?"

"I'll do that. You call me if you need anything..."

"It'll be okay. Go."

They kissed, and then Emma was gone, leaving Jayce with a little under half an hour to prepare another coffee, and her speech.

Elvis watched her attentively while she paced the kitchen, talking to herself. Aware of the cat's intense gaze, she stopped.

"You're right, this is silly. It's not like anyone can make that decision but me. And I made it, right?"

A meow was the answer, as much of an affirmation Jayce was going to get for now.

This was a somewhat odd situation. The lieutenant had never been to Jayce's home. It was the first time Jayce saw her in casual clothes like this. This might make the talk easier—or harder. They'd find out.

"Thanks for having me." Chomsky shook her hand, taking a look around. "You have a beautiful home."

"Thank you. Can I offer you something? I made coffee."

"I'll have one, thanks. Can I help you with anything?"

"No thanks, I'm okay."

So much for the initial niceties. From the kitchen, Jayce could hear Chomsky talking to Elvis in a soft tone, something that made her smile. This might be easier than she had expected. She had good reasons after all.

Jayce returned to the living room with two cups of coffee—she knew Chomsky took hers black—and a plate of cookies on a tray.

"You're probably wondering why I asked you here," she said.

"I think I know. It's not much of a secret that you were looking for a change of pace. Given the circumstances, I understand. The situation got out of hand."

"Yeah. I don't blame anyone, but maybe I didn't make myself clear the last time. It was different before the halfway house. I don't feel like I have anything left to prove. That's on me, though. I understand that you might not be able to accommodate my wishes in the long run, and if that's the case...respectfully, I will resign."

She could tell from the way the lieutenant's eyes widened that this news came unexpected.

"You have thought this through."

"I had a lot of time to think."

"I imagine. I know you've wanted out of the undercover assignments for a while, and. Believe me, I understand. I didn't get the impression you didn't want to be a cop any longer."

Jayce suppressed a sigh, taking a sip of her coffee for a moment of stalling.

"That's not the point, not for me. But I'm aware I can't pick and choose all the time, and I've realized...There's too much on the line. I don't have just me to consider any longer."

"You've earned the right to pick and choose a little—but there's something else I wanted to run by you. Perhaps you'd be able to make time to study."

"I'm not sure I understand what you're saying..."

"I'll be leaving at the end of the year. Don't worry, it's for another job. This is a great opportunity, and I don't see why I shouldn't create them for someone else if I can. I'll miss this unit greatly, but it would be a great relief to know it's in good hands."

Jayce stared at her, speechless. A moment ago, she had talked about the possibility of resigning.

This was life-changing as well, in a completely different direction.

"I kid you not, dealing with the higher-ups and politics sometimes can feel like an undercover job—but they aren't going to shoot at you."

"I hope not." Jayce wasn't sure if it was okay to laugh at the joke—or what to say, at all. If she got this right, it would be an amazing career opportunity.

"Would you leave the coffeemaker?"

"Don't get ahead of yourself," Chomsky warned, but she sounded amused. "I value your work, but where I go, the coffeemaker goes. All right—what do you say?"

Work kept Emma busy, even though she found the time to check her cell phone at regular intervals. There was no message from Jayce, because, realistically, Jayce would be fine by herself for a few hours. Still, she was relieved when, at the end of her shift, she could grab the folder with the samples and head home. Emma was happy that after the harsh detour, they'd be able to shift the focus back to their immediate plans for the future.

There was one more thing to solve first, but that would have to wait until Jayce was cleared to go back to work. Jayce had told her not to worry. Emma worried a bit, because she knew Jayce was passionate about her job, and if she couldn't negotiate for the changes she wished to happen, would she find something else she could be just as passionate about? Emma had changed careers, because she didn't have a choice, and it hadn't always been easy. She had to admit that her first job, moving money around for people, hadn't been a vocation. She'd been fairly good at it and made a comfortable living before everything else went downhill. At this point, she wasn't worried about money. She had a job she liked going to every day, and she wanted the same for Jayce.

She was surprised to see the dining table set for a candlelight dinner.

"Hey."

Emma turned around to see Jayce leaning against the door frame.

"I'm sorry nothing's made from scratch, but we need to go through all the meals Kitty made us. Based on last week, I'm sure it's going to be delicious."

"Yeah. This looks great. I brought the samples too."

Emma put the bag on the coffee table and walked closer to carefully embrace Jayce.

"You can hug a little harder," Jayce said, laughing a little. "Lieutenant Chomsky made me an offer that's going to be hard to refuse. Well, in fact as long as I pass the test, it's a go."

Emma pulled back a little, trying to make sense of what she'd just heard.

"What kind of offer? You won't have to leave the unit, will you?"

"No, she's the one who's leaving, for another job. Someone will have to do hers, and she thought I might be good at it."

"That's amazing, congratulations!"

"I know I said harder is okay, but...ouch."

"I'm so sorry. Sorry." Emma stepped back, sending a prayer of thanks to whatever higher power had listened. This was better than anything she could have hoped for. "This is such great news. Lieutenant Finney."

"Well, not yet, but I do like the sound of it."

It was good being able to make long-term plans again, and not be afraid. It was something, Emma realized, that she'd been missing for a long time.

"I guess we have some work to do, then, planning the wedding and the honeymoon...But now I'm starving."

"Okay. Let's take a look at Kitty's Delicacies."

They had never planned a big wedding, so gathering their closest friends at the town hall, only a few weeks later, had been easy. They had found a venue for the reception close by.

While they were waiting, Emma's hand in hers, Jayce took a moment to regard the other couples, wondering if all of them were truly aware of the magnitude of the moment, not taking this day, and the right they executed, for granted.

The happiest day of all.

Jayce had never imagined she would marry in white, but gestures mattered. She and Emma deserved this, just like every other couple in the room. The dress, the cake, the wedding dance afterwards. And, of course, the ceremony and the paperwork to show that their city, their country, respected their marriage like any other.

"What are you thinking?" Emma asked, smiling, looking stunningly beautiful. Jayce let a few seconds go by before she answered, because otherwise, she might burst into tears. That, too, was unexpected. She leaned in to kiss her, quickly and spontaneously, because—who would stop her?

"You can't wait, can you?" Daniel joked.

"You got me."

"Stop harassing her," Kitty chastised him. "Do I have to remind you that when we got married, you were so eager to get out there, you nearly forgot to tie your shoelaces?"

The shared laughter eased her nervousness some. Jayce hadn't imagined how much nerves would come with this day regardless of the pure unadulterated happiness.

"Jayce, can I talk to you for a moment?"

"Of course. Be nice to my future wife," she advised their friends and followed her supervisor to the corner a few steps away. There hadn't been much of an opportunity to have a personal conversation with her boss since the last time, but Jayce could imagine what was on her mind these days. It hadn't been easy for Jayce to get where she was. The path had been even harder for Chomsky, a woman of a different generation.

"I'm glad you're here," she said. "That means a lot."

"I'm happy to be here. I wasn't sure you had all your old/new/borrowed/blue items together. Well, I can see the blue. Here's something borrowed. They belonged to my mother, and I'm sure she would be proud."

For a few seconds, the image of the intricately made earrings blurred in front of her eyes. "Thank you so much," Jayce said. "I'll be honored."

They had chosen light blue for shoes. The dresses were new, each of them had some older jewelry, and Kitty had taken care of getting them both something borrowed. There was no way a person could ever have too much good luck.

"Good. I think it's your turn now."

In retrospect, the minutes flew by, and Jayce didn't remember all that much except for the pure joy on Emma's face, her eyes welling up at the magical words "I do."

Finally, she could kiss her again, this time with the cheering of their guests.

⁂

Suitcases were packed, and a cab brought them from the party to the airport where their flight to Prague took off a couple of hours later.

After checking in and a short nap, they spent the first day discovering tourist destinations, enjoying a pastry and coffee near the Old Market Square for lunch, crossing the Charles Bridge and walking up to the castle after.

They had lunch in the area and walked back the same way. The now illuminated bridge was packed with tourists this time, but they didn't mind the slower pace, jetlag starting to catch up with them. It made the beautiful scenery almost unreal, like a dream. Holding on to Jayce's hand, Emma felt assured of the place they were in now, and the commitment they'd made to their shared future.

A few streets from their hotel, they stopped at a bar for a nightcap, tired, but unwilling to let the day and its magic end yet.

"It's strange," she said after they'd sat down in the corner of the bar and ordered. "For all this time, I always felt like I had to make up for the time lost, like I was always running behind." That was as good an explanation as any why she'd had such trouble dealing with Caren—or dealing with her situation. Luck and determination, meeting kind and caring people had brought her here. In love. Married, in a place she'd never imagined she'd see someday.

"And now?"

"I've changed direction. I realized I can never get that time back, and I've stopped trying, because there's so much I look forward to."

"I know the feeling," Jayce said softly, as she took Emma's hand and placed a kiss on the back of it. "No more looking back."

⁓

The plan had been to start the day early. They had set the alarm, and Jayce was studying the instructions of the coffeemaker in her room, reminding her of the bold proposition she'd made to her supervisor. Oh well, if everything worked according to plan, a coffee station like Chomsky enjoyed would be well within the budget.

She smiled when Emma came up behind her, embracing her.

Emma's words from the previous night had resonated deeply with her. The struggle to prove herself, wrestling with an uncertain future, lay behind her. She could approach new challenges with a new outlook.

"You know, I was thinking..."

"You'd like to change the itinerary for today?"

"Sort of."

"Okay..." Jayce drew a sharp breath when Emma's hands wandered underneath her shirt. "I think I know where this is going."

"Who says the wedding night has to be...at night?"

Jayce turned around to kiss her, making sure Emma knew she was on board with the idea. All the places they were going to visit would still be there in an hour or two.

"No one. It's up to us."

This new freedom was even more precious since they were in it together.

About the Author

B arbara Winkes writes sapphic crime drama and Christmas romance. She loves writing characters who get the job done, whether it's stopping a predator or saving cherished traditions—while still making time for love. She lives with her wife in Quebec City.

barbarawinkes.com

Also by Barbara Winkes

The Crossing Lines Trilogy
Undercover
Redemption
Vengeance

The Connected Series
Promised to the Queen
Drawn to the Enemy
Tempted by the Protector